"Is anyone gonna overhear us, Em?" Jethro glanced to the physicist for a moment. Even as Emmett shook his head, his friend added, "'Cause we can step outside, or wherever you think would be the best place?"

Both a quick exhalation and a smile brushed simultaneously over Emmett's lips. "Nobody will be hearing us, Geddy." The background noise of the rambunctious club seemed to lower of its own accord, as the physicist devoted his full attention to his friend. It was as if the two had water clogging their ears, with each vocal tone blunted and distorted by the time it reached them.

This assurance didn't prevent the older, mustached man from leaning forward and speaking in a soft tone; and despite the vividly animated, energy-filled club Emmett could hear the elder's breath as it rattled his vocal cords without difficulty. "I'm sorry, Emmett, I thought you'd told her."

"What could I have told her?" Emmett took another drink, wincing for a moment as the flavor of the lemon mingled with that of the glass' contents. His voice nearly cracked from the burning sensation, and he shivered delicately. "She knows the gist of what I did, there, and the details would only make things worse. I just tell her that the trauma keeps me from remembering."

Geddy shook his head. "M'Wife knows. She knows damn near everything. We like to use it for vacations, y'know? Marge made sense of it, after a while."

Emmett lowered his chin for a moment, gazing at his feet through the wooden, veneer-coated table. Then, he looked Geddy square in the eye, inquisitively. "How did she take it, Geddy?"

The Black man raised an eyebrow in dismay. "Terrible!" he laughed softly, then, looking up to the sky. "No, you right. You need to tell her when *you're* ready, not when I think you is. 'Til then, you forgot."

Physics Incarnate
A novel

Jesse Pohlman

Pohlman Press   Freeport,NY

ISBN-13: 978-0615591568 (Pohlman Press)
ISBN-10: 0615591566

www.jessepohlman.com

This novel is dedicated to all those who
offered their support toward its production.

Thank you for your faith in me. You are too many to name.

View the complete list at:
www.jessepohlman.com/thankyouforpi

Chapter One
Autumn in the Catskills

It was nearly the middle of October and the deciduous trees were beginning their yearly metamorphosis; their coats destined to shift from a festive green to a banana-like yellow, then to a rust-like brown. Before long, their garments would fall off altogether, and the trees would survive the winter naked in what was a curious paradox. On the other hand, the region's conifers remained green and clothed, seeming to ignore January's cold bite entirely. On mornings such as this in upstate New York, the scent of burning firewood was ever so perceptible in the chilly mountain air of the Catskills; yet by the afternoon, most would take to their T-Shirts – an unrelated parallel to how trees reacted over a year, taking place within one day of a human's life.

Within this region was a scholastic establishment lovingly called "Triple C." Its proper name was Catskill Community College, a school which had a strong focus on preparing students for larger, grander institutions through a rigorous two-year program. In some fields there were options to achieve Bachelor's degrees, of course, but most students moved on to obtain their credentials from elsewhere. It was surrounded by woods, and in homage toward the pioneering spirit of the Empire State its architecture was a combination of older buildings and throw-backs to older buildings. Log cabins dotted the gently rolling hills of the facility, and to an unaware observer it might well appear as if the entire school was made of nothing more than oversized frontiersman's huts – and, quite fittingly, some of the structures had indeed been just that, until they were expanded and modified for a modern age.

One instruction hall in particular, however, broke from this mold of neo-woodsman modeling; it was three stories tall and fairly long, equipped with a basement, and adorned with heating and cooling equipment. Wood-paneled steel beams provided integrity, while double-paned glass provided a window toward the forests outside. A large placard its central entrance depicted it as Louis DuBois Hall, named after a French Hugenot who had helped lead the colonization of New Paltz. It was, as its students were well aware, the science building for the college; and, as a result, it took the most modern and cutting-edge approach to its appearance as possible, reflecting the inexorable march of science's so-called progress.

Within DuBois Hall, classes were taking place. In room 201, a clock facing the room ticked to 3:48 while gazing upon twenty two students, all of whom sat staring up toward the front of the room. Twelve were female, ten male; six were Black, two Hispanic, one Asian, one Native American; one wore a gay pride shirt, two who sat next to one another had on wedding rings; thirteen wore crosses, one wore a Pagan pentagram and one a Jewish star; and, of course, twenty out of twenty two had either blonde or brunette hair. The average age was nineteen and two thirds.

One of the girls in the room let blue eyes drift over a pair of glasses in front of her; those glasses were made up of lightweight titanium frames and lenses formed mostly of silica. These, in turn, were composed of nothing more massive than molecules; tiny, tiny amalgams of atoms held together by nearly magical seeming bonds that allowed them to function not as the tiny spheres of a child's ball pit, but as a solid object. There was motion in those molecules, but it was mild at best – vibrations in the face of sound, perhaps.

Dr. Emmett Eisenberg felt every last twitch of that sort upon his face. The metal was high-strung and tensely bound together, while the glass hung suspended before him and, if he paid it any mind, was far from as firm. For a moment, he allowed himself to drift into the soft caress of the vibrations.

The soft serenade of sliding substances was swiftly driven from his mind. He blinked his eyes, glancing his student body over, and he smiled. His hands were covered by thin, brown leather gloves; his index finger extended as his left arm gestured to the centerpiece of his classroom – a "smart-board." This proprietary equipment was a combination of a gigantic touch-screen and a projector setup. The system was designed to project a carbon-copy of a nearby computer display onto the touch-pad; a user's touch would then be relayed to the computer and interpreted as the click or drag of it's mouse. With his gloved index finger's first knuckle he rapped the exterior, thin layer of molecules in order to connect it to the electrically-conductive substances behind it; this triggered the mouse to toggle almost exactly where he'd asked it to – a large arrow on a slide show pointing to "next."

On the screen flashed the man's next subject; Newton's Third Law of Motion. He first presented it as it was originally given, in Latin, with very few stumbles: *"Lex III: Actioni contrariam semper et æqualem esse reactionem."* A second touch and a rough translation emerged below the original: *"Law III: To every action there is always an equal and opposite reaction."* Emmett smiled as he looked toward the classroom; most of the students hadn't begun writing, yet, but he didn't have even the slightest inclination to suggest that wise of a course.

"So, most of you have probably heard this one. Not so much the first version of it, but the second." A scattering of grins and perhaps one genuine chuckle; but he wasn't here to be a comedian, just to make rudimentary physics available to liberal arts students who, for the most part, had little interest in sciences. "Anyone want to venture a guess at what Sir Newton was talking about with this one?"

He'd already addressed the first law – the concept of inertia, wherein an object in motion would remain in motion until an external force intervened; and, of course, he'd wrapped up the second one on the previous week, detailing how an object's movement is altered in proportion to the amount of force applied to it from an external source. Emmett wasn't surprised when a hand rose up; it was Sonia Monterrey's, a sophomore whose grades were decent and who had routinely expressed an interest in his class even though she was a Psychology major. His colleagues had briefly kicked around the idea of trying to "convert" her in the belief of pursuing a scientific degree, but he'd had two reasons for declining this proposition. The first was a simple distaste for interdepartmental politics, a fact he'd made quite clear at the time. The second, as he'd told his fellows, was personal. Nevertheless, he gestured toward the girl and called her name.

"It means that if you push on the wall, the force you use on it doesn't just disappear – it has to go somewhere. I'm sitting in a desk right now," she said, tapping the surface of it, "and that's pushing it into the floor, which pushes down into the ground. Am I right?"

Emmett grinned a bit, nodding. "More or less." He glanced at his watch; he only had a few more minutes to work on the lesson, but it would do. "But even more than that, guys, that force is also returned to *you*. Lets do a little experiment – put your hands on your desks and push down a bit. Tell me what it feels like."

Another student, Brian Wilcox, quickly looked up after doing as he asked. "It kinda hurts." Emmett knew that Brian was on the swim team; the kid should have grasped this concept before he even proposed it, but apparently Brian hadn't studied his art as well as he should have.

The instructor shrugged indifferently, his left hand raising toward his ear. "Yeah, it might, but more than that – what's it feel like the desk is doing, Brian?"

"It feels kind of like..." His hands slipped, and the desk vibrated a bit as the wooden plank swung upward so violently that it nearly rocked him out of his seat. He shook his fingers vigorously, staring at Emmett with irritation plain in his expression. "Fuck, that hurt!" A few laughs around the room were silenced by a glance from the teacher.

Then, paradoxically, the professor chuckled – though it seemed to be theatrical in nature. "Language," he softly cautioned. Then, he continued, "Its like a diving board, right?

The force you exert is returned to you? When you release it, it reacts in an equal but opposite manner. So when you push against the wall, the wall pushes against you. And with that," he looked at his watch again, "our lesson is complete!" With a collective sigh of relief from the majority of his class, the students began to form a chaotic line at the doorway.

In Emmett's mind it was a perfect metaphor for a radioactive substance; the various atoms were quickly dissipating, one part of it after another leaving the central mass and going its own way into the universe. Perhaps the subatomic particle would find a new home – or, at least, give someone cancer! But his eyes caught his pupil Sonia's approach and he offered her a nod. "How can I help you?" he asked with a welcoming lilt.

Her eyes suddenly left his face, looking away as her cheeks grew ever so rosy. "Oh, I just wanted to say I thought it was a good approach, Doctor Eisenberg. Hands-on;" she quipped, "I'm learning about that in my educational psych classes."

Emmett blinked, his mind racing to do calculations that had nothing to do with the physics he was so enamored with. He had black hair with tufts of gray starting to creep in ever so slowly; a color that matched the same exact hue of his eyes. He was tall, about 5'11, with a frame that showed a bit of muscle seeing as he weighed in at 173 lbs on the dot. When it came to style he had just enough; brown pants and a suit-jacket over a light-blue shirt and tie. His aforementioned gloves always fit into the style of clothing he wore, whether it was a black suit, a white one, or even a green one. This raised questions at times, but he had never been seen by his students without them on - in fact, he kept a mental list of who had asked about them and who had not. He made it a habit not to be loud and boisterous; his voice was damn near a whisper at times, yet he always made sure he was heard, and his gentle tones were clearly enough to have held his classroom's attention - and then some.

She, on the other hand, was perhaps twenty years old, maybe a little above that landmark. Sonia had never asked about

Emmett's gloves. She was shorter than him and slender, with a sharply angled face and blonde hair. She couldn't be insinuating what she appeared to be; yet her posture hinted at something devious, her feet angled away from one another in an all-too-welcoming fashion. Her eyes looked back to his; and something in the bright blue orbs stirred a memory deep within Emmett's mind.

"Yeah," he finally answered with a polite smile, wary of taking too long to script his response while at the same time recognizing the imperative of not sounding like he was blurting his thoughts out, "I suppose it was! I'm just glad the lesson came across properly. I know my subject is a bit difficult."

She shook her head. "I don't think so. People just need to study instead of swim." The reference to Brian caught Emmett off guard and he laughed softly. "Its not so bad, your class." Her posture adjusted again; no longer was it even slightly suggestive, but merely conversational. He'd imagined it – and he'd preferred it that way.

"Well, thank you for that!" His laugh was gentle, and she nodded and joined the crowd of dispersing particles as a mere curiosity, a building block of matter that returned to next to nothing, its last half-life finally eclipsed. With the room emptied, Emmett logged out of the college's computer system. He took a memory stick out of the school's computer and opened his laptop case; a black journal was shifted to the side and a pouch was opened, allowing him to conceal the data-stick inside. Finally, he took his bag and slung it over his shoulder. Gravity tugged the various supplies contained within it to the ground, but this effect hardly impacted him beyond a bit of pressure being applied to his jacket.

Dodging the dozens of students in the corridors of DuBois Hall, Emmett escaped into the slightly chilly winds of the Autumn air. He gazed about, passing by the central plaza of the campus and moving toward Hudson Hall. It was primarily used to host the liberal arts section of the school; History, English, and other such subjects. It also had various other offices, as well, including the department that his mark worked in. Named after the famed explorer whose moniker adorned a number of New York facilities, Emmett hardly had the chance to glance at his watch before he heard a warm voice call his name.

"Punctual as usual, Maria!" He smiled, his eyes turning to gaze upon Doctor Maria Montclaire, a slender, 5'5 woman with blonde roots and the most striking strawberry-shaded strands of hair the rest of the way down. Her eyes were a natural shade of green, and though she was only four years Emmett's senior she was six years into her time at Catskill Community College's psychology department – in fact, she was threatening to lead it within the decade! She wore a green blouse with a knee-length skirt, with stockings helping to keep her legs warm – it gave her the impression of looking young and "hip" yet also professional and intellectual. It was her favored style of dress, one that fused welcoming and wise intonations.

She stepped up to him, a hand finding his hip as she leaned in and upwards, delivering a gentle kiss to his lips. "Of course, Em," she abbreviated, "how was your last class?"

"Fine enough," he replied casually, a grin creeping across his face. "I did my hands-press-the-desk gag again; someone always seems to irritate a fingernail, or something. I'd feel a little bad for them, if half of 'em didn't claim to have taken high school physics at some point." At Maria's dry smirk, he continued, "It isn't really rocket science, that Newtonian physics thing."

"Well, dear," she countered with a warm tone, "I can relate. Today I had to teach a lesson on Gestalt therapy and some of the class brought up obsessive compulsive disorder. I can see where they get it from, but just because we call something 'fixed' doesn't mean that its something the person is consciously aware of doing."

Emmett was too polite to ask his girlfriend for clarification; after all, in the year since they'd gotten together, he couldn't even remember how many times he'd asked the question – let alone the number of different, enlightening, and ultimately forgotten ways she'd explained it! For example, he grasped that this method's interpretation of depression revolved around the vague nature of "unsatisfied needs." On the surface this made complete sense; it was even a boring conclusion! Of course a lack of fulfillment led to depression, because if a person wants what they can't have then they only want it more, and they grow frustrated! Yet somehow in Gestalt therapy this notion of "fixed Gestalts," if addressed improperly, could lead to serious repercussions if handled poorly – the old "if antidepressant are poorly provided, they could give a patient just enough energy to kill themselves" conundrum. Emmett supposed that simply giving a person what they wanted, then, could be a very bad idea, but he certainly couldn't be sure of that.

"This is true," the scientist responded warmly, opening the door into Hudson Hall after a cold wind blew by. Maria nodded her appreciation as they entered, but as her head bowed she shot a glance upward at him that caused him to stand up just a bit straighter.

"You still have no idea what I'm talking about, huh?"

Emmett laughed, his hand slapping the back of his neck and scratching at it slowly, as if he had a bit of an itch. His mind raced with surprise as he attempted to formulate an answer, but sadly none could come quickly enough. "You forgot, didn't you? I guess I shouldn't be surprised, I feel the same way when you talk about quarks and muons."

The scientist merely studied the psychologist for a while after they were both good and inside the building. "Geniuses indeed, but in our own fields, don't you agree?"

She laughed, her shoulders rising and falling in an amused shrug. "It took us how many years to get a doctorate degree? How much work? Its no surprise we don't get what the hell the others' subject matter is about. Its a dichotomy between the left brain and right – I'm more sociable and creative, and you're just a smart troll that writes formulas on a chalk-board!"

At Maria's giggle, Emmett slipped an arm around her and pulled her close. He used a touch of strength, just enough to apply a little pressure in his squeeze. It drew a soft squeak from her lips, while his fingertips gently stroked her shoulder. The two walked along, the larger man leaning ever so slightly the smaller, slender woman; they headed up a stair case and toward a small office – Maria's.

As the building was one of the oldest structures on Catskill Community College's campus, hallways squealed and screeched with each step the two took. The narrow, wooden-surfaced walls eventually gave way to a small alcove with a doorknob guarding it. The wooden way-gate opened with a creak into a rather tiny room that came complete with an even tinier closet and a few aged, wooden chairs with thin pads for students to sit on, accompanied by one lone old wooden cabinet for the office holder's usage. The professor's desk and chair were all procured by Maria herself; a nice, red mahogany desk with multiple locked drawers and a red, felt, soft chair to boot. She had a higher-end desktop computer, red wireless mouse, and a pair of red file cabinets, each with a class listed. There was a mini-fridge in the corner, along with a number of do-dads including a glass globe with electrical plasma within – the kind one places one's hand on top of in order to attract the static toward it as if one was in control of lightning itself.

Emmett stared at this particular globe for a moment, watching each individual strand of energy; it spread in a semi-consistent pattern, little tendrils emanating from the central power generator right until it struck the glass that contained it. They dissipated quickly after that – but with one touch to that outer shell, the bio-electricity from a human finger would send this mostly stable system not into disarray, but complete subjugation. The plasma arcing inevitably toward the point of contact – it was like a lightning rod. He'd always marveled at those sort of things; in most circumstances, when a new entity was introduced, grew less consistent! Then again, that was only true when more energy was added; many times, if a binding agent were added to a mixture it would help form a more stable compound. It was something of a conundrum that ran through his mind for a moment; it was more interesting because he grasped the processes at work in such a profound manner, and not in the least because he was clueless and mystified by physics and chemistry.

His gloved hand caressed the globe softly, and there was no apparent disruption to the network of lightning lattices. Emmett's eyes were jerked up toward his girlfriend, however, when she giggled. "Oh come on, you know you're supposed to use your bare hands. I promise it won't shock you."

She'd done it again; made a way to mention his persistently gloved condition. "Oh, I know, dear," he responded, fingertips slowly reaching underneath the darkened leather and lifting it upward over his hand. With a great deal of effort he touched the glass globe and the electricity aligned as intended; the plasma pulsed into his palm. Nobody was scarred, nobody exploded, nothing went wrong. He smiled a smile that nobody could notice.

"See! Just fine," she laughed, stepping over toward him and placing a soft kiss on his lips. He closed his eyes, relaxing into the swift exchange. After a few fleeting seconds they disengaged with an affectionate touch and Maria reached underneath her desk and withdrew a bag. She had a meaningful glare in her eyes as she began to peruse it, reaching around and rattling various instruments within. She finally grinned. "Aha!" And she withdrew, of all things, a book! It was a marble notebook that had at least a dozen small plastic tabs bobbing about as she moved it, and she opened up to one of those pages and began to read.

"Emmett, dear, can you hand me '*Case Studies in Delusion*,' by Michael Transeau, and '*Lucid Delusions*' by Cathrine Tobin?"

Emmett walked over toward her book-shelf and thumbed through. "Sure," he added to ensure she was aware that *he* was aware of her request; Tranesau's book was easily found, as it had a standard-seeming black cover with silver lettering pronouncing its name. However, it wasn't long before Emmett's voice called for assistance; "Tobin's book, umm, what's that look like again?"

"I think its green. Also, I need '*Delusion and Depression*, *a Corrollational Circumstance'* by Peter Fisch. That's got a red cover," she added as she heard the physicist shift some books about, "and it has black lines in it that kind of make it look like an acid trip, to be honest. Its supposed to represent the tone of the book's conclusion, or something."

This book was found more quickly than Emmett could track down *Lucid Delusions*, however that wasn't hard – it was actually on Maria's desk, which is where he oh-so-conveniently placed the book he'd honestly located. After Maria politely asked, "any luck?" while searching through her records, Emmett managed to locate a blue tome! He grasped it, flipped to its cover and, upon seeing a completely unrecognizably Russian name (as compared to "Tobin," anyway), he shelved it and found a second azure book.

Taking it in his hands, he set it down in the pile. "Got them all," he added cheerily, looking the spines of the three books over casually. "I take it you've going to be rather busy, tonight?"

She laughed, setting her marble notebook down and looking Emmett over for a moment. "Why? Jealous? I promise it won't be *all* night, hun."

"Good! I was thinking we could go to a Hibachi for dinner. I believe there's a new one opening in town, and I'd like to try it."

Her laughter only grew a bit more sardonic, and she rolled her eyes playfully. "Yes, you told me. I don't know how many times you've told me! But before we go, I do need to get some adjustments done on this project. The research from the Tobin book isn't going so well with the Fisch one, if you understand my meaning."

In one sense, the physicist understood all too well. The scientific method, to which both he and Maria adhered to some extent (he was a superior adherent, at least in his own mind), mandated that when doing an experiment one must collect data through the conduction of experiments. Experiments require controlled conditions – in physics, it was easy to have a "control" group in which the results were virtually predictable, accompanied by a "variable" category in which a single something was different.

Another requirement of data collection was to always have more than one example of the experiment; if in one instance di-hydrogen monoxide did not extinguish a burning match head, it would be a poor precedent to write a paper about the weakness of water against flame. Therefore, a given experiment needed to be conducted not just dozens, but hundreds of times in order to ensure that one variable is, or is not having an effect. Emmett especially derided the fallacies that this notion led to – medical studies were routinely conducted to "confirm" older, well-organized observations while the more interest quirks of physiology, such as the notion that Marijuana could prevent cancer, were quickly derided based on the idea that the sample sizes weren't large enough. The obvious answer of actually running a controlled study never seemed to gain approval, at least in his eyes.

Nevertheless, even Emmett had to concede that the method had its flaws; it could not, as it were, fully deal with the nature of Maria's occupation, psychology. Oh, sure, her ilk *tried* to subscribe to the methodology that the physicist took such pride in, but the inherent beast of psychological disorders made it difficult to ever establish a "control" in the first place. Mental disorders were difficult to pin down in the first place, as one diagnostician could mis-understand a symptom or, more likely, simply never have an occurrence to interact with one as a patient could withhold information. Therefore, the most effective kind of psycho-theraputical research was in the areas of psycho-pharmacology.

Three hundred people claiming to suffer from depression could be split into two groups, and half could be given a placebo while the other half are given an actual brain-altering substance. Emmett imagined this was as close to possible as a controlled experiment could get in this field. Yes, the exact illness might not be accurate, but at least the relief of symptoms could be attributed to the medication's failure or success, with only a minor degree of "incidental" outcomes such as the placebo effect. In his mind it was still a piss-poor reconciliation between the scientific method and psychology, but at least it allowed for a somewhat useful element of data acquisition.

The physicist distilled his thoughts in to a clarion comment. "Hard to accurately pin down where each author is looking in the data, when they pull their conclusions?"

"Something like that," she countered as Emmett lifted the book of case studies and began to thumb through – there were about twenty in all, each one richly detailed. "A couple of times, each one uses stuff from the Transeau work. I've got another collection of case studies at home, right now, but Fisch and Tobin don't draw from it as often. Those two *do* draw from three of the same studies, and come to some very different conclusions about just what the hell is going on in the client's heads."

Emmett shut the book and nodded. "So you're research is on the link between delusion and depression, right? How they can cause each other?" His first impression was that he was on the right track – then she raised her finger. That was a bad sign, because it implied that he'd gotten something, somewhere and somehow, completely wrong.

"They don't exactly cause one another so much as influence each other, and there's heavy undertones of schizophrenia involved in the works as well. I'll give you an example of what I'm dealing with," she specified. "Severe trauma can cause the brain to sort of defend itself by constructing an artificial reality. That's our delusional aspect – the patient's family is murdered and, in response, she begins to believe – truly believe – that she never had one. She'll claim she's adopted, because the incident was about more than death; it was the eradication of her entire family from the pages of history. Sometimes the patient won't even want to fill in the gap – she'll claim she never wants to get married, or doesn't want to do research into where her parents were from before she was adopted, orphaned, or what-have-you."

Emmett nodded dryly. "So how would depression filter

into this one?"

"Well, if the assumed goal of psychotherapy is to help the patient live in a healthier reality," Maria consoled, continuing into the difficult nature of the conversation, "The patient isn't depressed at that point, to be fair. She's just very far from the reality of the situation. Furthermore, its realistic that at some point, someone is going to contact her on behalf of her lost family – either funeral directors, bill collectors, or what-have-you. If the patient is reintroduced to reality in the wrong way, it's bad news; but even if she's brought back into it the right way, she's going to have serious problems for a long time." Maria sighed, her eyes drifting to the floor with sadness; one of her greatest traits had always been that, no matter how much the research aspects of psychology appealed to her, she was also extremely committed to the well-being of people in general; committed to the point where even the thought of unpleasantness befalling a faceless, fictitious person was unpleasant to her, as well. " At some point the therapist is going to have to make a decision to intentionally depress the patient in order to help them avoid worse pain in the future. It sucks, but its life."

Emmett mused on this; in a sense it was nothing new, but Maria's explanation brought the unnamed molecules of human existence to a new, painful light for him. People suffering to avoid worse later? That was easy enough to imagine – but for some reason or another the layered masks that Maria portrayed were all too close to home. The physicist exhaled. "And how do you think depression might lead into dementia, or delusion?"

Maria shrugged callously, her face turning grim. "Lets face it, the world sucks. Here's another example – omnipotent-esque banks are continually coming down on the common man, crushing his future and tearing him from his home. This regular Joe isn't going to see a company made up of individual people for very long."

"Especially with the way our government classifies corporations, imagining them as pseudo-people subject to their own class of laws," Emmett added, his tone reaching into a new, grim depth.

Maria gave him a thumbs up. "Right. Evil oil companies nearly destroy an entire ecosystem, killing a dozen or so employees in the process, and their executives still get paid. It doesn't matter if an accident does a lot of harm to the company as well; it becomes a conspiracy, a game where the real movers-and-shakers can cover up and effectively cancel out any economic damage before its serious. The depression of every day life, and all of the small little problems that companies seem to inflict upon the patient will lead to his impression that the world is against him. This usually manifests in Schitzophrenia in a violent way, but it can manifest in depression as well. And, its all a delusional belief based on the fact that the patient has been depressed for so long that they've actually sought out a false, but powerful 'cause'."

"So, basically people can start to believe that there's some magical powers-that-be that make the world an evil, scary place," Emmett concluded, boiling down such a complicated issue into a single, overarching theme. "And if these issues become permanent fixtures of a person's life it could really mess them up for years to come."

Maria nodded her agreement once again. "Pretty much. It can sometimes work the other way, too; people can get so convinced in their own abilities, or someone else's, and they can become sort of like a personal super hero – the politician who can fix *everything* wrong." The psychologist grew silent, finishing her packing and slipping her bag over her shoulder. Emmett donned his gloves once more and glanced down toward the watch on his left wrist. It was a simple Rolex; nothing fancy, nothing complicated, and it told the time. Its precision was its key attracting figure. Looking toward the physicist, she asked, "What time is the train tonight?"

Emmett looked back up at her and smiled. The two had important plans this weekend, as they intended to connect with an old colleague of Emmett's from his younger days. "Well, its about 4:30 now, and we need to be on the train at 7:30. We still have to stop home first, right?"

Maria's shrugged. "I don't really have to, but if your friend is performing then I'd like to look decent, as the guest of the bandie's friend," she remarked, fingertips curling through her strawberry locks; her bottom lip extended in an ever-so-faint pout. Emmett didn't need a map to gauge where she intended to go with this, and his gloved hand brushed over that lower tier with a warm look in his eyes.

"Dear," he whispered reassuringly, "you're always beautiful to me, but if you want to unwind for a little before we go, that is more than fine – we have the time." The term "chemistry" had been used to define the two, and there were plenty of ways to make solutions in that particular science – but very few chemical reactions were as exciting as the two of them, let alone so completely well-blended.

Chapter Two
New York By Night

The Hudson Valley was a prominent geographic facet of New York, located along the titular river that had, for centuries, been a vital artery for transportation throughout the state. The area itself was a mixture of the great and the greatly depressed; in some locations, old and dilapidated factories dotted the landscape while in others some of America's wealthiest denizens dwelled pleasantly enough. It was a region rich in history, and richer still in challenges – as New York City continued to change, this area so near and yet so far from it was pulled along for the ride.

Nestled next to the river, or at least rather near it, was a railroad line called the Hudson Line. It conveyed passengers from this lovely valley into that nearby city, toward – specifically – Grand Central Terminal. After their train had stopped into the station at 7:34, reflecting the MTA's traditional sense of timing, Emmett Eisenberg and Maria Montclaire had both nestled into a seat and headed south. The train was perhaps half full, with folks heading into the city for the night - many of them wearing sports jerseys reflecting teams they were likely en route to seeing. One small group had on black shirts with a wild-cat emblazoned on the back; each had the earbuds of an MP3 player practically stitched onto them. Once they settled in, the train began to move again. The trees of the Catskills passed by like the breeze as the pair quickly placed their belongings to the side and began the intricate, intimate process of research.

Well, Maria did, at any rate! She proceeded to reach into a black leather bag and withdraw those books of hers', hitting them with a speed to match the metal tube they were riding in; she folded her legs, feet covered in red heels and thighs just barely obscured by a thin red dress. Emmett, on the other hand, flipped open his cell phone and dashed off a quick text message, his gloved fingers moving dexterously over the dial. With a quick adjustment and the redirection of some electrons he was on the internet, looking over the current events of the day. He returned to reality about five minutes later, overall unimpressed with both the bland news articles he'd found and the buzz of his reply.

"We're still good, right, hun?" Emmett asked, glancing toward his girlfriend. "We'll stop at the hotel real fast, first, and drop our things off?"

Hardly even looking up, Maria nodded and muttered halfway into a stack of index cards, "Sure, dear." He understood the pressure of writing, through his multiple submissions to journals such as *Interaction Monthly* and *Motion Magazine*. Science journals had adopted peppy-sounding names to attract wider audiences, although they still required a certain level of knowledge in the field to draw serious conclusions from reading.

Smiling, he tapped a return message to his friend and closed his eyes. It took only a moment for the subtle clicking and clacking of the railroad tracks to permeate through his body and he allowed himself to relax into the roughness of the ride.

With each turn, he could feel the change in velocity as well as orientation; he could taste the metallic friction between the train's wheels and the rails; and he could sense the multitude of electrons flowing from that oft-maligned third rail into the cars, a vital source of power for both the lights that Maria read by and the transmission of the train. Tiny micro-fractures could not escape his notice, but they were in no danger of destruction at the hands of the natural wear-and-tear of moving at speeds of up to sixty miles an hour. He could hear those points of friction flexing just as well as he could hear the whisper-soft words from the nearby music lovers' MP3, a familiar sounding, beyond-radio-perfect voice crying about how her lover "Tore us to shreds."

He only allowed himself to remain in this trance for a few minutes. The trip seemed quick enough; Emmett spent his time reading and playing games on his phone while Maria read up on her psychology and further formed her project's skeleton. Before long they were pulling into Grand Central Terminal, and grand it was – most notable for its massive main concourse, Maria and Emmett made their way through the crowd delicately, the bright lights creating an artificial daylight just as effectively as its golden-hued walls provided the impression of an entry into more than just a new city, but a new life. The massive concourse clock told Emmett it was 9:00, and the duo stepped outside to hail a cab.

      The extraordinarily expensive cab took them to a Marriott hotel on 30th street. A quick check-in to room 602 established that the room had all of the promised amenities – TV, a shower-massage shower head, hyper-inflated room service, solid curtains to block out the sun (Emmett had once been woken on account of nearly see-through curtains; he would never return to that hotel), an iron and a fold-up ironing board, a telephone, and most of all one ginormous king-sized bed. They set their belongings down and, assuring they were still as sharply dressed as ever, set off toward a second financially depressing cab ride.

      The location the two were destined for was a Jazz club called X-Quisite. Unlike most night clubs, it wasn't open to the public. Memberships were required, often towering over $400 per person for a year; or, lesser expenses for a month. Of course, at those prices drinks and smokes were cheap. Emmett and Maria had never been to X-Quisite before; they were getting in because they were friends with one of the club's preferred customers, paying a one-time fee of $30 each, and promising to keep their mouths shut.

      The exterior was simple enough; it looked by all accounts to be a warehouse, and upon entering one certainly wouldn't have a reason to believe otherwise. They found themselves in a small office with computers and filing cabinets, all befitting an import-export company that very well might have operated out of the facility once upon a time. They were also met with a friendly man sitting in front of a heavy steel door. Emmett divulged his "password," paid his money, underwent a quick frisking for weapons and stepped through the door, which when opened allowed the sound of a smooth jazz rhythm to flow from the facility's interior. Maria followed.

Inside the club was a completely different world. Dim blue lighting adorned the ceiling, giving the entire area a purple-ish hue as the beams of photons reflected off of a similarly-shaded wall. Intricate paintings of Jazz and Blues legends covered these walls, along with photographs of different acts that had performed at the club. There was a bar with no tender; it was self-serve. There was also a small buffet laid out, but by the time the pair of professors had arrived it was down to salad and bread.

The layout was simple enough – along the back wall of the club there were small tables and chairs, while in the center were large round tables as well as couches and recliners that faced toward the stage. A poker game couldn't have found a nicer home. There was a bit of smoke in the air, mainly from a large man in along the back wall that was seated with a lovely girl in a black dress. The smoke consisted of decaying plant matter; it irked Emmett's nose, but the tar and nicotine did no harm to him, nor to Maria.

He found a seat across from the stage and glanced toward Maria. "Interesting place. Would you like a drink?"

"I'm not sure," Maria began, glancing over the building slowly. "There's a lot of guys here, a lot more than there are women." She glanced the room over; indeed, the overwhelming majority of the guests at the moment were male, and many had liquor in their hands. "Where's this friend of yours we're supposed to meet, anyway?"

Emmett smirked a bit, glancing the room over. Maria wasn't wrong; but a lot of the girls were simply in a different part of the club, or across the room from them. There was no way to overhear them; the sound waves coming from the musicians was overwhelming, with the various differences in pressure clearly obscuring any attempt to discern sounds from another area. With a gesture toward the stage, however, he singled out his accomplice.

"Huh?" Maria looked at the group; though it was dark she could clearly make out a bass guitarist, a lead guitarist, a drummer, a keyboardist and a singer with a guitar of his own. "There's, like, six of them up there. Want to be a bit more specific?"

Emmett reoriented his finger toward the keyboard. "That's him. Jethro Marx. We call him Geddy, actually; he's a genius. Really, I mean it," came the high praise.

Maria's eyebrow raised, and she observed the man; it was hard to tell behind the sound equipment, but he was definitely a black man with only slight tufts of curly gray hair hanging on for dear life over his ears. The man was approaching fifty years old and he was tall, yet portly. He had a gray mustache, and as the tendrils of smoke cleared before her she managed to see his movements over the keyboard were both precise and chaotic – he never missed a note, but he almost seemed to spasm in tune with the bass guitar.

"What's he do?" Her question wasn't snarky, but simple, and devoid of the deeper meanings Emmett was accustomed to. "I mean, you've never really told me about Geddy before, so I'm still kind of stunned we've come all the way to the city to meet some stranger. Is he a musician?"

Emmett shook his head. "No. He's in construction, actually, and--" he stopped right in tune with the last vibration of the cymbals. The song ended and people applauded.

"Alright ya'll," the singer's baritone voice echoed over the club's PA system, "we're gonna take a bit of a break. If you wanna come up an' jam, be my guest, but don't touch my guitar, y'hear?" With that proclamation the band disbanded, and without fail Geddy offered a slight wave to the group as he headed to the bar. A few minutes later he returned with a tray; the first glass was a green concoction with a cherry sticking out of it, the second was a tall glass of water with a lemon in it; and the third was, judging from the smell, unadulterated whiskey.

"That one's mine," the deep voice of Geddy Marx remarked as he pointed to the dark substance. "And Emmett told me you like the sweet stuff. Its called a Midori Sour, try it."

Emmett grinned and looked toward his girlfriend; she

rolled her eyes and nodded. He took the glass, took a quick sip, and handed it to her. "Yeah, its pretty good."

"Damn right it is, Em. How you been, man, I ain't seen you in years!" The big man extended a fist toward the small professor; Emmett returned the favor, bumping knuckles briefly.

"I'm good. Getty, this is Maria Montclaire. Maria, Geddy."

She extended her hand, and Geddy received it gently. "Good to meet you, Maria. How you liking the club?"

"Its dark, actually. Not really what I'm used to. Speaking of," she added, taking the glass from the scientist and sipping at it just as he had. She blinked twice, then tilted her head back and took a longer swig. "Okay, its pretty good, I admit it."

"Told you!" the big man chuckled, sitting down next to the pair. He was an imposing enough presence, and his eyes turned to Maria. "And Emmett's told me a lot about you! You're a shrink!"

Maria coughed once, then shook her head. "Not exactly. My big thing is research, really. I take studies and process them, figuring out what the best ways to help every day people are. And I understand that you're in construction?"

Geddy nodded. "Yeah. Emmett and I worked together at Connor Point." The comment was off-handed, followed by a simple, "But, now I run my own company." It was innocuous enough, the tone in the older man's voice; as if intimating that the two had met at college, at a meeting, or at any given nightspot much like the one Maria was meeting him at, now.

The professor's blood ran cold; he looked toward his friend with widened eyes, and only managed to avert them when Maria looked back toward her boyfriend with surprise.

"Em never mentioned it to me." Her eyes, filled with a sudden sadness, glanced back toward the musician, downright apologetic toward her boyfriend's friend. "I'm sorry, Jethro, I really didn't realize. It must have been terrible."

The two men exchanged a swift glance, and Geddy laughed. "No no, call me Geddy. It ain't your fault, sweetheart.

Now, you mind me askin' what Emmett -has- told you about the place?"

Maria studied her boyfriend, who by now had finished half of his glass of water, and sighed. "Nothing much. I know he was there, and I know that it was a real disaster. It was bad, and some things happened that Em still won't talk about." With this, her hand reached out and took his gloved fingertips, her hand's warmth just barely penetrating through the leather veneer.

"Well," Emmett began, grasped gloved hands wringing one another nervously, "its like this. Geddy was one of the lead engineers at the reactor. He didn't handle the nuclear physics himself; just the architecture of the buildings and their structural integrity. He helped build the place brick by brick, and if it wasn't for his work, his solid planning, and that quick thinking when it came to how to take the place apart, I'm afraid the melt-down would have been complete. Anyone else's name on the blueprints and it was all downhill from there."

Geddy shook his head, his eyes showing just how at-odds he was with the professor. "Nah, man, your quick thinkin' helped save a lot of lives, when you think about it. If I'd built the damned place better maybe we wouldn't have had the problem in the first place. You the one who made the right call!" There was something in the elder's voice that indicated a serious amount of respect for his friend.

Maria exhaled slowly before she took another sip of her green concoction. "I don't know what to say, Em. Connor Point was damn near twelve years ago, and I know it still hurts you, but its okay to talk about it." Her voice was reassuringly relaxed; there was no judgment, not even in the lines on her face; her green eyes simply looked at her beloved. "I love you, Emmett, I just wish I knew more about things." At the physicist's continued silence at this invitation, Maria's green eyes widened. She was afraid of something, clearly. "I'm not mad, I promise, I just want to help."

"I know, dear," Emmett sighed. "I mean, you know the gist of it, right?"

The 'gist' had become something of a public policy nightmare. Connor Point was a research facility located in central Africa, on land that had been purchased by a collective of humanitarian agencies who saw an opportunity to bring in some good business and, simultaneously, accomplish a lot of research in a far-off area; the kind of research that "NIMBYists" (as Emmett called them) decided was a bit too dangerous for populated areas. Emmett's particular role had been running (along with others, of course) a nuclear breeder reactor, while performing some of his most cutting-edge research on Trans-Uranic elements - those with atomic numbers greater than Uranium's 92.

If Emmett hadn't already accomplished his doctoral degree he would have earned it within weeks of working at the site. Trans-Uranics were exceedingly rare and almost exclusively man-made, with Plutonium, Neptunium and Californium being three of the only frequently-used such substances. Oh, there were plenty of others, ones with atomic numbers topping well over 100. In Emmett's more tricky projects, and with some serious applications of physics, even the threshold of 200 atomic masses had indeed been crossed! Emmett helped create multiple new isotopes, many of which were unstable while many others showed promise. But such work was unfathomably rare and incredibly difficult to perform – except, perhaps, for Emmett Eisenberg

Then, as these stories typically run, came the accident.

Of course, nobody could point a finger at what *exactly* what went wrong If someone could, they'd kept their mouths shut for good reason; the reactors went critical, and as Geddy had said all that was known to the greater world about the facility's fate was that some quick thinking and hard sacrifices had led to the errant reactor being cooled down before a major radioactive incident happened. The facility was shuttered almost overnight, and the place was dismantled just in time for Emmett's severance check to clear. He, Geddy, and the bulk of the other researchers got clean bills of health and went on with their lives; the world at large had only noticed for a few minutes that something had even existed. It had been the safest major disaster in nuclear history; cement was flown in, the reactor was entombed and no radiation was detected outside of Connor Point's gates at any time.

"Yes," Maria affirmed to the physicist, "but I didn't know you were still in touch with anyone! Or that I was meeting someone who was so deeply involved in things. What was it like, your research?"

Emmett rubbed his forehead for a moment, searching for an explanation, then shrugged. "Complicated. I was making a lot of super-heavy elements, the sort of things with extremely brief half-lives. Clearly it was dangerous. It was a lot of work that I don't think the world of nuclear physics was ready for. Hell, we bailed out of Thorium in the 60's; if we'd have taken the less *selfish* route, maybe we'd have avoided this whole global warming crisis."

A soft chuckle came from the other man's lips. "'Ol Emmett, always the crusader for that Thorium stuff. The way you talk about it, people'd think you invented it!"

"Oh, god, yes. Emmett loves his pet little conspiracy theory!" Maria's tone was flirtatiously patronizing, warm yet chastising.

The physicist glowered for a moment; though he smiled quickly afterward, it was hard to tell which face – the jerk or the joker – was authentic. "Well, I know an answer when I see it. Its brilliant; the uranium isotopes involved are practically useless as weapons, the original test reactor didn't have to worry about melt-downs because it was built to fail safely. It needs some refining, but at least countries as far advanced as *India* are putting some serious effort into it!"

Maria frowned a bit as the ramble grew more eccentric. "Hun, are you alright?"

Emmett blinked twice, then nodded. His hand slipped over her shoulder. "Of course, hun. I'm good. I guess I'm just tired, I didn't really expect this conversation. How about you, dear? The music was awesome, by the way, Geddy. I've never been a jazz fan, but you guys are good."

"Oh thanks, thanks," the engineer responded, "I'm just an amateur, man. Most of these guys just wanna play once in a while, so we get together on jam night. Bobby in the lead is a pro, so's Sam on the drums."

"Really? I really wouldn't have known." Maria's compliment brought a smile to Geddy's lips; and Maria patted Emmett's hand softly. "I'm going to head to the ladies room. Jethro, would you mind telling me which way to go?"

"Really, now, call me Geddy!" The engineer's gruff remark was met with a gesture toward a dimly lit but rather wide hallway, just behind a pool table and an arcade machine – a fighting game. "Right down that way, second door on the left."

Maria nodded, and the two gentlemen rose along with her. She placed a delicate kiss to her boyfriend's lips then began down the hallway with her tight dress sharply covering her curves. As she disappeared, the two took a seat and Emmett tapped the rim of his glass twice before pulling a quick swig down.

"Is anyone gonna overhear us, Em?" Jethro glanced to the physicist for a moment. Even as Emmett shook his head, his friend added, "'Cause we can step outside, or wherever you think would be the best place?"

Both a quick exhalation and a smile brushed simultaneously over Emmett's lips. "Nobody will be hearing us, Geddy." The background noise of the rambunctious club seemed to lower of its own accord, as the physicist devoted his full attention to his friend. It was as if the two had water clogging their ears, with each vocal tone blunted and distorted by the time it reached them.

This assurance didn't prevent the older, mustached man from leaning forward and speaking in a soft tone; and despite the vividly animated, energy-filled club Emmett could hear the elder's breath as it rattled his vocal cords without difficulty. "I'm sorry, Emmett, I thought you'd told her."

"What could I have told her?" Emmett took another drink, wincing for a moment as the flavor of the lemon mingled with that of the glass' contents. His voice nearly cracked from the burning sensation, and he shivered delicately. "She knows the gist of what I did, there, and the details would only make things worse. I just tell her that the trauma keeps me from remembering."

Geddy shook his head. "M'Wife knows. She knows damn near everything. We like to use it for vacations, y'know? Marge made sense of it, after a while."

Emmett lowered his chin for a moment, gazing at his feet through the wooden, veneer-coated table. Then, he looked Geddy square in the eye, inquisitively. "How did she take it, Geddy?"

The Black man an eyebrow in dismay. "Terrible!" he laughed softly, then, looking up to the sky. "No, you right. You need to tell her when *you're* ready, not when I think you is. 'Til then, you forgot."

Emmett nodded once more, glancing over his shoulder – Maria wasn't on her way back quite yet. He sighed and took a thin straw, stirring his drink up. The countless water molecules of the ice brushed against the bulk of nitrogen atoms that comprised the majority of the air he was breathing. This interplay chilled the gasses just above the liquid while the warmth transferred into the drink. Of course, heat was really just a matter of kinetic energy in a substance; cold and hot were relative, and even solid objects moved on the atomic level. Sometimes, it comforted Emmett to think of simplistic concepts like 'hot' and 'cold,' and not the specific nature of the physics involved. The relaxing mental vision was as pleasant as it was vivid. His train of thought was not going to progress unmolested for terribly long, however.

Geddy's voice had an unusually grim tint about it. "I always wanted to ask ya one thing, Em, before you go forgettin' about it. I want to know just one thing. Why'dya have to do what you did to Garrett?"

Emmett's heart sank; he bit the bottom-right corner of his mouth with his canine and applied almost enough pressure to rupture a blood vessel. He had honestly expected much worse out of his friend, but for some reason the question stabbed a particularly sensitive portion of his palate. His mind continued to reexamine the situation; the damage to the facility, the circumstances of the structure's demise, the nightmare come back to life once more.

Finally, he responded. His tone was almost void of emotion; it was a natural defense mechanism for a scientist to sound logical about a stressful issue, and it could not fool a man of even average intelligence – let alone someone so deeply connected to the incident as Jethro Marx was. "I did what I thought was right, at the time," the physicist breathed disdainfully.

"I'm so sorry," Geddy replied almost too quickly, but with an incredible and unadulterated sadness, "I really wish things was different, man."

Emmett's head bobbed up and down, though his heart was pounding like Sam's drumming had been just ten minutes ago. "Me too, Geddy, me too." The physicist's eyes glanced over toward the hallway Maria had departed down; sure enough, she quickly came back into view, swaying toward the gentlemen and sitting down. Emmett nodded toward Geddy once, then tilted his glass back toward his lips and drained it. He let the glass fall back to the table with only enough friction from his gloved fingertips to guide it; he winced at the sound as his surroundings began to rise in volume, in direct proportion to the attention he paid toward them.

She barely seemed to notice, though she instead folded her arms and rubbed her shoulders, face screwing up in surprised displeasure. "Huh," she exhaled, "that was a nasty draft."

Geddy's eyes closed as he offered a sagacious nod, looking at his hands before rubbing them together. "You know what it is? Some idiot probably left the door open too long, that's why you got the chill just now."

Looking to his friend, Emmett shrugged. The psychologist gazed between the two gentlemen and raised an eyebrow, a faint smile finally touching her emerald eyes. "So what did the two of you do while I was busy?"

"Emmett asked me how the business was goin'," Geddy

replied casually. "Its called 'Construction Connections.' We do us a lot of contract work, you know?" As the question was rhetorical, he didn't let Maria answer. "Mostly tall buildings, them skyscrapers? That's my sorta deal. We started off small," he continued at the look of interest in her eyes, "after the thing at Connor Point. But I got me a good crew together an' we made it a point not to give bullshit time-lines for our work. If we said it'd be done in three months, it'd be done in three months! None of this cost-overrun nonsense. Straightforward. People didn't always like what they heard, but they liked the truth more."

At this particularly long explanation, she blinked her eyes a few times. It was clear she didn't buy Geddy's absolutely unconvincing story; and it didn't help that when she turned to look at Emmett, pinkish hair swaying side to side, he only nodded dumbly. "If I didn't know better," she insinuated in a teasing tone, wagging her finger from side to side at her boyfriend, "I'd think you were fibbing. I'd say you two were part of some conspiracy or something!"

Emmett's voice croaked upward, seemingly unbidden by its beholder. "Maria's research, ah, is on how depression and delusional behaviors can blend into one, and one of the aspects she's looking at are how people see conspiracy theories." He looked to his girlfriend as if praying for her approval; all she did was make a circular gesture with her finger indicating that he continue to explain. A quick gnash of his teeth later and he did just that. "The people who blame the government for 9/11, for example – they just want to see an all-powerful enemy that is so strong it can put *them* down, thus excusing them from their personal failures."

Geddy looked blankly back toward Emmett, then let his arms rise and fall. "Those people is crazy!" He put forth in agreement, "Its obvious they ain't use no TNT to bring those buildings down! I could tell ya that from one look at the film."

"Absolutely crazy," Maria concurred in a less excited tone; in fact, she was downright somber. "The fact is that some people truly believe those sort of things. Some of them are simply a little troubled, while some are completely insane. They utilize these conspiracies as validations of their own circumstances, giving them reasons to fight the 'system,'" she provided tiny air-quotes with her ruby fingernails, "while others use it as an excuse to do absolutely nothing – they figure they shouldn't bother if they're already doomed. There are even times when religious cults decide the world is going to end so they---"

Geddy shook his head. "Them poor bastards kill themselves," he remarked sadly. He was thinking of one cult in particular, but that didn't satisfy the psychologist.

Maria blinked her green eyes once, then shrugged her slender shoulders in a display of nonchalance. "I was going to say that they quit their jobs and give away their possessions. In fact, I recall that there was a group of people called the Millerites. They followed a man who predicted a date for the end of the world – and when it came and went and they were all still there, many of them just kept latching on to new dates thinking that *this time*, the man would be correct."

Emmett gazed his girlfriend in the eyes; he realized once again that there was a certain, unspoken connection between the two of them. He felt physics in a much more primal way than she felt psychology, of course! But, the pursuit of psychological studies was nevertheless ingrained in her psyche. Her orbs were alight with thirst – as much as she knew, she desired deeper understandings still. Emmett was the the opposite in that he had understanding and thirsted to simply experience his passion, instead; but they were *such* a solid compliment, much like the molecules in a solid substance were never quite merged into one continuous chain but were bound together by their similarities.

Geddy, however, seemed more than a little confused – or, at least, concerned for humanity. He looked at Maria askance for a moment, then raised an eyebrow. "So wait, what happened to the rest of them? The guys that sold all they things and ended up broke? When the world don't end after all what do people end up doin'?" This sounded like a deeply serious issue to Jethro, with his interest at a sublime high.

Maria's lips slipped into a firm, sly grin. Something about her seemed to truly enjoy seeing the outcome – even as her eyes showed there was indeed a touch of sympathy in them. "They called it the 'Great Disappointment,' and they all had to try to pick up the pieces of their shattered lives and move on."

The physicist stared at her for a moment. "You sound like you've practiced that line, dear."

"I have!" Maria countered with a soft laugh; she tilted her glass back and took a sip of her still-chilly drink, with beads of condensation running down it. "I have. I'm only writing a book on the subject, you know. Miller was a real whack-a-mole. Its not hard to talk down to people like that; its a lot harder to understand them. People of faith are pretty tricky," she continued, sounding quite like she might be an Atheist. "To live your life based on a book or the words of a priest is surrendering free will, no?"

The two gentlemen offered a confused sign of acknowledgment; of her authority on the subject if not her point's validity. "It is fundamentally unusual to surrender one's free will. Oh, it happens all the time – every day you're a passenger in a car, you've given at least a little of your freedom up to the driver. But," she raised an almighty index finger, "there is a clear difference between--"

A voice called out over the loudspeakers. "Five minutes and the band's back on! Five minutes and the band is back on." A smooth jazz track came on; it was low enough that conversation could continue, but the volume of this background music would make it harder to get lost in the midst of a discussion like the one the three friends were having. Geddy looked to the stage and nodded to his band-mates, most of whom were setting up for another round, drinks in their hands.

"Go on," the construction commodore commanded cheerily.

Maria smiled. "I could. There's a big difference between that small concession and letting a book that's clearly been printed within the last one hundred years dictate the way you should live;

no matter how many people say its the word of their God, its a big thing. That's why its so hard to be a true man of the book – you need to give *everything* over to that text."

    Emmett looked to his drink for a moment, wondering just how much of God might be in the substance held within the glass. Then, something struck him; his eyes met Maria's. "You said a man of the book, right?" The corner of her lip turned upward; he'd found a purpose-serving chink in her rhetorical armor. "People of the book end up following the text, but there are a lot of people that take only part of the book and follow what makes sense. Its kind of like the protestants kicking the Pope overboard and saying they can pray for themselves, yeah?"

    "Ummm, a little," Maria conceded uncertainly, "but you've got my point. People who really give up *that* much of themselves to a religion are going to be, at least on some level, susceptible to others that profess their religion. That's how you got people like Bill Miller – they just show up, say they've done some research on the Bible or what-have-you, and tell people they're all gonna die and they should change how they live."

    Geddy tapped his feet a few times; if anything, it seemed he was itching to get an understanding of Maria's perspective. She wouldn't have imagined the words that came out of his mouth. "Now, I believe in God and all that, but I ain't stupid! What was this guy's game? Get the money?"

    "Not quite," Maria countered with a grin, "but power - was- involved. People went to their graves thinking the man had a point. He had control over lives – people thought he was able to see the future. That's power on a scale none of us could imagine, and he had it." Emmett and Geddy gave one another a measured look, then grinned a bit. Maria went on undaunted. "Some people thought if they prayed hard enough they could stop it – and if he came up and said, 'hey, you've just postponed Judgment Day because of what -I- told you to do?'" She laughed softly to herself. "That power just gets deeper. It's a two-way street, then; you've got the folks who are deluded into imagining doomsday is coming, and you've got a megalomaniac getting his mental rocks off by leading his herd off a cliff."

"So get the money, but mental," Geddy repeated; Emmett laughed softly, and the two men stood up almost at the same time. "I gotta get back to playin'," Geddy stated dryly. Maria rose in response.

Emmett extended his gloved hand. "Its always a pleasure, Geddy. I've missed you."

Geddy didn't take the hand; not at first. This elicited a scrutinizing gaze from the physicist and girlfriend alike. Jethro's eyes were in fact contemplative, as if deciding something of grave importance and having very little time to do just that. "Emmett, listen. A couple of us, we've wanted to get together for a while. They weren't sure if you were interested, and I'll tell 'em--"

The physicist was stone-faced. "Who?" Maria looked over toward the band; it was still setting up, and their movement was soothing in the face of this emerging crossfire.

"Well, Sari for one," Geddy replied.

Emmett's expression softened tremendously, as if there was some unseen pain fleeing the man's body. Dr. Montclaire had no difficulty detecting the diminishing depression in someone she was so deeply tied to. Whoever this Sari was, she'd had some significance to the two men's mutual past. "That..." he began contemplatively, "if she's better, I'd be really glad to see her." It wasn't long before Emmett's face grew a bit firmer. "But who else?"

"Just Jim Lowery, Em." Geddy clapped a hand on the scientist's shoulder reassuringly. "An' he's fine, too. Don't you worry none. He's doin' great."

The Physicist smiled a touch. "Sure. If Maria's interested, I'd love to meet up with them. What's the game plan for that?" The two looked to Maria, who's face spoke where words didn't – she was thrilled to see this outcome.

"Ain't much of one," the builder retorted, "I think Jim said he'd wanna do one of them Hibachi things. They've got fire, an' that's all I care about!" The big man giggled gleefully, "An I heard the food? Is supposed to be great. Its got a show and everythin', man! Its gonna be awesome."

Maria snickered softly. "I've seen them before, Jethro, and you won't be disappointed. Plenty of flames, indeed, and my boyfriend has been meaning to go to one."

Geddy gave Emmett a glance at that statement and shrugged. The two said their parting goodbyes and, as the musician marched to the stage, Emmett and Maria chose to call it a night. They hailed a cab and, after paying yet another excruciating fare, returned to the Marriott in one piece.

The couple's entry into the lobby was nothing special – it was late, and the pair had parked in the facility's rear lot. There was a door straight into the lobby, slipping past the pool, but it was locked; and it took Emmett a moment's worth of fumbling around to find his room key in order to gain access. Stepping inside, the duo immediately turned toward the elevator bank to their right. They went up, heading through the cliche'-carpeted hallway and back to room 602.

He swiped his card again, electrons promptly flowing over the card as connections were activated. They returned exactly the result that the computerized sensors in the locking mechanism were looking for, sending new waves of subatomic particles into two directions. The first flowed into a light and caused it to blink with a green hue; the second flowed into the locker's motors, enabling various gears and widgets to turn. A loud buzz escaped the machine's confines and the handle was released from its bonds, allowing the scientist to push it downward and open the door, itself. Emmett entered the room and found it, much to his non surprise, exactly as he'd left it.

Maria set her bag down and stepped into the bathroom. The door was left open as the shower turned on. A grin touched Emmett's face. When sleep was finally ready to claim them, they rested in the same bed and, as Maria dozed off with an arm draped over the physicist's chest, he resisted the descent of his thoughts back into the earlier conversation with Jethro. For a moment, he considered running; if not from Doctor Montclaire and his life at Catskill Community College, then from his promise to his old friend for a reunion. No matter how tightly the molecules of "Emmett" and "Maria" had been bound together, the inferno known as Connor Point - the incident that haunted him every night, no matter how content he was - seemed destined to tear those bonds apart.

Closing out the image of Sari sitting silently in her wheelchair, of what he'd done to Garrett, and the barely-audible whispers about the emission of radiation, Emmett managed to finally fall into a fitful sleep.

Chapter Three
Theories of Relativity

"Albert Einstein wasn't the only genius of his time," Emmett boldly declared before his Intro to Physics students. "He *was* so good, however, that even his mistakes turned out to be true. At least partially." He smiled as his students stared up at him, stumped; their puzzlement was precisely what he'd wanted to procure.

His return trip from New York City had been just as eventful as his journey down. Maria had been buried in her books, occasionally throwing Emmett a reference to some historical event that she was planning to include. Whereas she'd discussed the Millerites with Geddy, she broke out of seemingly nowhere the unfortunate case of Jonestown; the source of the infamous phrase, "Drink the kool-aid." It was an incident Emmett had been familiar with in more ways than she knew, and it only fueled his depressive thoughts on his way back to the mountains.

Now, however, he was once more in his metaphorical element; he was teaching! A smile was on his lips! The recollection of where he'd been earlier that week crept in only as his mind snaked its way toward the point they had all been waiting for. "We all know about his most famous equation, $E=MC^2$." He gestured toward the smart-board, wherein a picture of the super-genius pointing to his formula was projected. "Who wants to give us a little recap of that one?"

A hand shot up; it was the resident aquatics expert Brian Wilcox, ready after his last performance to take another dive in the name of science. "Go for it."

"Energy is equal to an object's mass times the speed of light, squared." There was an uncertainty in there somewhere, but the answer was functionally...

"Correct," Emmett said with a proud inflection. "And for us, that means a lot of things. First of all it means that objects themselves have energy." He touched the desk of the student before him, a girl named Kara Linka; she was a B student at best, but her desk was made of the same wood that everyone else's was made of. It was coated in a plastic-like substance, and Emmett's gloved hand brushed over the tightly-bound atomic structures without putting a dent in it.

"The desk before you, for example," he explained, "is made up of molecules that are, likewise, made up of atoms. Then there's all of those subatomic particles - all of this is in constant motion, even as the object before you stands still."

Kara looked upward toward her professor; "Motion is energy, right? Like, temperature?"

Perhaps, Emmett reconsidered, *B+*. "Absolutely! Temperature is a measure of energy! And all of the mass in the world has energy. And it means something for Luke Skywalker too! Lets see if anyone can guess," he hinted.

With some degree of predictability, Sonia Monterrey's hand rose after a moment of thought. Eisenberg gave her the go-ahead nod. "I see the speed of light and I think about Star Trek, first of all," she quipped to the class' slight amusement, "and second of all I know that light is as fast as it gets. The closer an object gets to that speed, the more mass it gains and the more energy it needs." This answer satisfied the professor; he barely bit back his own thoughts as she continued on! "Eventually the object can't go any faster because adding more engines just makes it bigger and slower, so it peaks out. That's why sci-fi writers invented warp drive and other loopholes; because it can't be done."

A grin. "Aha!" Emmett laughed softly, shaking his head to accompany his contradictory outburst, "there is in fact a working equation for a warp drive! Alcubierre was the guy who came up with it, Miguel Alcubierre." Hopeful looks struck some of the class, while the rest looked more confused than consoled - then again, this *was* a scientific monstrosity in the sense that it confirmed science fiction as a factual construct. Einstein didn't seem to be so bright in Emmett's eyes at the moment; what with his universal speed-limits and his relativity!

"Its a mathematical formula that establishes for, you could call it, a sort of contraction in space that would hypothetically pull a ship forward, while expanding the area behind it in order to effectively propel it." At the students' stunned silence, the professor shrugged indifferently. "The problem is, we don't have any idea how to turn even a quite sound equation like Alcubierre's into a physical object like that, yet. It would take anywhere from the energy of a few of our suns to, in some estimations, ten times that which can be seen in the universe today."

Some of the students seemed disappointed, now, and it was easy to guess why! There always had to be a buzz-kill to every rush; a drag-down, a party-pooper. "See, Einstein's theories hold in the idea that you'll still need bucket-loads of energy to create the different bubbles and fields that Alcubierre predicts. But in the abstract, well, the theory *is* sound. Its just beyond us. And that brings us back..." Emmett stepped backwards and pointed to the picture of Al once more. "...To E=MC^2. Just like there are speed limits on the road, there's ways around them - only its not as simple as just ignoring the big white signs telling you to *slow down!*" The class laughed weakly at the bad joke.

"Now," the physicist continued, "here's another trick; everyone knows that little formula and knows the term *Relativity*," Emmett portended ominously, leading his class to wonder exactly where their leader was going to go, "but its actually part of a theory called Special Relativity. In essence, this can be broken down into two points!" Emmett tapped the smart-board twice; first came a short slide reiterating the exact theory Einstein had evoked, and second came the points.

"Our first statement is that the laws of physics are the for all observers in what we call 'uniform motion' relative to one another. In other words," he summarized, "if we are all moving at the same speed, the laws of physics are the same for us. Where's the catch in that, guys? What jumps out at you as weird?"

Sonia again raised her hand; the physicist looked around, but as she was the only one volunteering his left hand reached out in her direction. She smirked. "You mentioned relative motion, and that tells me that if the motion *isn't* relative it will mean the two observers will see different things."

"Very good!" Emmett exclaimed. "At the risk of being called a nerd by your classmates, yeah; if someone is going very, very fast they might see the laws of physics as different when compared to a person standing still. That's a whole different, complicated mess; and as you can see we still have a second principle of Special Relativity! Someone want to read it for me? I'm tired of talking!"

After a confused moment, Kara volunteered to lead the class for a bit. She read the words fluidly, though her tone indicated she lacked a complete grasp of their consequences. "The speed of light in a vacuum is the same for all observers. It doesn't matter if they are moving, or if the source of the light is." She looked to the professor for confirmation.

"Bingo," he grinned, "and that's a *big* deal. It says that the speed of light in a vacuum doesn't ever change. It tells me that it stays constant - and that's what makes $E=MC^2$ such an unpleasant associate. It leaves you stuck at that speed unless you have either a way around the speed limit, like Alcubierre, or more than an infinite energy supply. So now that you know about how powerful Einstein's smallest formula is, lets look at something else he implies."

Another tap to the smart-board. "General relativity!" And he tapped it once more, advancing it forward. "Its a great deal more complicated than the special sort. In essence its a theory that explains how gravity works, how time works, and a bunch of other things; and the very first thing you need to know is that it *still* doesn't explain everything. It has particular trouble with quantum physics - when you're looking at the very, very small subatomic particles that compose the world."

The class nodded at this idea, though they were surprisingly silent for a moment. Emmett took this opportunity to stare at the wall and to remind himself of exactly *how* unpredictable the quantum states were. After all, observation - the only way to record data! - actually *altered* the closed system being observed; and this thought led Emmett to shed an internal tear for Schrodinger's Cat. The poor feline was trapped in a paradoxical state of both life or death, waiting until it's observation in order to find out, itself, which it was.

He blinked, then; the entire room was staring at him. "Essentially, Einstein predicts that space and time are tied together. It predicts that mass is the primary source of gravity - your black holes?" The students nodded. "That's part of how we know Einstein wasn't wrong. They have unbelievable gravity and can even alter one's perception of time. Light itself can't escape! Physically they're tiny - a mere singularity, as small as things can be! Their power doesn't come from size; just density!" At this, Emmett took a moment to look every student in the eye; there was a fundamental difference between size and density, and he wanted to confirm that he hadn't lost any of them at it.

Quickly satisfied with the lack of puzzled faces, he continued. "And one prediction it makes is that the universe is *growing*. And what's more, its growing fast. *And* Einstein himself didn't know what to make of this. There's a whole formula!" The physicist touched his screen again and a long string of numbers and symbols emerged. Mouths dropped to the floor at the alienesque symbols. "You can copy it down and investigate it if you'd like, but you don't need to know the details. This is still an intro class. Pay attention to the big points and you pass." Relief flooded the classroom and the professor continued to work his craft.

"The universe is supposed to be expanding, right? But Einstein himself didn't want to get on board with that concept; he added something called the 'Cosmological Constant' in order to balance the equation and make the universe stick together. He just smacked some numbers together to make his equation balance and damned the consequences of its source. Sounds fun, right? It was about as effective as sticking, what is it? Lipstick on a pig?" His reference to politics elicited many laughs from the history majors trapped in his class. "Well, he went on to call this his greatest mistake ever."

Emmett crossed the room, calmly gazing about. "So the deal is this; ya got Einstein debating Einstein and it doesn't take long for one of them to get proven wrong. Eventually, proof came along that the universe -was- getting bigger after all, and the constant was scrapped. Fifty years later, Einstein's 'mistake' is being proven to be accurate - just not in the way he intended. To wrap this lesson up," he said much to his students' relief, "there's actually some evidence that the universe is speeding up! Instead of being something that held the universe in a stationary form, the Cosmological Constant actually exists to push it apart."

With a glance to Sonia, he grinned at his students. "Now," he began, "for the writers in the room - you're wondering what's gonna come next! This expansion of the universe is a big enough problem, but when you're worrying about it getting bigger, faster? Oh yeah - that'll be interesting. See you next time!"

As the class began to file out, Emmett's eyes scanned across the room and found Kara Linka. A hand flashed out quickly and brushed effortlessly through the various molecules making up the air in front of her. She stopped, startled by the sudden gesture, and he smiled to capture her attention. "Kara," he began, "I just wanted to say I was impressed with you, today."

"Oh? Well, thanks," she remarked in reply, her feet angling inward and her arms folding across her chest. "See you around," she added, then began to wander away.

Refusing to stand in her way, he gazed next toward that familiar presence behind him. "So, Sonia, as always you're doing a great job for an intro student. Next semester, think about taking something more challenging; you might like it." For a moment, he thought back to the previous weekend where he'd worried about attempting to recruit the young English star; part of himself winced inwardly at the notion that he'd broken his previous inclination to avoid getting involved, but he quickly consoled that psychological aspect by making note of the girl's incredible potential as a *writer* of *science* as opposed to a simple scientist.

"I probably will, if *you're* the teacher!" The physicist blinked; his eyes found hers' for just an instant before he looked toward the wall. The innuendo was there, and he had to figure out a way - *quick!* - to deflect it.

He put on a broad grin, shifting his black, leather-bound journal around while packing his memory stick into its appropriate pocket within his laptop case. He offered the student a mere two individual laughs in a way that seemed just barely forced. "Oh?" A third, now; a third chuckle to seal the deal and he looked back toward her. "Mind if I ask why you say that?" It was supposed to interrupt her train of thought, to make her reconsider whatever was going on - and, if it was simply a misunderstanding, it would elicit surprise.

"Huh?" She blinked with a moment's worth of confusion, then batted her eyelashes swiftly. Emmett's genius plan fell apart as she expressed both surprise and seductive inclinations. "Well," she remarked in a drawn out tone, "you just explain things in such a nice way. Other teachers sound like they're talking at us, while you sound like you're talking to us, you know? Plus, you actually *know* what you're talking about! You've got a unique grasp of presenting the material."

Now, the physicist studied her intently. "What's that mean, exactly?" His mind began to race with her exact intentions; had she looked up his new papers? His *old* ones? It turns out the answer was far more simplistic than that.

"For starters, you knew *not* to try to detail every little bit of general relativity." Her words were innocuous enough. "Its a complete mess; I don't understand it one bit. Special relativity is easy by comparison. You figure it'd be the opposite!" she put forth a girlish giggle. "So you just focus on what's easy for us to understand and we get it. I like that in a professor!"

He could just hear it now; that is, hear the other things she liked in - or on - a professor. And he damn well knew the inner conflict that was about to brew. "Well, good. I'm glad I can reach you guys. Sometimes I think I'm alone up there, rambling on about stuff you youngin's don't really understand."

"Well, once in a while!" She giggled more; and she wasn't going away! Emmett slung his jacket over his shoulder, shut down his computer terminal, and gave her a nod. He looked away for a moment, started toward the door - and she hadn't left.

He gave her a smile, intending to try another angle; a much sharper one of rejection, that was. "I'm heading over to Hudson Hall, actually."

"Oh? I'm not up to anything right now, mind if I join you?"

His blood ran cold. He was headed to Hudson to make his usual rendezvous with Maria - and as innocent as this might seem to *her*, this wasn't going to go over well. Or would it? She might be useful! In fact, Maria would serve exactly as a control rod to the reactor that was the girl before him. He didn't need to have any more trouble with the young woman, and putting her face-to-face with his girlfriend might just--

His phone buzzed. "Excuse me, ahh, I have to take this," he said, pulling his phone from his pocket and looking at the number. He'd expected Maria, as she was probably already growing tired of waiting for him - and what he saw instead was the number for James Lowery.

"Your girlfriend?" Sonia asked teasingly. There was just a hint of anticipation in that voice.

Emmett couldn't lie; no matter how useful as a lie might be at the moment! He held the phone to his ear, not yet triggering the call. "No, an old friend of mine. I'll see you next week? No classes after today, right?" Nodding as an affirmation of his statement, the girl turned and walked away.

Emmett flipped open his phone and put it to his ear. "This is Emmett Eisenberg."

He'd expected a snarky tone to greet him; instead, he got a deep, feminine voice that most definitely did *not* sound like his friend. "Doctor Eisenberg, this is Katrina," came the slight hint of a Russian accent, "Please hold for Mister Lowery!" It was a secretary? Emmett was stunned; he frowned to himself as he listened to the phone click over toward a new speaker.

This voice was much more along the lines of what he expected, and the man on the other end of the phone could just as easily have been speaking through a time machine; it was a sly sounding speech, one always covered with the potential to be deceptive and one with just a speck of Irish heritage concealed within. "Dooooctor Eisenberg," began his old friend, his intentional drawing out of the man's first name serving only to control the pace of conversation - at least, that's how Emmett had always viewed it.

"Jim Lowery," he retorted in a neutrally pleasant tone; the foil to James' legendary kookiness. It was just like the old days. "Its been a long time. How are you?"

A soft chuckle came up in response. "I'm good, I'm good; and yerself, physics-boy?"

"I'm doing alright, actually," Emmett answered, "though I quite doubt that 'boy' is the appropriate term. Just calling to check up, I take it?"

Lowery let the line go silent for a moment, then he opened with a laugh. "Boy! Things really don't change with us, do they? Dead on, Emmett, dead on! Yes, I'm confirmin' that you'll be joined by Doctor Maria Montclaire at the *Konichi-Wa* Hibachi on Friday night, at 8:45 PM."

"Sure. Couldn't you have had your secretary make this call?" Emmett's warning shot was fired; and Jim, true to form, laughed it off like so much of a joke.

"I suppose," he confessed, "but I mostly jus' wanted t'hear yer voice for meself."

Emmett's smirk, at least, was invisible over the phone. "Why am I not surprised?"

"It sounds like y'have some doubts about comin'? I know Jethro felt the same way. Emmett, I promise that it'll be alright. 'S just me, me ladies, you an' yours, Geddy an' his, an' Sari."

Emmett looked at his fingers; he counted them up to five, then counted two more, then raised his pinky finger as an oddity. "Wait. These tables typically sit eight, right? I counted only seven."

"Y'mis-heard me, Physics-Boy. Check yer phone's acoustics - I said my ladies. Plural. I'm bringin' Katrina an' Lark. It adds up t'eight. If you weren'taken, I'd even suggest you give Lark's sister a look-see. Maybe I'll suggest it t'Sari."

Emmett laughed weakly; he knew that, to Jim, this was as good as coming out and telling the man his thoughts - and they were about their mutual friend and the trials they had all gone through together. "How *is* she, anyhow? I'm sure she's not looking for *that* kind of company," he said in an attempt to be funny.

While it remained that slippery little speech pattern, Jim's voice did cut down on the amount of cockiness that it had previously borne - the Irish lilt seemed a touch less pronounced. "I wouldn'be so sure, Doc. She's pretty interestin' these days. She sure talks a lot more'n the last time y'saw 'er."

At this, the physicist's face softened swiftly. If there had been one image that haunted him both during the waking hours as well as his dreams, it was the image of the young Hindu woman all but confined to her wheelchair, silent and hardly able to move. At the time it had inspired so much rage and despair - it had driven him so far from his center of balance that he was nothing more than a raw gamma ray burst gone wrong; or, perhaps less ominously, he'd fallen into being a rogue black hole drifting through the cosmos of Earth, heedlessly wrecking everything he'd come across.

"That's..." Emmett trailed off for a moment. "I can't wait to see you guys, honestly."

Jim didn't miss a beat, as if he knew exactly what Emmett planned to say from the exact pattern of his voice. "I'm glad t'hear it, Physics-Boy!" He chuckled softly as he chided the scientist, seemingly back to his old self. "So the *Konichi-Wa* at 8:45. Be prepared to take a cab, there'll be a lot'ta booze."

Emmett coughed. "I don't drink," he replied as casually as he could.

"Sure, Doc, keep tellin' yer girlfriend that," Lowery

retorted, as if he'd been inside of Emmett's head the whole time. "Jus' like I bet ya still wear those leather gloves. Mmmhm," he said in a mocking tone, "Dooooctor Eisenberg, y'haven't changed all tha' much, after all," Jim finished conclusively.

Emmett was quiet for a moment; when he spoke, his voice was more certain than he realized - and it wasn't a forced firmness in the least. "James, there's a lot that's changed in me. I bet you've changed, too, and I hope its for the best - I hope its like Sari and Geddy have."

"Well! Maybe Physics-Boy *has* grown up - a little!" Jim's grin was audible. "But, then again, I wonder if tha's just you havin' selfish hope tha' we *all* could change. Take care!"

And, before Emmett could even begin to demand an explanation of that charge, his friend was off the phone. Blinking twice, he looked up and found himself not just in front of Hudson Hall, but in front of Maria Montclaire as well. Her emerald eyes studied him up and down and, with a broad smile, she slipped her arms around his waist. His right hand pocketed his phone even as his left draped over her neck, allowing the weight of that limb to pull her in toward him as he leaned forward. A gentle kiss was all they spared before they both stood upright again.

"A tough conversation, love? You almost bumped into me," she chided, looking the physicist in the eye, scrutinizing almost as well as Jim might have been able to.

Emmett could see a entire, green cosmos within those orbs of hers. His eyes measured hers' as they started up toward her office. "Kind of. That was actually Jim, confirming that we'll make it on time."

"And?" The one word spoke volumes, compelling more explanation.

"He's very good at getting in peoples' heads, hun," Emmett confessed. At the look of surprise - and the visage of a protective girlfriend - on her face, he explained further; and quickly! "Not that he was picking on me," he continued, feeling stupid to even reference that train of thought, "but he was giving me a lot of things to think about."

The psychologist studied him for a while. Her gaze was like the sun at the equator - of Mercury, searing him into a tiny crisp as it exposed his soul to the cosmos. "Well," she finally broke the silence, "introspection isn't a bad thing! In fact, I told Doctor Marceau the same thing. He was beating himself up over his split with his wife."

"Marceau?" An image flashed into his head as neurons fired in his brain; the man's features were vaguely defined and blurry, as if he were intangible. He definitely had on a suit on all of the occasions he'd seen the gentleman around, but other than that he couldn't clearly remember a thing about him. "Isn't he the chair of your department?"

Maria smirked mischievously, reaching up and rubbing Emmett's head. His black strands of hair were easily tossed around, with a few of the grayer locks getting caught in his glasses and threatening to remove them from his face. He quickly reached up and secured them with one gloved hand, his other taking her palm and tickling it savagely. "Yes, dear," she answered, "things aren't going very well for him, and we just had a short conversation to try to cheer him up. I convinced him to try marriage counseling, so hopefully that can help."

Truthfully, Emmett didn't know the guy from Adam; however, he smiled warmly and let his voice fill with undue cheer. "Good!" he falsely celebrated the semi-stranger's potential fix to his love life, "I hope it works out for them." His arm slipped around her waist, pulling her closer; he was far more interested in how *she* was feeling, anyhow.

"So, Em," she began casually enough, "another train to NYC?"

He smiled in response. "Yes, dear, another train to NYC; we're set to check in to the same hotel, then we're going to head to the restaurant. That sound like a good plan to you, dear?"

"Of course, babe," Maria responded; she had just a hint of sadness in her tone. "Just one thing, I guess. This Sari girl you're seeing - she..." The psychologist trailed off, and Emmett knew exactly where this was heading. "She's not an ex-girlfriend of yours, right? I mean, I know you all worked together but that kind of thing..."

There were two reasons one could be defensive about such a question; the first was guilt in the face of a lie, while the second was offense at the suggestion. It was very hard to tell them apart, as both entailed nearly identical, involuntary responses to the same stimulus. Given the nature of his relationship with Sari, given the images in his mind of the girl's state after her time at Connor Point, all he could manage to do was shiver and exclaim, louder than he'd intended, "Never!" Maria shrunk back slightly. "No! Its...Its not that she isn't beautiful or anything in her own way, its just that I, uhh, its just not like that. It never could be, and it never was. I promise you."

Maria smiled slightly; and Emmett, ever the expert of the physical interactions matter, couldn't tell whether or not she believed him - or whether or not she had any particular disposition toward either reason for defensiveness. In the end, it didn't matter; she was once again on the train headed toward a night at the *Konichi-Wa* restaurant.

Chapter Four
Konichi-Wa Means Hello!

"Doctor Eisenberg? Doctor Montclaire?" The young girl's voice was gentle and welcoming; immediately reminding the scientist of the stereotypical portrayal of a Japanese school-girl fetishist. It wasn't that he had some kind of bias against them! But, between the flowing pink kimono and the perfectly-primped hair, Emmett couldn't help but imagine he'd stepped into an archaic brothel. Why precisely those two images clashed in his head was a matter for his subconscious to work out with itself, though he felt a pang of guilt within his inner depths for whatever strange things he must have seen to implant the idea in his memory.

Maria gazed between her boyfriend and the young girl and nodded. "Yes, that's us." Maria's voice was loud, but only as a response to the distant, yet echoing sound of pots, pans, spatulas, forks, and knives colliding with one another and with a metallic table - part of that performance bit that Geddy had helped sell the trip to his friends with.

She smiled invitingly, gesturing toward a seat in the waiting room. The receptionist's eyes were fixed on a computer terminal built into a waiting platform, one that was clearly intended to keep track of the myriad guests and their checks. "You are with Mister Lowery!" This was clearly a welcome thought. "He is a great fan of our place. Please, sit down; your party of six can be seated soon."

"Six?" Emmett blinked in surprise. "I'm sorry, miss, I think you mis-counted? We should have eight tonight." He was polite, but there was just an ever-so-faint amount of concern in his voice. This inspired Maria to turn toward him, but she refrained from speaking on it.

The girl looked at her screen again and shook her head. "No, I'm sorry. Mister and Missus Marx had to cancel their reservations. But, because you're with Mister Lowery, we've kept your private room reservation."

Emmett turned ever so slightly pale; Maria looked on with concern as the worries about being alone in a room with his old friend kicked in. He took a deep breath; *No, Emmett*, he thought, *you won't be alone. His secretaries wouldn't know, and he wouldn't be an idiot in front of Maria. It'll be fine*! He slowly sunk into a seat, his hand reaching up to carefully take Maria's and gently guide her down next to him on the long, yet comfortable bench.

She didn't resist; but she did lean in toward him and whisper softly, "Em, are you sure you're okay? You look worried."

It was at that moment that he took the opportunity to assess his beloved; her hair was starting to grow in, revealing naturally blonde roots that quickly grew into first pinkish, than light-red strands falling down over her face. She wore that hair in a dark-red bun - one vaguely reminiscent of the waitress', save that it was braided - and she matched this with a red vest over a similarly-shaded red slip dress. Her heels were as crimson as Dorothy's legendary slippers, and her green eyes were only sharpened by this contrast.

As Emmett fumbled for an answer, he could practically feel the door opening behind him; the hinges on the steel frame rubbed against one another and friction generated a tiny amount of heat as the gateway parted to the tune of footsteps - three sets, to be exact. Two of those sets were wearing high heels, as evidenced by the louder, more staccato taps on the floor. The third? It was accompanied by an all-too-familiar voice.

"Well! Its the doc! Doctor E! Eisenberg'imself!" James Lowery's slippery tone matched his appearance, though his Irish accent didn't; he had short, cropped blonde hair that was gelled backwards in tiny half-spike, half-string configurations. His eyes were a sharp blue hue that penetrated into anything they gazed upon with laser-like precision, and he wore an expensive-as-hell-looking blue suit over a white button-up dress shirt, covered by a blue tie. The man had once said that blue was the color that was best to wear when trying to influence people; and that's what Jim was outstanding at.

Emmett rose to his feet and extended his hand. Jim made a cursory attempt to place his atop the physicists, but Emmett would have none of it. This was a response both had clearly anticipated, for Jim grinned broadly and shook as equals. "I knew it! Th' man is still th'man! And what's this?" Jim gasped in mock surprise, his eyes on Maria. His hand reflexively extended; when the psychologist offered it, he kissed the back of it delicately. "Th' lovely Doctor Montclaire, in th' flesh. I've heard *so* much about'ya!"

Emmett resisted the urge to raise an eyebrow, and saw that Maria did it for him. To the best of their mutual knowledge, Emmett had never told James all that much at all about his girlfriend; to do so would have been inviting catastrophe, as Jim was nothing short of excellent at stealing that which didn't belong to him. Maria's confusion quickly melted away as James raised both of his arms. "This," he stated delicately as two women seemed to manifest out of nowhere and insert themselves under his limbs, "is Katrina, and this's Lark."

The woman on Jim's right hand was tall, brunette, and Russian all over. Easily six feet tall, Jim's arm wasn't so much around her as on her shoulder and tugging him upward. Her lips were pouty, her eyes were brown and she carried herself with just a hint of aggression to match her knockout physique.

Lark, on the left, was average in height, freckled, and had a strange meekness about her that made her seem momentarily docile; yet, her eyes held a fierceness that rivaled Katrina's. She was less endowed, but her hips had a subtle curve to them that made the woman virtually irresistible. She had naturally red hair, but she wasn't stereotypically pale; she had a hint of color about her.

"Its a pleasure to meet you," Maria remarked, looking

slowly toward Jim as she shook the hands of the two ladies. They responded with equal pleasantry, and Emmett shook hands with the two second.

After the introductions, James turned his attention toward the woman in the kimono. "Hitomi! Hi! 'S our booth ready?" His hand extended toward her; Emmett caught a flash of green concealed between his friend's thumb and his palm.

The girl extended her arms, took the hand and nodded softly. "Yes, Mister Lowery. Thank you so much for returning! Everything has been held for you as you requested. Please, follow me!" The girl swiftly grasped six menus - each wrapped in a thick, gold-painted binder - and began to march through the restaurant.

The quintet followed behind. Hitomi weaved and wavered through the tables; first, the more conventional wooden circles that were covered with red tablecloths. There were patrons eating what appeared to be a delicious combination of sushi and meats; the smell of the food assaulted the senses, only increasing one's appetite. It wasn't long before they reached the Hibachi tables; the restaurant had two whole rows of them, and as they slipped between the tightly-packed tables the group was assailed first by the loud clangs of one of the chefs who was beginning his routine. To his left, Emmett felt a sudden increase in temperature as another chef lit his cooking slab aflame.

Looking back toward their guide, Emmett winced internally as she nearly walked into a door! It was a wooden frame with what at least appeared to be paper covering it; she reacted quickly enough, however, sliding the door open with ease and entering into a surprisingly spacious booth that was, at least according to the plan, private. The centerpiece was the hibachi table, where their meal would be prepared specially for them in a performance of culinary excellence. The wall was decorated with paintings of samurai, dragons, and castles as well as a number of tapestries with sayings in Japanese.

Six plates, six chopsticks and six menus were laid out around the table. Emmett and Maria selected the position closest to the sliding doors, while Jim and his "assistants" slipped into the positions next to them. That left one slot open for their final guest, who would be arriving shortly.

Hitomi smiled and conjured from within her robes a small notepad. Her voice was high-pitched and chipper; "Would you like any drinks?" Maria, perhaps recalling her previous weekend with Geddy, ordered a Midori Sour. The ladies each ordered a glass of Plum Wine, while Jim ordered glass of high-end vodka as well as a lemon soda.

"So! Doctor Montclaire!" The quick speech of Jim Lowery emerged over the fray, "You're a psychologist, now? That must be interestin', ever do any work within the institutional system?"

A blonde eyebrow raised as Maria studied the man; that was to be expected, when such an unusual question was asked. "I've done studies and spent some time in them, yes. I've even visited them for work on my next book."

Jim leaned back in his seat, staring at the mental health professional as if she were insane. "A book? Get out!" He turned to Emmett, incredulous. "You didn't tell me you were datin' an author, Physics-Boy!" At this, Maria couldn't help but conceal a chuckle. "Tell me, shrink, what's the book about?"

Maria blushed; Emmett did as well, but while she was clearly flattered he was more frustrated. "Its on the co-occurrance of delusions and depression, and how fantasies influence peoples' mood."

The secretaries looked toward their boss; Jim, on the other hand, blinked stupidly for a moment before he leaned forward, hand cupping his chin and smiled. His face was completely calm, and if one was looking into his mood they'd instantly assess that he was intrigued - and nothing else. "Well, Doctor Montclaire, I don't suppose it'd help if I told you what I do for a living?"

"What -do- you do, now?" Emmett asked abruptly.

"I," James began, "am in the security business." Emmett's face found his palm. "I did some freelance work after Connor Point, actually; gave m'contacts a guarantee 'o success in exchange for their cash. The CIA figured some things out, but they only knew enough t'know I was the real deal."

Jim took a breath to continue, but Maria's voice interrupted him with disbelief in her voice. "The CIA?" she asked with dismay, "I'm sorry, but isn't it illegal to talk about any work with them?"

"Oh, no, not in th' abstract! I worked for the CIA. I didn't tell ya I broke int'a some facility, shot some guards, an' walked out with millions'a dollars worth o' information; I jus' told ya I worked for the CIA." Lowery's tone was one of complete and total dalliance - he might as well have said he walked on the moon! Yet, taken at face value, he also sounded surprisingly sincere; as if he truly believed he had worked for the CIA.

"Now I'm workin' corporate jobs. My company, Lowery Security Services," he produced a business card, "sells assessments an' counter-measures to the kind'a intrusion I can perform; to a limited extent anyway!" He winked over at Emmett. "I can't give away all m'secrets, now, can I?"

Emmett turned to Maria slowly and shrugged. "James is kind of what you'd call a Mentalist. He's a fast-talker. He can tell what you're thinking through your body language and the way you present yourself. Your tone of voice." Despite Emmett's seriousness, Maria seemed to be a skeptic.

"A'course," the slick one stated, "now that you've told 'er, it won't be quite as effective. She's a shrink!" Jim sounded half-dismissive and half-appreciative of the profession Maria'd chosen. "She'd be a tricky one t'read, no matter what. People like'er are very aware of their subconscious emotions, and cover'em up effectively."

Maria nodded her understanding, her eyes drifting over to Lowery. "So what you do, then, is you talk your way into a place? Trick people?"

"Most of the time, tha's the easy way in. Sometimes y'have to crawl through an air conditioning duct, an' sometimes its a bit more complicated. The point is, I--"

Maria held up a hand. "Wait wait wait." she halted him

mid-speech, her tone laced with disbelief, "Air-conditioning ducts? Like, in Die Hard?"

"Mmhm," James confirmed in his Irish lilt. "Exactly like that, yeah. I do whatever I need to t'find out what I need t'know. Now, though," he remarked idly, "I'm more interested in securin' businesses against intruders of my level. If y'can keep me out, you aren't gettin' compromised. 'Less your employees fuck up, o'course." The spy's voice was perfectly neutral; it was totally impossible to tell if he was lying or not. Maria clearly didn't believe him, but Emmett certainly seemed to!

The conversation might have continued, but Hitomi returned with a tray covered in filled glasses. Emmett and Maria were first to receive their drinks; they took them with softly issued thanks. Then came the ladies and their wine; and finally came Jim and his liquor. Emmett had expected a shot; at most, a double-shot. Instead, James received what he called a "pony-sized" glass filled to the brim with vodka. He sipped in a bit of his lemon soda then a touch of his vodka and smiled to himself as the two flavors intermingled.

"Jesus," Emmett stated with dismay as James tripled-down on his concoction, taking gulps out of both glasses in the same order, "are you going to be able to drink all of that?" The physicist removed his gloves for a moment as he idly crushed up a lemon and poured it into the water before him. They were then replaced.

Swishing the mixture around in his mouth, James grunted an unintelligible response as he shook his head. Swallowing, he exhaled softly. "Ah. No. Most emphatically no. At least," he trailed off with a grin, his head canting to the side slightly as his ear twitched ever so subtly, "I'll'ave some trouble gettin' it done. But we'll see how things go, t'night. Our last guest is approachin'."

The girls looked to James and giggled softly, but Maria simply turned toward the paper doorway. "I can't see a thing through this; how do you know?" After a few seconds, James' theory was surely borne out. He merely grinned as Maria waited, then turned and gazed at her boyfriend's friend smugly. "Mr. CIA, our guest isn't here yet, is she?"

Emmett, however, remained silent. James looked down toward an expensive, diamond-encrusted watch on his wrist then held up three fingers. Then, he dropped one to leave two up. Then, another. Then...

The doorway slid open and the booth grew a touch brighter. At first, it seemed like the private section had gotten some of the light from the main restaurant; but even as the door shut it was impossible to doubt that something had definitely gotten *lighter* in the place. Odds were that it had to do with the Hindu goddess standing among them; she wasn't particularly tall, only about five and a half feet, but she was slender and had legs that created an illusion of height to go with her perfectly sculpted hips. She wore a violet dress and a matching scarf that looked much like a traditional head covering, only she wore it around her neck and not her head. She did have a small pair of lines drawing into a U-shape on her forehead, the traditional *Tilaka* as worn by the Hindu Brahmin, or priestly caste; however she didn't carry herself as particularly haughty.

In fact, if Maria had to judge based solely on facial features, this gorgeous girl harbored serious self-doubts - that much was clearly evident in the sad, yet stunning brown eyes hanging just below that mark, while her full, luscious lips had the slight inroads of frown lines running into them. Other than these subtle characteristics, the woman looked younger than many of Maria's college students; far, far too young to have worked with Emmett and Jethro, and far too young to have happily suffered the accident that had happened at Connor Point. Her face was angled just right; not too sharply, making her look like a shark, but not so roundly as to give her a plump face.

"Sari!" exclaimed Jim, waving with a dumb, already-buzzed grin on his lips. While Maria had been watching the woman's entrance, James had downed at least two more gulps of his booze. Upon seeing the CIA-Wannabe, however, Sari brightened and smiled, the markings of her stress seeming to melt away. Then, the newcomer took a look at Maria's boyfriend and drew in a sharp gasp of air.

"Emmett!" She immediately charged the man, wrapping her arms around him as he fought to get up in order to hug her properly. After much to-do, he managed to stand upright and clasp his hands around the slender girl's back, patting it tightly.

His voice was choked; one hand was that of relief, and the other of sadness. "Oh, Sari! Sari! Its so good to see you again, and you look so..." Emmett trailed off, pulling back to look at her. He closed his eyes tightly. "I'm sorry, I don't have any right to say this, but you look great! I'm so glad you're better."

Sari licked her lips and spoke with a distinctly American intonation in her voice. In fact, though she had all of the vestments of a native of India, she seemed to only have the slightest of accents - as if she'd been raised in America her whole life. "Doctor Eisenberg, please, it isn't your fault and you know that." She reached out and touched his forehead; he relaxed, slightly. "You have tortured yourself for far too long. This *beautiful* woman here would not be next to you, otherwise."

Maria stared at the young Brahman and canted her head to the side, then rose to her feet and offered her hand. Sari took it with surprising firmness and shook it. "You must be Doctor Montclaire."

"That's me. You can call me Maria, if you want." She didn't sound suspicious, but she did seem a bit intrigued at something. Her next statement made clear she wasn't worried about her boyfriend being stolen away. "I'm sorry; I must confess, you're a lot younger than I imagined. I guess you're like Emmett was, a prodigy child."

Sari blinked a few times, then looked behind the psychologist. Emmett turned his eyes in that direction and confirmed what he'd suspected - Jim gave the Hindu a subtle shaking of his head, confirmation of what Emmett already knew and what their mutual friend had apparently decided to leave to chance. Sari smiled an acknowledgment of this fact, looking toward Emmett. "Yes," she began, "he and I were both rather advanced students. I am thirty two years old, a few years younger than Doctor Emmett is. I was in my residency when the, ah, accident happened."

"Oh." Maria sounded flattened; her tone sympathetic. "I understand." The paper doors slid open once more as Hitomi brought Sari a glass of water with a lemon in it. She proceeded to quickly take peoples' orders. Emmett took a steak and chicken combination, while Maria sacrificed the lives of many shrimp in exchange for that of a cow. Katrina and Lark, both women remaining eerily silent throughout the course of the conversation, each placed an order for chicken. Sari requested a pair of sushi rolls, and James? He effectively ordered the whole restaurant - he requested their surf-and-turf special, a combination of Filet Mignon and lobster tail.

"So, Sari! Tell Physics-Boy what y've been up t'!" James ingested another shot of his vodka, forgetting the lemon soda. His speech was impacted slightly, but it seemed that the booze hadn't quite hit him yet. "It'd be a blast t'hear how y've all been workin' on changin' the world!"

Sari moved to Jim and, after hugging both himself and his secretaries, took a seat at the far side of the table. She crossed her legs elegantly, her eyes measuring James for a moment before she looked toward Emmett. Her voice was soft and polite. "I have not done very much since we last met, Doctor Eisenberg. I recovered from my wounds by finding my center of faith once more, then I began to study medicines from around the world that incorporate my talents."

Emmett nodded slowly; he remembered those talents rather well. "Good!" He nodded his head. "I'm glad you've found some faith again, you needed it."

"Well, if you don't mind me asking," Maria interjected, "are you actually Hindu? A Buddhist?"

Sari seemed honestly stunned by this question - for a second. She let her shoulders rise and fall, but Lowery seemed more than content to interrupt the darker-skinned woman, as if speaking for her was somehow appropriate. "Sari 'ere ain't got a particular faith, really. She's a mish-mash o'everything plus a pinch o' secular humanism, or somethin' like that."

"Oh?" Maria trailed off, glaring at James with disappointment before she returned her gaze to the girl. "And, again, if this is hard please don't let me push you, but," Maria paused, letting the gravity of her introduction ring home. "What injuries did you experience at the facility you all worked at?"

Emmett looked at his girlfriend without surprise; he'd figured she'd eventually ask this grave question. Sari, on the other hand, blinked twice and looked to James. Jim didn't seem so quick to help her this time, so she took matters into her own hands. "I was traumatized by the stress, Doctor Montclaire. I am sure you have seen similar conditions in your practice. I was very much incapacitated at the time, but I am now so much better. I owe this recovery to my friends, as much as my faith, which, if I am to pin it down," she added, "coincides most forwardly with Hinduism."

Maria inclined her head deeply. "If I can help, if you just want someone to talk to, I can offer that." She sounded sincere, offering her therapeutic support.

"Thank you," Sari responded, "but I recovered long ago, and do not have lingering problems. However..." she trailed off, her eyes shifting to Emmett. "I wonder if you are the same?"

Emmett shrugged his shoulders indifferently, as if to put it off. "No," he answered frankly enough, "I'm not, really. I think about it a lot, about what happened to you and the rest of us."

"Speakin' of," Jim interrupted, earning himself a downright menacing glare from Sari, "I gotta ask this. We both kinda do, and it ain't easy, but I wanna know - Garrett. Why'dja do it?"

Maria slowly turned toward the physicist, who lifted his glass to his mouth and took a sip of the cool water. He caught a bit of crushed-up lemon in his lips, swallowing it down and exhaling slowly afterward.

"Doctor Eisenberg, it is alright," Sari offered with a true sadness in her voice. It was painful staring at the Hindu goddess' eyes at that particular moment. "What you tell us is up to you."

Emmett took another sip then calmly, carefully wiped his pink tiers clean of the moisture covering them with the thumb of his glove. "I did..." he trailed off, looking once more at the woman who had suffered such grievous injuries at Connor Point. "I did what I thought was right, back then. I had to do it." He knew what was coming next; a smart-ass remark from Jim, a statement of reassurance from Sari, and with a quick check he'd already confirmed the confused and concerned look from his girlfriend.

Just then, the door slid open and a savior wearing a white apron with golden trimmings stepped in. On his head rested a hat with a similar color scheme, and his belt was seemingly made of the precious metal - and he carried a knife on it. He was almost six feet tall and most likely in his thirties; he was also Asian. "Hello!" his heavily accented voice declared as he wheeled in a cart with a bonanza of items on it; two large containers, a number of small bowls, a series of squeeze-bottles, various utensils including a spatula and a two-pronged fork, and a second tier of the cart contained a large ice bin filled with meats and other fine foods.

He moved to the center of the table and bowed; then, he began to check orders. He started with Sari. "You wanted the Tuna and California rolls," he queried, turning to Lark after receiving confirmation. "You want Hibachi Chicken." He looked toward James afterward. "The lucky man wants the Surf and Turf." A soft barrage of chuckles. "How do you want the filet?"

"Almost rare," Jim responded with slurred speech; his vodka was halfway gone. "Just enough t'kill anythin' inside of it."

The chef nodded, then looked at Katrina. "You wish for the hibachi chicken," he asked; then he gazed at Maria. "For you the shrimp and chicken," he stated delicately and then, once the psychologist's order was confirmed, he pointed at Emmett. "And you have the cheeseburger."

Emmett raised his hand to protest; James nearly fell out of his chair with laughter. Instantly, it seemed, the man shook his head, leaving a confused physicist unsure of what exactly was going on. "No, no! Only kidding! You want the chicken and steak! How do you want me to cook it?"

Emmett visibly relaxed. "Medium, please," he stated with a sound of relief. The chef nodded and bent down, and the sound of a valve opening could be heard. He held his hand over the metal cooking surface, then looked up to a ventilation shaft and tested it with his fingertip to ensure there was an adequate exhaust. He dipped a rag into a container of water affixed to his cart, wringing it out to dispose of the excess moisture. The half-cook, half-performer then readied his spatula. Then...

He threw the rag into the air much like a pizza chef might fling raw dough! He caught it with the spatula and slowly guided it down to the table. A soft sizzle escaped as water was boiled away; the molecules grew distant before Emmett's eyes as bubbles turned to thin white steam. The chef applied pressure, the heat radiating through the cloth and into the wooden handle of the utensil. He swiftly, carefully cleaned the surface of the grill, every inch of it being cleared off; any debris was guided carefully toward a small indentation on the chef's side of the grill; from there, it was slid into a hole that presumably led to a garbage can.

Next came the inferno; the chef poured what looked like oil in a large circle on the grill. Then, he placed two dots at his side of the table and added a crescent on the patron's side - he created a smiley-face! He gave the man a single little strand of hair, then reached into his pocket and fished out a lighter. He sparked it twice, got a flame, and declared, "Watch out!" He touched it to the oil, and the flame quickly spread over the grill and went skyward. Emmett could see the chemical reactions taking place, could watch as the liquid was downright explosively oxidized and its vapors flew up into the ventilation ducts.

His attention was broken as metal collided with metal and the chef performed a quick percussion routine with a twist - his fork and his spatula flew into the air at different intervals. Once, he caught the spatula with his hand behind his back and, once, he spun the spatula with the fork itself. Emmett looked over toward

Jim, who applauded wildly. Maria, for her part, seemed entrapped in the show. Her hand slipped down toward Emmett's leg and he took it softly, cradling it with care.

With one final flip he stopped, then he took out a large bowl of rice and placed it on the table along with a series of vegetables; onions, broccoli, zucchini, carrots, mushrooms and bean sprouts. He began to flip the rice into the air, turning it over and ensuring all parts of it were heated by the hibachi table. Next, he formed it into a circle; and then used his spatula to cleave a small wedge out of the top. He'd created the image of a heart. He then pointed the spatula at Maria and Emmett. "Hope you stay like this," the heavily-accented chef spoke.

"Kind of like this..." He stuck the spatula underneath the compressed rice and lifted it slightly. "Beating heart! Of love!" He repeated this a number of times, then smiled warmly. "Hope you no have...!" Then, he flipped the spatula and, coming damn close to spraying rice all over the diner as he said, "Broken heart!" The entire table applauded except for the professors, who nestled their heads upon each-other as they watch.

The show continued; in the end, however, they were left with nothing short of a fine meal. Each received a pair of dipping sauces - ginger and mustard. Then, as they ate, Jim spun his chopsticks quickly and then pointed one end of them at Emmett. For a man who had imbibed about six drinks in less than an hour, James had incredible dexterity. "Its a damn shame Geddy couldn't'a been 'ere today, Physics-Boy. He would'a loved it. We'll'ave to do this again some time!"

Sari nodded her head and smiled; she was busy indulging in the seafood she'd ordered. Emmett looked at Maria, his mouth full, and grunted a response while giving his girlfriend a thumbs up. She patted the back of his hand and turned her eyes to Emmett's old friend, then answered, "Of course."

James took another bite, then looked toward Sari. "What do ya think?"

"I think..." She trailed off for a moment, perhaps startled to be asked anything. "I would certainly love to see you both tomorrow night, if that is possible?"

Emmett blinked his eyes, and exchanged gazes with his girlfriend. He swallowed the bite of ginger-covered steak. "Ummm..." He seemed confused; a sip of his chilly water was all he needed to right himself. "It sounds like you guys have something planned?"

"We're going t'the Wildcats concert tomorrow at the Midtown Ballroom. If y'want, y'should come." James held up a pair of tickets he conjured from seemingly thin air; the slender paper slips were wiggled delicately. "Its totally up t'you two, if y'can handle it."

Maria nodded warmly, reaching her hand out - she took the tickets from the spy and smirked. "I happen to love music, Jimmy. We're in."

"Are you?" Sari exclaimed happily, "I am so happy! This will be an excellent time!"

Emmett received his ticket from his girlfriend and slipped it in the front pocket of his jacket with one hand, while the other expertly swept up a chunk of steak. It was just about perfect on its own, and the sauces gave the meat an exquisite flavor; the ginger was sweet, the mustard was slightly spicy but not overwhelming. He looked over at James and gave him a thumbs-up. "I have to admit, Jim, this was a great idea."

Laughing softly, the spy raised his glass of sprite and took a swig. "Thanks, Physics-Boy. Y'know..." Suddenly growing dour, James looked over toward Sari ponderously. Upon her looking back at him puzzled, he turned to the professor. "I would be willing to offer y' a job, if you're interested. I could use someone with yer skills."

"What skills?" Maria interrupted, grinning broadly. "My boyfriend isn't so great at breaking and entering, and I really doubt he's ever had to *shoot* anyone before!"

Jim gazed at her for a moment, as if almost surprised she dared to speak up! Then, his eyes fell on Emmett's once again. "No, I'm serious. Emmett's a genius, and he 'as a gift that most people wouldn' understand with a decade's study. I could triple yer salary, Doctor Eisenberg. Y' do the math."

Emmett's silence - and the stunned expression on his face - was alien to most. Maria gazed at him in wonder, then quickly swept her hand in front of his view. The obstruction of light particles from his view didn't really seem to bother him, but it was the concoction of molecules that made up the air brushing over his nose, lips, and cheeks that caused his eyes to blink in a natural defense against the tiny torrent of wind created by the hand's passage. He turned and looked at her with surprise. "What's up, hun?"

"Well?" Maria asked, glaring at him as if seeking an explanation.

Emmett merely raised an eyebrow. "What are you --- oh." His face fell flat as James' question caught up to him. He began to grasp for an answer when Jim began to chuckle again.

"I suppose I can't blame you, Physics-Boy! That'd be too much like our old job, anyway!" He ran fingers through his hair, finishing his glass of vodka and chasting it with the rest of his sprite. The espionage expert leaned his head back, swallowed, and exhaled purposefully. Sari giggled delicately. "Ah! Can't beat a good drink!" he stated happily. "A good drink, a good meal, and good friends t' share it all with!"

He reached into his pocket just as Hitomi returned to the room. "And here's t' us all, a toast!" he said as he offered her his credit card as if she'd known all along the exact second she'd return. Emmett gazed at the man and wondered just how little he'd changed - and, paradoxically, just how much Sari had, as well.

Chapter Five
The Big Dummy

"Wow," uttered Emmett as he stared upward at the Midtown Ballroom. Located on a busy street and conveniently positioned right next to a large parking facility (pay-by-the-hour, naturally), the ballroom had extravagant architecture - sharp angles were accompanied by a series of gargoyles, making the dance hall *look* like an industrial-era structure, to be sure. Six large pillars adorned the facade, with a line for tickets wrapped around them.

Fortunately, he and Maria could bypass the line entirely. They walked right up to the doorman, and presented their tickets, ignoring the mass of people. "This place is huge," Emmett offered to his girlfriend. She nodded her agreement and the doorman - a muscular man with dark hair and tanned skin - smirked. He was Hispanic, with dark eyes and a name-tag that read 'Mark.'

"Damn right it is. Best place for a party this side of the Bowery and Webster Hall." He took the tickets, looked at them, then ran them through a scanner. The bar-codes on them each led to a chirp of satisfaction from the machines. "Yo. If you need to leave for *whatever* reason, make sure you get them re-scanned or you won't be allowed back in. If you want to drink you need a wrist-band."

"Thank you, Mark" Maria said as she slipped her arm under Emmett's and leaned on him. The physicist, stealing one from James' book, shook the man's hand for a price of five dollars.

The big man smiled; a gentle giant, perhaps. "Enjoy your show."

Emmett strolled in and glanced around - the place was currently sparse, with only one large crowd gathered around the bar. The stage was concealed by thick black curtains. Sizable, dark-colored couches and lounge chairs adorned the walls with tables, but there were no tables in the middle of the floor today. No, today they had set up barricades around those precious bits of furniture to make sure the revelers didn't inadvertently slam into those who were resting.

"Looks metal enough for you?" Emmett asked with a coy grin.

Maria responded by tugging on his hair flirtatiously, eliciting a yelp of surprise. "You of all people," she stated teasingly, "should know that I'm pretty hard-core when I need to be!"

He blushed slightly; she wriggled her eyebrows in amusement. The two staked out a couple chairs in the middle of the seating area. Emmett's phone buzzed and he looked down at it. "Ah, its Jim. He's with Sari and they're outside coming in now." His eyes darted toward the trickle of people coming in; they wore different kinds of shirts, many of them adorned with the band name 'Riki and the Wildcats.' Emmett stared at the name for a moment, then looked at his ticket and saw the same name. He rubbed his forehead.

"Are you okay, love?" Maria's hand cradled his face warmly, and she looked deeply into his eyes.

He smiled. "Yes, I'm fine. I just had a thought, that's all." His eyes didn't lie - he was alright, just deep in deliberations with himself. She nodded wordlessly, accepting his diagnostics as the two looked up to the door and saw Jim and Sari coming in on their own.

"Doctor Eisenberg!" the Hindu Goddess exclaimed, looking just as stunning as she had last night. The *Tilaka* hadn't changed, though today she wore purple robes. She opened her arms for a hug and Emmett provided the embrace. Then, she looked to Maria and reached out, pulling the psychologist into the lock. "Doctor Montclaire, oh! I am so happy you two decided to come tonight!"

"Agh!" Maria cried out as she was grappled, grinning at

it. "It wasn't anything, really."

"Dooooctor Eisenberg," James greeted him verbally, an outstretched hand matching.

The hand was taken and shaken. "Jim, hello."

"And Maria!" He took her hand once more and kissed it, looking her over swiftly. "That, my dear," he stated, "is a lovely shade o'blue you're wearin'. It's a perfect contrast t'the hair. My appreciation for your fashion sense is overwhelmin', very nice."

She blushed a bit, tugging Emmett closer to herself and smiling playfully. "You look good too, Jim." Emmett could just *feel* the threat James could have posed; if he'd wished.

"Oh! Doc! Geddy and his wife are comin' soon, they'll be in any minute." James' voice was relaxed; Maria raised an eyebrow, however, clearly suspicious of the spy's statement.

She raised a fingertip to her nose and scratched it idly. "Umm, Jim, aren't they not in town? Or busy? Whatever it was, that they weren't around last night?"

James looked at Emmett, then at Sari, then he shrugged. "They've already gotten back, probably, and're on their way here. Its cool, Doctor Montclaire. Trust me, it's cool." The Irish lilt of the espionage expert was convincing, but Maria didn't seem to be taking well to the tale. She glared at her boyfriend, who offered his own helpless rise and fall of his shoulders, then she looked back toward the door expectantly.

The crowd continued to trickle in, slowly becoming a downpour of new arrivals. Some staked out seats near the group, but they mostly managed to maintain their territorial independence in the face of the increasing influx of patrons. They were getting near to the show's start, and Jethro and Marge still hadn't arrived. A couple young couple, a duo of rockstar-wannabes who bore matching purple-tinted Mohawks, came over and asked if anyone was sitting immediately next to the party.

"Its about to start," Maria said with a look down at her watch, "are you still sure they're coming?" She eyed Jim up.

Emmett, surprisingly, answered. "They'll be here. Sorry, folks, these are taken." He looked over to a nearby wall, raising an eyebrow as he studied the pattern of people arriving. Just like any structure of independent bodies, crowds tended to have areas that were avoided and not even looked at for no ostensible reason. With a little observation, however, the structure quickly revealed itself - and, with a moment's effort, Emmett's eyes seized upon two chairs that were, as it appeared, conjured out of thin air. "There's two over there that might interest you," he drew their attention away from his party.

Sari stared grimly at Emmett for a moment, perhaps concerned about something. Her lips parted as she struggled to find the right words, then gestured to them. "Good find, doctor."

"Yeah," James said with a grin, a fingertip jabbing the physicist in the shoulder. "Good show, Physics-Boy, you've still got th' gift!"

Maria nodded to the pair as they moved over to claim the new chairs before someone got in the way. "Didn't even see 'em," she remarked, looking back at the other pair. "Hey. Are you okay, Sari?"

"Yes, thank you, Doctor," she answered politely, bowing her head to the shrink. Then, her eyes widened broadly. She was staring not at Maria, but at the space behind her.

"Sari? Oh! Hey, Geddy!" James extended his hand, eying the man up. The large Black man took the hand and shook it generously, then handed it off to a short, slender Black woman with mostly-gray, curly hair. As usual, Jim kissed the back of it. "Marge."

Geddy clapped her on the shoulder and pulled her close. "Jim, how you been? Sari! Hey hey!" He opened his arms for a hug; the young woman couldn't control herself and ran toward him, clasping her arms as far around his waist as she could. "Easy, there, Sari, easy."

"Its like a reunion!" the Brahman remarked, gesturing to Emmett and Maria. "We're all together again!"

Emmett stepped forward to greet his friend, but Geddy seemed unusually worried. "Hey. This is your wife, right? How are ya, big guy? Glad you could make it. What's..." he trailed off.

"He didn't tell you, did he? I can tell. You wouldn't be here if he told you." Jethro Marx's eyes looked at James for a moment. Then, he raised his hands in exasperation. "You big dummy! You gave him the tickets, didn't you?" Sari frowned, stepping away slowly and looking somewhat afraid. She practically shrank.

James stared his old comrade down and blinked a few times. "What tha hell d'ya mean, I didn" tell 'im? 'S Riki and the Wildcats, brotha'. Everyone knows 'em, these days! How'd you expect 'im not t'know?" The Irish lilt rose, now - and it had a subtle undercurrent of nervousness in it, a wholly foreign element to James Lowery.

Now it was time for Maria, who had already taken care of the pleasantries with Marge and had made a sincere effort to drift into a side conversation, to look at her confused boyfriend. Emerald eyes drifted toward Geddy's, and Geddy's in turn moved to Emmett. "What's so special about them?"

From the stage came the sound of a guitar strumming a chord. It was a low, melancholy tone, left to stand alone as if were a sound-check. In actuality, it was a call. The crowd responded, cheers rising up and reverberating against the ballroom's walls. Emmett's face drew a blank, then, going from confused to downright horrified. Maria blinked twice, the vibration of the string echoing through her very chest cavity. She immediately understood the perfection of the note, grasping without hesitation just how sad - and, much more subtly, tense - the sound was.

"Emmett, lets go." Jethro held out his hand to the physicist, and Maria cocked an eyebrow, staring at the strange offering. Even more disturbingly, Emmett lifted his palm as if seriously debating the issue.

Maria put her hands on her hips and stared at Emmett. "Hun, what is going on? Why are you all acting *very* weird? Weirder than usual," she muttered the last under her breath.

Suddenly, two notes heralded the start of a guitar riff. It

was a warm-up number, and fans began to cheer. It was a cautious bass-line, one that repeated over and over as the crowd began to scream, in tune, the simple name, "Riki!" From melancholy to excited, the slow burn grew louder and more energetic. A drum beat; a simplistic one, but one perfectly in tempo with the rhythm of the guitars served as a backbone to the tune.

Then it happened; the music disappeared even as the crowd clapped in tune with it, and all eyes were drawn immediately to the stage. As if by magic, there stood a gorgeous blonde woman no older than thirty years of age. She didn't quite out-do Sari in the beauty department, but she certainly came close. She was short, with slender hips and ample cleavage, and her eyes, piercing blue orbs framed by black highlights in her hairdo, were locked squarely on the pocket of the crowd where Emmett and his old colleagues stood. If Sari was a gentle beauty, she was a sharp one. Spotlights centralized on the female who wore a tight black corset, black stockings, knee-high boots and a barely-concealing-at-all frilly dress with slender garters left to hang down un-affixed.

Her voice echoed out alone over the reverberations of the instruments which, egged on by a simple cue - the outstretching of her left arm to the side of her body - cut off in the middle of a note if they happened to be in one. The silence would have been deafening, if not for the short, staccato words she expressed.

"There was a time,
Far back in the line,
When you were mine.

As memories fade,
The commitments we made,
Broke like cracked pavement in shade.

We tried to make the word burn,
For vengeance we all did yearn,

Yet only you failed to learn.

So, what, the feelings you had,
Drove you thoroughly mad,
And to betray us you were glad."

For a moment, Sari turned pale - and Maria wasn't far behind. She felt as if something was being torn from her chest as the soloist sang. She turned to her boyfriend - seeing his face locked upon the girl's - and tugged on his shirt. "Who is that?"

James answered briskly, in a strained voice. "Erica Hall."

Quick strokes of the guitar brought the entire band back into focus as the lead broke into a loud, sharp and swift solo, timed to interrupt the final verse of what seemed like a devastating introduction. "We need to go, Emmett! Now!" Again, Geddy extended his hand, shouting over the sound of the concert.

"Never before have I loved a man
With such an overarching master plan
Set without any regard for
Anyone
Other than himself."

A pair of quick strokes marked the arrival to the chorus, and the singer's rage and depression rippled through the concert hall and elicited shrieks from the crowd; fists pumped into the air twice with each strum. It seemed for a minute like Emmett might take the hand that the old construction worker had extended to him, though to what end was an unwrite-able story.

"But you broke me,
You ripped the love from my heart!
You crushed me,
A love doomed from the start,
You broke us,

You tore us to shreds,
With your violence...
I can't let this story end!"

Emmett lowered his gloved palm, staring at Geddy and shaking his head. He turned his eyes to the woman singing, glaring at her with an unusual determination. Her eyes met his for a moment, and they burned with an unparalleled fire. Sari practically nudged Maria out of the way, looking at her old friend pleadingly even as the song continued. "Please! No! You have to leave, this is just what she wants!"

"Who the fuck *is* that!?" Maria roared, drawing the group's eyes onto her.

Staring stone-faced at the stage, James Lowery issued the words nobody wanted to remember directly into Maria's ear, leaning toward her with uncanny balance as he whispered, "Erica Hall. She worked with us't Connor Point. She was Emmett's girlfriend. And..." he trailed off, Maria's green eyes locked in a death spiral upon Emmett's, and took a second to word things as best he could. "She blames 'im for i'tall."

It was almost impossible to blot out the music thumping, or to ignore the crowd-surfing and the jumping and the waving hands, but Maria managed to do so long enough to shove Emmett in the chest. "Why didn't you tell me!?"

Finally fixing his attention back to his girlfriend, he bit his bottom lip purposefully. "I'm sorry, Maria, I didn't know she'd be here." His voice was well overloaded with exhausted sorrow and he gazed up at the older Black man before him. "We can leave, Geddy, but we won't go out like that. We don't even have to wait until the show is over. We leave; and that's that." Jethro looked at James; the spy nodded, and Geddy shrugged his acquiescence.

"You damn well better, Emmett!" shouted the slender psychologist, fighting back tears. "And when we get to the hotel?" Maria left the question hanging expectantly.

Emmett picked it up effortlessly, well-enough seasoned to the situation. "We explain everything. Every little thing." His friends nodded meaningfully. "Is that fair, dear?"

Despite her expression clearly reflecting her disagreement with that statement, she eventually softened slightly and exhaled, slipping her arms around his waist and pressing her head to his chest. "Okay, Em. That's fair. You deserve that much. Lets go."

The group headed for the doorway, and sure enough they were the only ones heading there. They made it as far as the main gate of the Midtown Ballroom. The large Hispanic man who had taken their tickets, stood in their way.

"Excuse us, Mark?" Maria asked politely, if insistingly, as it allowed her to take charge of *something* in the face of this catastrophe. "We're going to leave now. Here's our tickets, we don't need a refund." Despite James looking as if he was quite annoyed he wouldn't be getting his money back, Maria's charge was sure to be successful. It wasn't at all unheard of for people who didn't like a concert to leave early, after all...

...So that's why the man folding his arms and shaking his head in refusal was unusual. At this, Sari closed her eyes and shook her head. Her voice was exhausted and sad. "Oh, no," she whispered ruefully, "its a trick, is it not?"

"Riki," the man said with a warm smile on - one that completely deceived onlookers to his devilish motives, "told me she would like to meet your group back-stage after the show. I can have Little Stevie here escort you, if you'd rather not stay for the performance?" The man gestured to a large, bald White man with tattoos on his muscular arms. Sure enough, his name-tag read "Little Stevie."

James cocked his head to the side, looking at Emmett with disbelief in his eyes. Calmly and without any sense of hesitation, he looked the large doorman square in the eyes. "An' did Erica tell y' what would happen if y'tried to stop us from leavin'?"

"Yes, she did. She said it would be a very big scene *you* know you don't want to go down," Stevie spat back daringly, as if encouraging a confrontation.

James gazed over to Emmett for a moment, brushing the bouncer's threat off with sheer amusement, and the physicist shrugged in response. Maria didn't seem to like this particular response, but the other doctor in the room seemed inclined to let this play out. "I guess they'd be right, Em. We don' want th'show ruined. We'll go back-stage now, an' we'll wait for Riki."

Mark nodded once, firmly. "Stevie will escort you, then. For what its worth, you're nice people, but Riki gets what she wants." He extended his hand, and in it was the green slip of paper that Emmett had given the door-man when they first met.

Taking the hand, shaking it, and receiving the return on his investment, the physicist merely sighed in preparation for their adventure back-stage. "That's what she says, anyway."

*****

The performers' lounge of the Midtown Ballroom was luxurious, albeit small; the walls were a soothing, deep violet color and the hint of tobacco (and other intoxicants) lingered in the room despite the presence of a number of incense burners that had clearly seen heavy use. There was a small clutch of leather couches, a mini-bar for refreshments, and a table with a bevy of sandwiches and chicken wings on it.

'Little Stevie' was a perfect gentlemen, inviting the six to take whatever seat they found comfortable and to help themselves to the refreshments that were available. Never one to pass up a deal, James broke for the bar. Pouring himself some Gray Goose, he looked over his shoulder at Emmett. "So! Physics-Boy! Want a drink? Y'might need it, if y' wanna do this."

"Water with a lemon, since you seem to be tending," Emmett replied casually. He took a seat on a small couch and slipped an arm around Maria. The psychologist seemed more than a little nervous; her anxieties were building up rapidly. "And Maria will have---"

He was cut off. "The same you're having, Jimmy," she responded in a meek voice, glaring up at Stevie. The bouncer didn't seem to notice.

"Sure, Emmett. Water." James' statement was sharp and

harsh, as if he didn't believe the scientist truly wanted to stay sober. He poured the drinks as requested, his eyes darting up to the larger man in the room. "Oy, Jethro! You wanna get us out o' this one, already?"

Geddy and his wife, the thus-far-quiet Marge, found a pair of reclining chairs. She sat next to him and slipped her hand upon his, while he kicked his feet back and reclined "Not really, no" he answered, "I say its up to Emmett to make the call on that one. Its his problem, its his ticket out to punch."

Maria raised a curious eyebrow at the engineer, then gazed at her boyfriend in amazement. "I told you, earlier" he retorted in a dry, emotionless tone, "We can not leave like that. We're going to deal with this head on. Its been a long time coming."

Sari whimpered softly and found a seat on the couch, gazing over at Geddy as if she wanted to force him to change his mind. Her orientation shifted toward James, then, and she folded her hands in her lap. "Mister Lowery, please," she pleaded almost pathetically, "make him change his mind."

"Tha's *her* bag, kiddo," James answered regretfully, handing Emmett and Maria their chosen drinks. "'T'in'nit mine, I'm afraid, and I don' have any leverage on 'er. We'll 'ave to deal with it th' way't comes, I'm 'fraid." He tilted his head back, refusing to even gaze upon a lemon soda to off-set the burning of the booze. "Speak'a the devil."

Maria's utter confusion was brought to a head as Stevie stepped to the side and the singer walked on through the door. She looked each and every person in the room over with disdain in her beautiful blue eyes, but it was when they fell upon Emmett that she brought her hand to her stomach slowly; a subconscious tell that caused James to wince visibly. She lowered the limb, gazing over to Jim with a sinister glare in her expression; she had the appearance of a corpse.

"Can you hear my heart beat, James Lowery?" she announced more than asked, "Do you feel how I do?"

Maria glared at the woman - her anger finally came to a boiling peak and she stood up, pointing at the shorter girl's chest.

"How *dare* you have us held here! This is illegal imprisonment, and we'll have your pretty little ass arrested."

Erica stared at the psychologist, and for some reason the half-vacant, half-enraged stare nearly brought Maria to her knees. Then, almost like a robot acquiring a target, she turned her head to Emmett. "So, she has no idea, does she." Once again, she made the question a statement.

The psychologist's face grew long. "Of what?" Maria asked weakly, exhaustion creeping through her body.

Sari looked up at the singer and issued yet another plea even as her eyes were filled with endearment. "Miss Hall, please. Stop this. You do not need to get revenge to be happy, you know that! You have been able to get by."

"I can't forget, Sari," she looked to the Brahman, and for just a moment a hint of emotion flashed behind the singer's own eyes - sadness. Pure, unbridled sadness. "I'm glad you're looking so well. You're talking. That, I'm happy for. But," she echoed Emmett's very language, "this has been a long time coming. It has to happen, and it will happen this way."

James walked over to the songstress, next, and he lowered his posture. He stared her dead in the eye, blank-face to blank-face; then, suddenly and just for a second, Jim smiled widely, flashing his teeth before resuming the blank face. It was a curiosity that cased Maria to screw her lip upward in dismay.

"What do you see?" the singer asked mockingly, "What do you smell? What do you hear?" Erica wasn't taunting him, as her fingertips reached up and caressed the skin over her carotid artery. She took her own pulse. "My heart is beating at a regular pace, perhaps slightly elevated. I'm sweating, but that won't give you much because I was just performing. My voice?" She shook her head. "The strain of singing so recently is too much for even you to hear through. That leaves my pupils - and you can see exactly what is coming, as the eyes are the window to the soul."

Licking his lips dryly, James reached behind himself and - with a few quick gulps in rapid succession - finished his alcohol right off. "She's determined. No two ways about it, folks, this is goin' down tonight. She already forced it on 'im," he said with a despondent look at Emmett, "I jus'hope you know what yer up to, Erica, because there's no goin' back on it." Sari couldn't fight back a tear in her eye.

"You don't *have* to do this, Riki," Jethro intervened, his hand softly running through his wife's hair. She had her eyes closed, as if half-asleep or at the very least trying to shut out the reality of what was going on. "We can still leave, and we can still walk away with our lives together."

High-heeled boots carried Erica to a chair directly across from Emmett, and she sat down daintily. She unzipped them and removed them, leaving stockinged feet spread apart as her legs folded over one another. In a way, she looked very much like the consummate businesswoman. In a way, she looked like a succubus preparing to seduce someone. In a way, she looked like a murderer just about to slay her prey. "Eisenberg, I'm the mistress of emotions. I can tell you how you *will* feel, let alone telling you what you presently feel."

Maria blinked incredulously as Emmett nodded. "You are. So do it, already, if you haven't already. Do whatever you plan to do to us."

"They all had the same questions, you know. Even Marge - and I am so sorry, Marge, that you have to be here, for this," she added with a look to the elder, who didn't even begin to match the half-dead gaze of the singer. "But even you surely wonder about the truth. I would not be surprised if they all asked it, Emmett Eisenberg, in the backs of their minds. Why did you do it?"

Maria whispered softly to her boyfriend, staring into his eyes and seeing a strange determination that she had never quite viewed before. "Do what?" It seemed for a moment as if he became a breathing corpse, as his eyes drifted elsewhere.

"Say it, Erica," Emmett retorted vacantly, as if he was compelled by a force outside of his own mind. "Be clear. Why did I do *what*?"

She scrutinized him, her eyes boring into his like a drill tears into the first chunk of a bed-frame. "Why did you kill

Garrett?"

Maria gasped and retreated from the physicist. "Kill?" Sure, James had asked about Garrett before - but never had he implied that her boyfriend had done something that terrible! That unforgivable!

"I did what I thought was right at the time, Erica." It was a voice suddenly laced with pain, but a voice that was honest. Maria closed her eyes and began to rationalize, swallowing the saliva in her mouth in a stereotypically loud gulp. They worked at a nuclear facility together, there was an accident; the man must have had...

"I get it. It was radiation poisoning," Maria blurted out; Erica turned to her, glaring at her fiercely for a fleeting moment of weakness. No longer was she emotionless - she was infuriated! And this caused Maria to nod slowly. "During the accident, he must have gotten poisoned. It was a mercy killing, to keep him from the pain!" The group looked at her, now, but she couldn't see the disbelief in their eyes. "Emmett..." She looked at him.

Erica began to laugh then; it was a cold, alien and half-human guffaw born of pure sadism. "She really loves you, Emmett! Just like *we* did, isn't that right?" she asked nobody in particular, for nobody answered as her hand rubbed her stomach. "Lets make a deal, Emmett. I tell you if you tell me - we used to play that game, together, didn't we?" Maria's face grew beat red. "You tell me. No! You tell *her!*" she pointed at Maria accusingly, a sudden flare of hatred in spite of Erica's otherwise calm demeanor.

"Miss Hall! Please!" Sari pleaded. James just filled his glass up and took another drink, and Geddy and Marge merely hugged each other with deep care. Even Stevie looked like he was having second thoughts about imprisoning these people. "Think about what you are doing, what you're risking. If you make this happen, if you torture him with this, if you tell him, we know too well what may happen!"

Erica gazed at Sari. "It has to happen, Sari. This is for his own good, for all of ours. Emmett Eisenberg!" she charged him;

his eyes widened as he felt himself unable to come up with any lies or even any reasons against confessing. He didn't even want to. "What really happened ten years ago, at Connor Point?"

Chapter Six
Unpleasant Memories

The alarm bells were ringing incessantly, and the sound of the steel blast doors breaking joined in to create an unbearable cacophony of noise that none could hear themselves think over. The gateway between the reactor chamber and the outside world groaned under the stress it was under, as mechanical women screeched over and over again, "Blast Door Breach, Blast Door Breach. Level Three Emergency, Level Three Emergency. Blast Door Breach..."

Finally the portal collapsed, the heavy steel seeming to disappear into thin air. A loud Irish lilt exclaimed, "W'need t' cut this shit out, now! Get on it!" The first man through was a muscular blonde figure adorned with multiple bruises and lacerations, and he stumbled into the reactor chamber looking like he'd just come from a horror-show. His face was sliced wide open, from the chin to the forehead, and blood poured from the wound into his left eye, obscuring his sight.

"I...I couldn't stop them!" the man exclaimed, fingertips pressing up against a second barrier between the intruders and the reactor's core control panel. With the door collapsed, the sound of stone being pulverized was clearly audible, accompanied by subtle tremors as various layers of the ground were punctured. "Its up to you, now. I will hold them as long as I can!" His voice was hardly audible over the whining alarms.

The intruders, as they were, stormed into the room. They were led by none other than the Irishman, James Lowery; only he carried in his left hand a bowie knife and wore a jacket that read "Connor Point: Omega Security Chief Lowery." A name tag, embroidered with bar codes and thickened with an internal radio chip, as well as a small black slip of radiation detecting material, repeated this sentiment. He was no older than twenty five, and he spun that knife around between his fingers in a superhuman blur. "Its over, gentlemen," he stated plainly. "Give it up. We're all friends, yeah?" He sounded welcoming, but there was an overwhelming undercurrent of tension in his voice. "Lets solve this thing together, lets not go through wit'this."

"What? Through assassination?" The wounded blonde issued back, blood spraying from his lips as it caught the wind of his words. The sound of drilling was overwhelming, and combined with the alarms the people in the room had to scream to be heard clearly. "Through single murders that don't make up for anything they've done to us? We need to break the cycle!"

The next one to enter the room, covered in sweat and looking more than his share of tired, was a tall Black man who was a little bit chubby but equally muscular. His ID tag remarked that he was "Connor Point: Omega Engineer Jethro Marx", *and he flexed his fingertips. "Garrett, you done went off the rails. Whatever we do, man, we do for a reason - this don't got no reason. It needs to stop."*

Bringing up the rear was a slender, blonde beauty. The woman also carried an ID tag, one that read "Connor Point: Omega Psychologist Erica Hall." *She brought up the rear because she was willingly burdened by the duty of pushing a wheelchair along; a wheelchair bearing a hospital-gown wearing girl no older than twelve years old. It was dark-skinned girl with a golden* Tilaka *engraved in her forehead, one who was half-slumped in her seat and staring blankly into space.*

"Please," the blonde shouted, imploring those already in the room to see reason; or, at least, the ones who had been in the room before her friends' unwelcome entry. "Stop it! Stop! We need to talk! That's all we need to do! We can just talk, and..." Then, her face grew thoroughly horrified. "No. No! Don't! Please! No!"

Garrett's face suddenly grew relaxed, as if accepting of the multiple wounds it had endured - and then, with no warning to those who didn't understand, the man's body broke down. It was as if he was suddenly crushed to death by the very air around him, and he was reduced to little more than a nauseating puddle of flesh. Erica grasped her shoulders and began to tremble, nearly losing all of the strength in her legs. "Oh god, oh god, oh god," she repeated, reaching for her face as if afraid she might lose her stomach. She rocked back and forth, a hand slowly drifting from her face to her belly. Jethro? He looked away, gazing at the wall before he closed his eyes, shaking his head.

Even James, the man with the blood-doused knife, winced. His accent was without control, as was the rage contained in his eyes. "Tha'was cold, man. What t'hell are y'thinkin'?! What th'fook are y'doing?! Drop th' god-damned wall before I break through it an'break your fookin' face!"

*"Impossible," came a half-muttered remark. The man's ID tag read simply enough, "*Connor Point: Omega Physicist Emmett Eisenberg.*" His gloved hands relaxed from their clenched position as he turned away from his friends, looking down the hole he'd dug. There was no equipment, but the sound of stone crackling echoed off of the walls of the reactor chamber. It was massive, leading down further than the eye could see. "For all of your balance and agility, you don't have the strength. None of you do. This is over - this world is over."*

James raised his knife and slammed it into the air six feet away from Emmett's body. Three times he swung; three times the man was rebuffed by nothing more than the wind, or so it seemed. "Damn! 'Is barrier is too strong. Emmett! What th'hell d'ya mean, over!? Y'just murdered Garrett! You've---"

"Murder?" Emmett looked over his shoulder, his dark hair just barely catching the corner of his eye. His tone was gentle as it had ever been, but it was devoid of any clear feelings. "You're one to talk, James. Three people, I believe, were shot or stabbed? You even made the news." It was true; a businessman's recent assassination was most certainly chalked up to the security chief, and not the patsy that had been arrested. At least the find of child pornography on the 'perpetrator's' computer had probably been legitimate. "And how about you, Jethro? Jumpers? I bet their fall was terrifying, especially since they

weren't at the top of a building the moment before the ground disappeared on them." Slowly, he even turned to the crying woman behind the wheelchair. "Even you, Erica. You kept it from me, too. And, you caused your victims to enter suicidal depressions, until they carried it out."

This inspired a loss of control in one of the four intruders. "You seen what they did!" Jethro roared back, raising his hands as a suddenly-appearing blue light began to shine from the place where James had tried to stab the air. The glow radiated across the room in small, tiny rings; ones that stretched across the width of the chamber and bounced off of the walls harmlessly. "They deserved it! They did this to her! We's just payin' them back! But this ain't the way, man!"

Emmett turned to face Geddy, stepping toward the glow and looking at it. "Insufficient. You're removing the barrier, true, but not as fast as I form it. Moreover, you aren't even correct about Sari." His reference to the limp, wordless girl in the wheelchair bought another wince from the security chief. "They didn't do this to her; we did it to her. We are part of this, Jethro. All of us - Humanity. That was the reason for it, so that's what must end. What happened to her cannot be allowed to happen again. That pain cannot be imposed on this universe any longer!"

James marched forward swung for the physicist's face; his hand broke as it hit the force-field, flecks of bone spewing across the room. He ignored the agony, clenching his teeth. "God fookin damn it, Emmett! Yer insane! Yes, what they did was wrong!" He shook his fractured fist, adjusting the bones even as he tried to scream reason to the man behind the bubble. "What're you gonna do, jus' collapse everythin'? Make it a fookin' black hole? Y'can't do that! Even you have limits, Physics-Boy! Just because y' can rearrange matter doesn't mean y' can pop a fookin' planet!"

Emmett folded his arms, sounding every bit the professor he would later become. "I cannot do it from the outside, true; but all I need to do is get to the inner layers. All I need to do is *transmute a few elements, and its over. Murdered Garrett? In six minutes it won't matter, he'd have died anyway. At least he died painlessly."*

"Geddy?" whispered the singer desperately, barely able to manage speech through the tears streaking down her face. Coherence was difficult; elegance, impossible. "Geddy, please. Get through it, please. You have to help me stop him."

The engineer looked at her incredulously. "No Erica! If I push that hard, it'll..." he watched as she shook her head, rocking in place and rapidly repeating her request. He sighed, surrendering to her demand. "...Okay. Fine. It has to be." Geddy's arms spread apart as if he was doing the breast stroke in a relaxing pool, and the blue light expanded from a speck to a sphere. Emmett, for his part, merely narrowed his eyes and turned around once more, looking at his friend.

"You're distracting me," he uttered in feigned disinterest to the intrusion. "And, there is radiation escaping. Alpha particles - nothing critical, yet, but it isn't going to be pleasant, either." Sure enough, the tags on everyone's ID badges were slowly starting to change color.

Geddy roared in defiance. "Fuck that, Eisenberg, I ain't your bitch! All I need t'do is give her a window!" The blue sphere of light continued to expand, but it was an inconsistent and tenuous growth that frequently threatened to recede.

"Emmett, give i'up!" James pounded on the force-field with his knife using his only stable hand. The other hung at his side uselessly, with blood dripping from it to form a pool on the floor.

His head lowered. When Emmett spoke next, he did so in a hushed whisper that was drowned ten times over in sadness. "I can't, Jim. I can't take it. I can't accept it. What they forced that child to do was wrong - way, way beyond the pale. We have these gifts for a reason; this is mine." He raised his head, looking forward into nothingness. His voice flattened once more. "Now, you're distracting me. The sooner you acquiesce, the sooner the pain ends."

The sphere nearly collapsed; it began to regain territory, but slowly. "Please, please, please, you need to know, he needs to know," whispered Erica, rubbing her stomach softly as she waited helplessly in the face of the two men's stand-off.

"Alright then," Geddy obliged, and with another shout of exhaustion he pressed his hands forward. The sphere became a ring. Suddenly, Emmett's shoulders slumped and he fell to his knees. The ring expanded immediately, dissolving the barrier. The grown physicist began to cry softly. Geddy walked up to the reactor core, ignoring the still-shouting alarms and closed his eyes. Suddenly the entire damned area of the facility disappeared, and dirt began to fill in the hole that Emmett had dug. The Incident at Connor Point was over.

*****

"...So that's it," Emmett Eisenberg stated ten years after the fact. "That's the truth, Maria." The flat, evenness of his tone made it clear he wasn't lying; the fact that Geddy and Marge sat there quietly and didn't deny any of the far-fetched facts was telling. Erica expressed no joy or satisfaction, and she looked as devoid of emotion as she had looked the minute she walked into the room.

The psychologist had tears streaming down her face, the cheeks of which were puffy and plumped with the red signs of stress. Everything she'd heard was so impossible to believe. "You...You...That can't be true, it doesn't make sense."

James had long ago finished his second glass of vodka and abandoned all pretension to level of class, taking a swig directly from the bottle. "He was a super-villain."

"You *all* were!" Maria cried out, rising to her feet. "You all murdered people! Left and right! You caused them to kill themselves, teleported them into the air, or just plain fucking *shot them!* How could you?! What possible reason could you have for that kind of behavior?!"

Emmett opened his mouth - he didn't get a syllable out,

because his response was downright predictable. "You did what you thought was right?! Huh?!" his girlfriend screamed toward him. She flung her half-full glass of vodka at the wall, leaving a nifty mark in the purple paint. "Right?! You have no god damned idea what right is, coming up with a bull-shit story like this one! Goodbye, Emmett!" She grabbed her purse and stormed for the door; Little Stevie didn't stand in her way, didn't even try to stop her. He merely stared at the physicist. Yet she never made it out of the room.

"So, Maria, does -he- know?" Erica issued challengingly. The psychologist stopped and stared at her boyfriend's former lover.

"Does he know *what?* You think I'd know? I don't know!" She very nearly stormed toward Erica, taking a step forward but quickly turning to face the door again. Her hands found her hips and she began to breathe rapidly. "I don't know anything and I don't know any of you! No, wait, I do! You're all fucking crazy!"

Suddenly a mouse-like whisper emerged from nowhere in particular. "He couldn't know, Miss Hall," Sari whispered delicately. "He doesn't understand why you hurt so much."

Erica stared at the man, cocking her head to the side with that ever-so-stoic expression on her face. "He couldn't," she answered with careful measure, "because he didn't ask. He didn't talk to me for ten years, Sari. Will you tell the coward? Or shall I?"

"Y-You may, Miss Hall, please," the girl whispered weakly, not in the least wanting this show-down to continue. Maria's impatience was overwhelming.

Erica nodded without any form of pleasure in her soul, it seemed; she merely looked into Emmett's eyes. "Radiation poisoning, Emmett. It wasn't enough to poison any healthy adults, but unborn children?" The physicist paled - his eyes reflected a mental struggle against the truth that was hanging down over his head like the Sword of Damacles, much as Erica's hand hovered over her belly. "Our unborn daughter? I miscarried, Emmett. And *you weren't there.*"

It was subtle, but James reached down to his ankle; to something hidden there as he kept his eyes on the scientist warily. Maria screamed in astonishment and bolted from the room without hesitation, but Emmett? He only grew very pale, tears forming in his eyes. His lips moved, but their trembling was too tremendous for him to speak. It seemed for a moment like he might break, but finally he closed his eyes.

"I'm sorry, Erica, I'm so, so sorry. I didn't...I couldn't handle it."

A female's voice spoke up, then. "Geddy tol' me," Marge offered with a strong Cajun accent, breaking the silence that she'd indulged in throughout the night, "that tha reason you weren't told was because they was afraid you'd snap."

Jethro held his wife closely, gazing at his old friend and nodding. "You was the most idealistic of us, Emmett. You couldn't take it, an' we knew it. We should have told you, but we was hopin' to keep it a secret. We was all dumb, we was all wrong."

"Yeah," James relaxed in his seat, then, no longer worried for the lives of those in the city, tonight. "Like y'said back at th' Point, we were all murderers. Even you, Erica," he remarked in the face of her refusal to look at him while he spoke.

Sari stood up, taking quick steps over to Emmett and wrapping her arms around him, hugging the man. "I was just a little girl, then. I was abused. I was a victim," she said as she seized the man's gloved hand and clenched it tightly, "but I never asked any of you to follow that path of revenge."

Erica stood up and walked over to Emmett. She looked down at him without any pity or emotions in her face whatsoever. "Your violence tore us to shreds," she quoted her earlier song, "and killed our child, Emmett. My revenge on you is the fact that you know what you destroyed, and its both of us knowing that you won't even have the balls to show some dignity and kill yourself for it - I won't let you.. Maria? She is just an unfortunate casualty of my plans. Like Garrett, of yours, and that

will only make your pain greater. Goodbye forever, Doctor
Eisenberg." Turning on her bare foot, she sat down long enough
to slip on a pair of high heels. She slung a bag over her shoulder
and walked out of the room, with the intention to never be seen
again written clearly in her stride as she shoved past the stunned
Little Stevie.

Emmett, for his part, only sat there; he was reassured by
the young girl whose suffering he'd gone mad over so many years
ago, her hand brushing over his shoulder warmly, and he was
swiftly joined by Geddy and Marge, each of whom hugged him
hard. James? He walked over and patted the physicist on the
back, then looked over at Stevie. There was a loose end in the
room; a silent, stunned loose end, and a loose end that required
tying - or cauterizing.

Slow, deliberate steps carried the slender Irishman over to
the much larger man. He looked the bouncer in the eye, and his
visage left no question that not only could he manage to take the
behemoth down in a physical fight, but he wouldn't even hesitate
to kill him. "Now then, Stevie, d'ya understand why Erica said
it'd create a scene we didn' want? Cuz she came six inches from
drivin' a human atomic bomb insane, y'dipshit, an' any one o'us
could kill ya wit'out a secon' thought - 'part from the man's wife
over there, o'course." He gestured to Geddy in the mass of mortal
depression. "A scene we didn' want? Only 'cuz it'd reveal
th'truth, an' that don't help us. So here's the deal - yer takin' a job
wit' me company, an' y'start tomorrow. Don't?"

A coy little smile touched his face as he reached up and
patted the bald man square on the head. "I don' teleport people. I
don' heal 'em. I don' change emotions, an' I don' re-arrange
matter. I jus have great balance an' supernatural senses, an' I can
use that alone t'kill ya fifty more ways than any'a the others. So!"
Defying his grim tone, he broke into a broad smile and clasped
the big man called Little Stevie on the shoulder. "You start
tomorrow, at sixty G's a year plus health care an' other bonuses.
Two weeks paid, plus twenty sick and some bereavement an'all
that jazz. No tryin' to fuck me secretaries, they're *mine*, but Lark

has a sister y'can make a move on if ya want. Sound good?
Here's me card. Lowery Security Services. 9:15 sharp."

   The big man didn't blink, and he didn't show an ounce of
fear in the face of the shorter, slender, well-dressed blonde
Irishman, but he *did* nod appreciatively and accepted the
proffered, thin tab of cardboard. "See you tomorrow, boss."

Chapter Seven
Just Another Madman's Monday

When he'd returned to the hotel he found that Maria had already left. A hand-scrawled message testified to that much, adding that she was going home and didn't want to see him again, not for a very long time if ever, at all. Emmett didn't dare leave the hotel room for fear of what any sort of stress might do to him - he instead poured coconut rum from the faucet, for after he was finished with it? It was more than a capable intoxicant.

After about two glasses, he managed to gather the strength to rummage through his luggage. He found his laptop case and nearly ripped it open, searching for a particular item. He found it quickly; a black, leather-bound journal with a tiny lock upon the fabric. He removed the leather glove from his fingertips and touched it; the fused metal of the locking mechanisms were adjusted on the molecular level and it parted for him. The glove was replaced and he opened it slowly. No dust had gathered on the bindings, and as he flipped the pages he remembered the various things written down within. They were rare, sometimes written half a year apart and focused solely on the more secretive aspects of his life. He'd kept it with him at virtually all times, just in case someone grew snoopy. *"Too late for that,"* he mused. Finally, he found a new page.

He reached for a pen, the kind that hotels provided to their guests (complete with logo, address, and phone number), and began to write. He began with the date, then moved in to the actual body of his entry into his rarely-used journal.

"It's been a long time since I gave in to temptation. It began innocently enough; the shifting of atoms from di-hydrogen monoxide to ethanol for personal pleasure, or the creation of sound-proofing so others couldn't overhear an important conversation. Then, it progressed to selfish agendas - making

chairs appear for people to sit in so they didn't have to bother me. Can it turn into more? I've never thought of it as an addiction.

I know my limitations have softened, though living flesh is beyond my control. I feel as though I could manifest a small star if I chose. Erica, oh Erica, her skills have improved too. She can influence an entire room and sing at the same time. I imagine Jethro, Sari, and James have all seen similar gains.

Maria knows, now. Maria knows, and I'm afraid I've lost her. She won't return my phone calls. I'll try to see her after classes on Monday, and I hope she understands by then. I didn't know the depth of what happened at Connor Point. I've read through my journal entries on the year after the incident and I wondered how I was able to write coherent English. I went all over the world seeking answers and inner peace. I guess I'm not the only one - but was I really so impossible to reach that I couldn't have been told, back then, what was going on?

Or did I just refuse to listen to reason, like I always did back then?

Whatever the case, its over now. The jig is up, and its time to answer the questions."

Setting the locks back upon the journal with a single flexing of his mind, he spun it around idly one time and slid it back into his bag. He looked to the rum and sighed, walking over to the mini-fridge and grasping a can of cola. He poured it into the liquor, stirring it up with a hotel-provided straw and taking a slow, long pull from the glass. He shivered at the burning sensation of the booze and relaxed into his seat.

It wasn't long before he found himself asleep; and not long after that, or so it felt, he woke up in the middle of Sunday afternoon to multiple voice-mails from his former co-workers at Connor Point asking how he was holding up. The only one who didn't call, predictably, was Erica - and he was glad for that little fact! He rubbed his head, half-wondering if the tingle he felt there was due to a hang-over or the emotional stress of the situation, as he went through the phone tree and punched in his identification number and listened to the recordings.

"Emmett, its Jim. I wanted t'see how you were, see if y'were holdin' up well 'nough. What happened last night was six shades'a fucked up, so if y'need someone t'talk to, I'm here any time. Katrina or Lark'll put y'through no matter what I'm up't, promise. Jus don't do what I did an' drink yerself into a stupor. I know y'don't wanna let that 'appen, but I know ya got'ta deal wit' it somehow."

The second message was from Jethro, and it was a vast contrast to the one from his sly friend. "Hey Emmett, its Geddy here. Me an' Marge wanted to apologize for everything that happened. I should'a grabbed you and taken you out before that woman could start her voo-doo. We all was responsible for what happened to you an' Maria, an' I hope you an' her get your problems worked out an' move on. I'm here for you, man. I'll look ya up soon."

His final message was indeed from a lady, though it wasn't exactly the lady he had in mind. "Doctor Eisenberg," Sari's slower, softer speech squeaked, "it is Sari here. I really hope you do not let Miss Hall's need for revenge destroy you This was a terrible tragedy. I know you have trouble with inflicting blame upon yourself for the things that happen around you. Do not punish yourself for her actions. She did not have to do what she did to you and Doctor Montclaire. I shall pray for the both of you."

He called each one back, starting with James, and left reassurances that he was, in fact, *not* dead due to alcohol overdose. Jethro's message had been much more reasonable in its concerns, and he responded by indicating that he didn't hold his friends accountable for the issue in the least. Lastly, there was Sari's message; and to her he simply apologized, perhaps ad-nauseum, for the way things had turned out and demonstrated his repeated appreciation for her help with the Erica situation.

Finished with letting his friends know he had gotten their best wishes, he took out his laptop and looked up the next MTA-North train back to the Catskills. He discovered that it was in about five minutes, and he was in no shape to make it. The next bit of work he did was to discover whether or not there was a second train; it was in two hours. Emmett smiled to himself weakly - at least there was a little bit of luck in the world!

After a relaxing, headache-dispersing shower he put on a fresh pair of leather gloves and re-donned his favored brown suit. Each button was swiftly fastened. His still-graying hair was touched up and combed into a slicked-back position. It took him a moment, but he was able to isolate a few new, bleached tendrils. Biologists imagined that it was a testosterone imbalance which caused the initial loss of color and, over time, the eventual loss of the colorless hair. Emmett didn't know - or particularly care. He imagined, perhaps as a defensive mechanism, that the chromatic shift resulted in a more wizened visage.

Next he slid on a pair of pants and fastened a belt around his waist, tucking his shirt in. A tie was affixed around his neck, with each tightening serving as a portent to just how badly this return trip could end up. His glasses were the last thing to be donned, and behind the safety of those lenses he quickly forgot the momentary spike of emotional instability he experienced from the pressure around his neck. He was ready to take care of business! And that business? It was the train to the Catskills!

*****

Maria had never answered any of the calls he'd left her, but he wandered his way through Catskill Community College's campus and made for Hudson Hall room 109, where Doctor Montclaire was scheduled to teach Introduction to Adolescent Psychology. He found the door to the room closed and he waited, standing about aimlessly for nearly fifteen minutes before the doorway opened and students began to filter out. One or two, he recognized; most he didn't, but once the flow slowed to a drip he gazed into the room and saw...

...Not a strawberry-haired woman at all. There was a dark-haired man there, instead; a substitute professor. Emmett frowned and slipped away, making his way toward the offices without (hopefully) being detected. Each footfall brought him closer to Maria's office, up a staircase and to that thin door in the small office. He knocked three times.

He received no answer, and knocked three more. Upon not getting an answer a second time, he turned and headed for the Psychology office itself. The receptionist there, a gentlemen who was sitting behind a name-plate of 'Lesley Robins,' didn't quite look like he belonged. Emmett's eyes didn't narrow but he took a moment to survey his surroundings - and they all checked out.

"Lesley?" he offered hesitantly, expecting that the man was merely a fill-in.

The man looked over his shoulder and nodded. "Yeah, that's me."

Parents had sick senses of humor, sometimes. "Hi. I'm Emmett Eisenberg, I work in the Physics department."

Again, the receptionist nodded; he smiled softly, professional as could be. "What can I do for you, professor?"

His posture shifted slightly, his eyes looked over toward a wall. "I was wondering if Doctor Maria Montclaire was in today? I was hoping to talk to her about a student we both have." The lie slipped from his lips effortlessly. It wasn't the most common request on the campus, but it wasn't entirely unusual either. College professors sometimes discussed the schoolwork of their pupils, but only when they had a clear reason to be concerned, such as a project the youth was working on, or a recommendation or other official proceeding. Lesley didn't seem to register any surprise. "Umm, no. She took a leave of absence, actually. I--"

"She what?" Emmett burst out in alarm, eliciting a raised eyebrow from the secretary.

"Ummm," Robins replied suspiciously, "I can leave her a message that you came by, if you'd like?"

The floorboards underneath the physicist's feet creaked, and he felt the metallic atoms of the nails holding the deceased organic wood (all conveniently concealed under a thin, artificial rug) strain as they bent to support the weight. Emmett's fingertips twitched instinctively; he was already agitated, and that twitch was all too close to becoming something more.

He turned to see that suit-wearing chairman psychologist, Dr. Marceau. The man was bald, in his late forties perhaps, and he sported a muscular neck that was likely accompanied by a rather well-developed build. Emmett nodded to the department head with what respect he could gather. "Good evening, Professor...Marceau, was it?"

The head of the Psychology department offered his hand; Emmett took and shook it. "Right, you are!" He had a heavy accent; French, to be sure, but perhaps from one of its old colonies, such as Algeria. "And you were Doctor Eisenberg, of the Physics branch of our school? Yes! I had expected you to come by. Please, step into my office."

Emmett frowned - Lesley smirked as if he expected the physicist was going to get a stern talking to, while the two professors made for the director's desk. Marceau sat down and gestured in the direction of his door. Emmett shut it compliantly and took a seat across from him, moving the chair ever so slightly forward to close the distance between the two men.

"I just want to say my piece," he opened dryly, "and that's all. I know you are close to Doctor Montclaire, Professor." The man's tone was stern, but with a certain level of compassion in it; as if he understood the circumstances on one level while disliking them on another. "I have never really made it my business to get in my employees' personal lives, but this is an exception. Whatever happened to you two has seriously hurt Maria's heart."

Emmett winced internally; and he must have shown some external signs, because Marceau leaned forward and folded his arms underneath himself for support. "She is on a leave of absence for however long she requires it. I can sympathize with your own feelings, and your closeness to her, but it does not escape me that she aches because of your actions. You," he stated rather firmly, "are to refrain from contacting her."

Some people thought they were good at reading others; body language was undoubtedly a good clue as to how someone would react, and if anyone could get an attitude right it would be a trained psychologist. Someone who specialized in the recognition and understanding of human thought patterns, feelings, emotions, and cognition would almost certainly know when to push an envelope and when to let it rest.

Marceau, however, had no way in hell of knowing what Emmett was capable of. Slowly, the scientist leaned forward and stated Marceau dead in the eye. "Or what?" he countered fearlessly. At Marceau's look of astonishment that someone would stand up to him, Emmett leaned back in his char. "Your best shot is to try to get me brought up on harassment charges, but the bottom line is that you aren't the person to make 'em."

"Doctor Eisenberg," he remarked with a frown, "this isn't a threat. It is a request, but a very serious one. Disrupting the harmony of this school is an offense that can lead to your dismissal. Do not pursue this, please. Your career is too promising to--"

Emmett laughed caustically. Marceau seemed annoyed. "What is so funny, professor?"

"Please," the physicist answered with what appeared to be undue boldness, "my career isn't what's in jeopardy here. I'll make you a deal - I'll forget we had this conversation, and you'll leave me the hell alone, understand?"

Marceau reddened substantially, and for a moment it seemed like he would start screaming at the scientist. It took only a moment, but he relaxed and leaned forward again. "Alright," the psychologist finally stated, sounding none too pleased about the way the discussion was concluding, "pursue things as you wish, and I will do the same."

"Deal," Emmett said, offering his hand indignantly. The department head raised his eyebrows and produced his own through a well-honed reaction. Emmett shook it, briefly, then strolled whimsically out of the office and out of Hudson Hall, his mind not registering a single face as he half-stormed toward the parking lot. He made it about half a building's length before he began to breathe more regularly. Searching briefly, he quickly isolated a bench and sat down upon the uncomfortable pine, closing his eyes. *"Deep breaths, Emmett. Get yourself together, because you're no good to anybody like this, like some power-addicted buffoon."*

He envisioned a water flow; envisioned a river flowing peacefully through a valley. That valley, despite his best wishes and attempts, was swiftly inundated by rain. The resulting influx of churning liquid was chaotic and tumultuous, its banks running over. He stepped into the frame of this mental picture, and his psychic self raised his hands. The water droplets were too small and random for him to effect, but the flood itself? With but a thought, he began to rapidly spread the molecules of di-hydrogen monoxide apart, instantly vaporizing the overflowing torrents and returning them to the air.

His eyes opened slowly and looked to the sky. It was a sunny enough day in the early hours of fall, and aside from a chilly breeze there was nothing that even threatened rain in the next few hours. Maria? She was the only thing generating a storm today, and that was merely an internal one. He had every reason to be upset, but he could have handled affairs differently, no? *"Surely,"* he contemplated internally, *"things will work out the way they're supposed to."*

"Doctor Eisenberg?" a soft, feminine voice pronounced nearby. It was a familiar tone; friendly, but not at all related to the storm in his mind. He gazed upward from his seat and took in the sight of Sonia Monterrey. Draped upon her form was a neat blue dress with a thin, dark blue sweater over her shoulders to ward off that cold. Her hair was tied back in a bun, making her look far older than he knew she was. She looked all too familiar to another particular blonde from ten years ago - and he had to fight the urge to look down upon seeing her.

"Hi, Miss Monterrey," the physicist answered with feigned warmth.

She didn't wait for an invitation; she sat down next to him and looked him over. "Call me Sonia. If I had to guess," she began innocently enough, "I'd say you're lost in thought about something. Have a rough weekend?" Emmett could only nod in the affirmative. "Pegged it!" she said with a half-jovial tone; the other half was layered with concern. "Was it more than rough?"

Was it ever. "Yeah, I guess you could say that. Its really alright, though," he brushed his concerns off, eager to change the topic. "How are your studies?"

"Great, actually," she said with an idle shrug. "Mid-terms are coming up sooner or later, but what can you do about it other than study and pass, and maybe snort some Adderall?"

This thoroughly common nightmare of college life was a welcome relief to the professor's face. Mid-terms *were* a trying time, and for many they were overwhelming, but in the face of Emmett's personal life it seemed perfectly trivial - and that generic disposition of a threat, when compared to the students' look-alike with the power to control her victims' emotions and sporting an overwhelming desire for revenge, was reassuring. In essence, it proved the world would carry on, which was something Emmett himself had once aimed to prevent.

"That sounds like it must be tough," he replied with a friendly look. She nodded, then began to wiggle her fingers. "Go on," he invited.

"Nuh-uh," she taunted teasingly, "you're not changing the subject. What happened this weekend? What has you so down? And *don't* say its nothing," she chided preemptively, "because I can tell you're sad."

He sighed and rubbed his forehead for a moment, looking down at the pavement. "You wouldn't believe me," he remarked accurately enough. At the dubious look he received, he ran his fingertips through his salt-and-pepper hair. "You really wouldn't understand, but to make a long story short?" He smirked darkly and looked at his left shoe. "My girlfriend met my ex," he explained plainly; at her horrified look, he continued, "and that's just the easiest bit of nonsense. A good time out with some old friends ended up with me spending the night alone and, well, you get the sense."

She looked at the spot between her feet, her knees coming

together in a defensive gesture. "I'm sorry," she finally said, looking up at him. "I guess we don't know that much about each other. I don't even know why you wear those gloves you have on."

Looking down at the brown leather, he grinned inwardly and added her to the list of people that *had* asked, as opposed to the ones who didn't. He looked her over indifferently. "I guess I'm just neurotic, I feel like I just want to have a barrier between myself and the world I interact with." It was the most honest answer he'd ever given, as he'd usually say that he felt kind of cold, or just simply enjoyed wearing them as a distinctive style. Rarely did he ever disclose the truth behind his defense mechanisms; and never, ever to a student. Clearly, he quickly reasoned out, he wasn't in his right mind.

"Why do you think you need one of them?" she asked gravely. "A barrier, I mean? Did the world hurt you, or did you hurt the world?"

He answered without hesitation, "Both," lifting his hands and looking over the thin leather. It was indeed brown, with brown stitching that held it together. There was an ever-so-thin layer of fur covering the inside, mostly intended to absorb any moisture that might manifest itself. It sported five fingers (he *was* human), with a wrist-covering that reached down into his suit-coat. He lowered his hands, offering her an innocent smile. "I guess you can say I've caused as many problems as I've solved, and I've had a lot thrown my way, as well."

"How? I mean," she asked politely, "you're a physics professor. Have you always been involved in schools, or..." She trailed off when she saw his intention to speak.

His voice was soft, like always, only now it sounded truly sad. "My research wasn't always great, and a lot of it was really painful to perform." At her disturbed look, he raised his hands wardingly. "Oh, no, I don't mean anything like *that*, like, you know, involving people! I stayed away from that madness!" He sounded more than happy with this dubious fact. "I did a lot of Trans-Uranic work, which is to say I worked on atomic substances that are heavier than Uranium."

"Huh," she stated confusedly; even an ace student like Sonia had to reach her limits at some point, and clearly Emmett found them. Sci-Fi focused on warp drives and laser guns, and far less on the minutiae of atomic structure and molecular physics.

"I guess you can just say that I've seen some of my research abused; at least the way I feel about it." He shook his head, effectively extending the sincere truth into the domain of Loki. "None of it could be weaponized, of course, but there's been some profiteering on the work I've done, the kind that shouldn't really exist for things that important to the future."

"Money makes progress, or so they say," Sonia replied with a shrug. Emmett sighed, and Sonia continued on. "Doctor Eisenberg, its true. Some of us hate to admit it, but Adam Smith had it right. The profit motive is pretty important. Greed is good, as long as its kept in check."

Emmett laughed, surprised that the clone of Erica Hall could make him feel that way. "That's the part of Smith's work people like to forget." He quickly grew dour, however, with his eyes blinking at just how depressing the conversation was; and just how much he was reminded of his time with the 'Mistress of Emotions'. "I never doubted that someone would make some money off that work, but I didn't like the way some of my co-workers handled the business end of things. I started off trying to save the world," he continued, returning to the realm of honesty once more. "But, I guess the way things turned out, I did a lot more harm to it than good."

Sonia reached out and took his gloved hands into her's; her fingernails were painted a bright blue, matching her eyes. "Doctor Eisenberg, you should never give up on trying to help out. Just because things went badly once doesn't mean you can't make them right a second time."

In his mind, he saw himself shaking hands with a man in a black suit; saw himself first arriving at Connor Point and walking through the various catacombs and construction sites on the 'grand tour.' He fell in love immediately with the various equipment and devices that were going to be at his disposal - not to mention his own skills! The promise was simple enough; human development. He was going to be part of a new revolution in science and technology that would save the human race! What was more, a woman who looked very much like the one in front of him took his hand in more than simple emotional comfort. The outcome, disturbingly, was something far more horrific, and a perversion of that initial fixture. Then, for just a moment, he started contemplating James' offer of employment. He sighed and shook his head clear of the very possibility, focusing again on the present.

"I've seen the way that an end can justify any means--" he remarked. It seemed clear he was interested in continuing his sentence. He never got the chance.

"Actually," his student Sonia intervened with a cocky smile on her lips, "That's kind of a poor translation of Machiavelli's work." Literature *was* her specialty, after all! The physicist recalled reading *The Prince* during his college days, but he couldn't for the life of him remember every nuance in the story. "His message was really more about just remembering your end-goals,"she concluded. At his confused look, her eyebrows raised. "But, do go on!" she invited hectically.

"Misinterpretation or not, its still true, here." His voice was grim. "The people I worked with started letting the ends justify the means, and my job went from performing cutting-edge research with unlimited positive potential to a total disaster, where everyone there was part of some large game that made no real sense to me. Now, I guess I'm paying the price for my optimism. It wasn't my goals that got met, so maybe that Italian you're talking about got my situation right." A gentle sigh escaped his lips as he shook his head. "Maybe his warning would have helped."

Sonia studied him for a moment, then stood up and grabbed his hands, pulling him to his feet. The physicist very nearly fell over as he got up. "That's it!" she announced conclusively, "you need to get out! Lets have a bite to eat!"

"Um, what?" Emmett managed to blather out, raising an eyebrow. "I'm not really--"

"No, and no. You aren't getting out of this. You need something to take your mind off of what happened, and that's that!" Her soft laughter threatened to echo across the grassy expanse of the campus and toward any of the nearby academic buildings. Emmett's eyes were understandably wide with surprise.

"Sonia, I don't think that's such a good idea," he began warily, backing away a step. He wasn't sure at the moment whether he was in the past, with Erica during those blissfully productive days and nights, or some distorted future where Erica was younger and he was somehow aged; one where he had met her so long after the disaster at Connor Point that it never had even happened. The present - the loss of Maria, the apparent death of his daughter at his hands, and the vacancy of his mental state - was hard to remain focused on.

She was quick to end his attempts to escape. "Doctor Eisenberg, please; its very simple, we go and get something to eat and call it a night. Simple, right?"

Exhaling softly in resignation, Emmett finally and fatefully nodded his agreement. "Good!" she declared warmly. She rummaged around in her sweater for a sheet of paper and a pen, then wrote down her information and slid it to her professor swiftly. He accepted and delicately folded it up. "I'll see you then!"

*****

Her choice of venue was nothing more convoluted (or costly) than a local chain restaurant. In the time between his ill-fated trip to the school and his arrival at the food joint, he'd done little more than re-read old physics journals and, where appropriate, make notations on the evolution of the field. It was part of an academic process that Emmett best described as 'studying progress as it catches up to me.' Simply put, theories from five years ago - let alone twenty-five - could either turn out to be bunk, be validated, or be dismissed only to re-emerge. Many an aspiring scientist had grasped an old, forgotten concept and given it a swift revision with newly unearthed data, obtained through the use of brand new machines, in order to come to new conclusions on their once denied validity.

Of course, Emmett's work never got proven false and only rarely got forgotten. He made it a habit to be right on the money, or close enough that he'd get some credit. Then again, Emmett had a rather unique view of the physical world, seeing as he interacted with it on a far more personal level than anyone alive - perhaps ever. He snapped himself out of his musings as the hostess looked up from an equally-obscure list of names and asked, in a polite but exhausted tone, "Hi, how can I help you?"

"Party of two," he stated, "the name'll be Eisenberg."

The woman frantically scribbled down the information, most likely misspelling his name, and reached into the podium she stood behind to procure a small, disc-like device with lights that briefly illuminated spastically as the mechanisms within turned a tiny turbine to create a vibration. She handed it to him and half-muttered, "It'll be about ten to twenty minutes."

He accepted the little machine and sat down on a rather uncomfortable bench, one with a nasty chunk of molding etching a mark into the flesh of his back, right below his neck. This was probably to make people want to get up and walk to the conveniently placed bar within eyes-hot of the waiting alcove. Fat chance; though Emmett quickly realized that the pain of the protrusion would keep him from drifting back into his daydreams. His fingertips tugged delicately at the wrist area of his gloves as he briefly contemplated changing the decor a bit; he decided against it due to the idea being a blatant abuse of power, instead contenting himself to grab and gaze over a menu briefly.

"*Huh. I'll be damned, this place actually serves steak,*" he mused, flipping through the whopping selection of five preparation styles; regular, spicy, cheesy, with onions and mushrooms, or on a roll. *"A steak-burger? I thought they called that a hamburger."* He smirked at his perceived wit, looking up from the menu and square into the captivating blue dress of his student.

Sonia's hair had been done up into a bun and she'd added a number of black highlights into the very tips of her blonde locks. It was a similarity that nearly caused Emmett to get nauseated, if not for the stark difference in the faces between the student and the cause of his current misery. The aforementioned azure garment began just above her cleavage and showed only enough to stimulate the imagination, and ran all the way down to just below her knees, where they met black stockings and short black heels. Emmett's eyes widened - she'd gained five years in appearance without aging a single day since he'd last seen her; and suddenly, for the first time his mind willed itself to recognize it, he wasn't just going out to eat - he was on a date. Moreover, it was one that he most definitely *wanted* to be on, resemblances to his past or not. He merely resolved himself to avoid, at all costs, asking her for her hairstyle's inspiration. Even if he wasn't in his past, he was certainly beyond his 'present.'

He stood and offered her his hand. She went to shake it and he, stealing a page from James' book, captured it between his palm and his thumb. He swiftly tugged it halfway to his lips, bending down the remainder of the distance and applying them upon the back of that dainty third second knuckle of her ring finger. He could tell by the way she stood up a touch straighter that she was probably blushing. "You look absolutely amazing, tonight," he offered both politely and genuinely.

"Wow. I wasn't sure I'd pulled the look off! And you always look that good, Doctor." Her voice was shaking, ever so slightly. The mild-mannered professor had never once approached anyone like that on school grounds, save for Maria; and how many knew that little fact?

He hesitated, her reference to his title calling his subconscious back to its kennel for just a moment. Clearly it listened, wagged its tail once while looking over its shoulder, then kept right on running away from him. He looked her in the eye, studying the galaxy of different pigments concealed within her iris. "Call me Emmett," the physicist quipped.

"Emmett Eisenberg," she echoed, crimson-colored lips leaving a second's silence replaced by a pleased pout. "A handsome name for a handsome man!"

He grinned slightly for two reasons: First, this only gave him more data to confirm his hypothesis about Sonia's intentions; and, secondly, he felt in the back of his mind the sudden approach of radio waves with every intention of setting off the chain reaction in his little remote-operated device that would tell them that, as Emmett stated, "Its time."

Sonia raised an eyebrow, then nodded as the beeper began to buzz. The pair returned to the hostess and were quickly guided to their seats. With a pressured pace, the woman ran down the day's specials - a soup Emmett couldn't care less about, some drinks he never intended to sample, and a deal on an appetizer platter that sounded none-too-appetizing. Emmett pulled out one chair and then moved to a second, earning a pleased smile from the other half of the table.

"So," Sonia opened, "we were talking about some things earlier and you were definitely upset. Your old work, I think?"

Emmett blinked; that's right! He *had* come awfully close to spilling a few beans, hadn't he? "Well," he began tentatively, "yeah. A lot of my old work was for the greater good and all of that, because science is our future and all of that jazz." The woman laughed gently. "And anyway, its like Oppenheimer and Einstein and their work on atomic physics. There's so much potential in that field, but it was all geared toward warfare because of the context it was discovered in."

The woman across from him sighed and let her head bob up and down understandingly. "I can imagine. What'd they say after Trinity? 'Now I have become death, destroyer of worlds?' It was from a Hindu text, I think?" At the look of appreciation from the professor's face, she continued. "It was a real shame. So you worked on a weapons program, then?"

"*Huh,*" he contemplated quickly, "*I never thought of it that way.*" His eyebrows furrowed and he shrugged. "Not *exactly*, no. But a lot of the physics I helped uncover have gotten really out of hand and they've been put into a bad light. I did a lot of Trans-Uranic work," he repeated; she nodded, "and either it ground to a halt or it's been used to dismiss other research."

"How?" Sonia asked; and Emmett found it rather hard to answer this question. After all, he was flat-out lying to the girl! It wasn't something he liked, and it wasn't something he was good at. In fact, with a conversation partner as perceptive as she was, there was every possibility she'd already figured this out - and widening the gulf between truth and fiction would only make matters worse.

He quickly conjured up a story, anyhow. "Well, I don't know if you've ever heard of Thorium?" When Sonia shook her head to the negative, he nodded; this gave him more room to manipulate his actual story, albeit slightly. "In theory, its an almost-entirely safe form of nuclear power, but its really underutilized. India is leading its development, to put it bluntly. Anyhow, one of the major reasons people are opposed to its continued development is that it can throw off Trans-Uranics, which are really hard to process and take a long, long time to decay."

Was all of this true? Did he care! It sold, and that's what mattered to him. "I see," Sonia responded. "Kind of like Machiavelli, after all. He got a bad rap as the guy who plotted the road map for tyrants, but he was truly just a Florentine trying to spread the word of the Republic long before it was the popular thing in Europe. *The Prince* was just satire that was taken too seriously by people."

"Like if people suggested Johnathan Swift *really* wanted us to eat children," Emmett added; both laughed, and before either realized it Sonia's hands had found Emmett's gloves. The physicist looked down and found this connection slightly alarming; and it typically led to just one request.

"Emmett," she began predictably enough; she didn't end it

that way. "What was your childhood like?"

Stunned, he recalled. *The older man looked much like* he *did today, though he had gray eyes and a rapidly receding hairline and was a good four inches taller than the physicist. The woman was a brunette; short and somewhat stocky, with dark eyes to meet her hair and a history of athletics etched into her frame. He could recall their disbelief when he told them, as a young raven-haired child, that he'd just-so-happened to* find *a gold coin buried a whopping foot and a half underground, one that could be dug up with his tiny, red, plastic shovel yet had escaped civilization during the neighborhood's development. Years later, he relived the man's eventual injury at the hands of a power-tool accident, and internally reeled in horror at the recollection of the infection that claimed his life spreading from severed fingers to his heart; his mother's passing had been far less horrific, death by a glioma-induced stroke in her sleep a year later.* Repression kicked in through his survival instincts.

"It was pretty normal," he lied once more, "my dad was a carpenter. My mom worked at a gym as an assistant secretary. I went to grade school and high school in Queens, New York, and I did my collegiate studies at MIT."

Sonia nodded softly. "Wow, I didn't ask for a job interview style answer, Emmett. Very professional!" she laughed and he followed her lead, seeing as there was little for him to say that would be honest, anyhow. Not that he particularly lied about his origins; whereas most men would embellish their pasts in the interest of fast access to a girl's pants, he played his down out of the interest of self-preservation as well as that of his friends.

"I mean, I'm a local girl from the Caramel area, you know?" she didn't sound particularly like she wanted to get into her own past, and Emmett quickly realized that this was perhaps the most logical and effective route he could have taken; not so much *playing* mysterious as actually just being blunt. Then, of course, he realized that he'd done pretty much the same thing only with a bit more detail. "I played volleyball a bit, and I took some fencing classes at a Y for a while. It was a good experience, but not quite my thing."

"Tell me about it," Emmett answered, "I was never that big of an athlete, either. I ran around with my friends when I was little, I passed gym class, and I never really tried to be a jock."

Sonia shrugged. "I didn't like getting changed for gym class, so I almost had to repeat it, once. It was lame."

With that, Emmett could agree.

*****

The quiet hybrid car approached a small apartment building made of brown brick, no more than three stories tall and containing, at best, no more than perhaps nine separate apartments. It was the sort of place that catered to university students with a little extra money to spend; a room of their own instead of a dorm, and a close proximity to the two great classrooms of the college lifestyle - academic buildings and bars.

As he shifted the car into park, he looked to the building and then to its inhabitant, his date. "Well, Sonia, this is the place, yeah?"

"Mmhm," she answered softly, looking the structure over for just a moment before pointing to a darkened window on the right-hand side of the building, one that was presumably on the second floor. "That's my writing studio. Want to come up? I'd really like to show you where I do all my work."

There it was; *the* invitation! He was being asked up to a college student's room for the first time since he was, in fact, a college student. Of course, now, he was a professor, and even still there was some little voice in his head suggesting that this was a terrible, terrible idea. It was quickly silenced. She hadn't had anything to drink nor, as far as he could tell, anything else to interfere with her conscious decision-making. She was an adult of legal consenting age. And, most of all, she was damn good looking. "Alright," he answered after an appropriately long gaze into her blue eyes, "lets head up."

He parked the eco-car on the side of the street and slipped

out, walking briskly to her door and opening it. She took his hand and he guided her up to the sidewalk, then up a short, wooden flight of steps into the main door. The interior of the apartment hallway was walled with wooden paneling and pictures of Catskill Community College hung throughout the building. Sonia opened the secondary door into the complex and started up a stairwell; Emmett followed, taking great care not to be seen. He'd already given himself over to something primal and dark, he figured - there was no sense in losing his job over it.

Unlocking a second door, Sonia stepped into a well-swept little kitchenette. There was a small stove, a combination refrigerator and freezer, a sink, a microwave and a toaster; one cabinet was open (Sonia quickly closed it) and it contained stainless steel pots and pans. Emmett cast his eyes straight ahead and saw a closed door with a cliched silhouette of a girl, distinguished as such by a triangular dress, that signified a restroom. To his right he saw a small, angled alcove with a closet that, as evidenced by an old television and an older couch, was Sonia's excuse for a living room.

As she led him inside, he saw that there was one further room within the area; that, he quickly surmised, was to be her main area to muse. Studio apartments weren't known for their luxury. They were known for quite the opposite, actually, but as she set her keys down on the kitchen counter and stepped through her living half-room into her bedroom, Emmett had to admit he was somewhat impressed. Hardwood floors gave way to a fairly substantial full-sized bed and two large dressers. There was a desk with a two-or-so-year-old computer resting on it, along with a large book-shelf covered in loose papers. A number of posters hung up in Sonia's room, scenes from movies she particularly liked - vivid, cinema-house grade, and concealed within glass frames.

"This is home," Sonia explained, her arms extending their full wingspan as she spun around the room to face him. "Away from home. What do you think?"

Emmett eyed the room over, his orbs resting on a poster of

a tall, proud-standing man in spandex who was looking off toward a setting sun as a cape billowed behind him. "You really are," he responded without any hint of an answer toward her question, "a fan of science-fiction."

She looked at the picture and nodded. "Saw it opening day. A really amazing film, really highlighting the moral choices people face when they give up their identities and become heroes." It was true, the man looking toward the future could just as easily have been a super-villain as a super-hero; he looked equal parts demonic and defensive. It hit home for the physicist.

"Yeah. Maria, she..." he trailed off, looking up toward her as if to seek approval; the last, absolute *last* thing he needed to do, now, was enter into a tirade about his girlfriend. "She studied this sort of thing. The man giving up his soul for the greater good," he remarked, trying to tie his lady into the conversation with his date.

She slinked up next to Emmett, gazing the poster over blankly as he did. She smiled a bit. "And what did Maria have to say about them?"

"She'd say that even the author of the comic book had unresolved issues dealing with power; that he was probably picked on as a kid." He turned to face her, hoping he hadn't offended. "I don't even know if I'd agree with that being the *entire* reason for a story, but she made a good argument for it. That's always what she was good at, getting in peoples' heads."

"Yeah," Sonia responded in kind, looking him over from head to toe. "Alan Moore didn't write his comics about kids being picked on, either way; he was much more influenced by politics and trying to make a point about them, although that's never the whole story for an author."

Emmett shrugged as indifference poured down his spine. "I wouldn't know, I've never read him, and I've never had much interest in the super-hero tale" he offered with perfectly calm fiction. Then, in spite of himself, he chuckled softly for a few seconds. "God, my life needs a sound-track." He sighed, then, and looked to the ground in resignation.

"Would today happen to be a song by The Police?" Sonia asked in a purposefully-delicate tone as she slipped her hand over his cheek. "Because then our sound-tracks might match up."

Emmett looked up, and she stole the opportunity along with any words he was planning to say when she stole his lips, as well.

*****

It was, as he recalled, a happy day. His fingertips danced through the air, and he weaved atoms into one another. A proton was removed, a neutron added, and a substance was ready for inspection. Satisfied with the outcome, he repeated the process en-masse, transforming ordinary air into a bar of metal - iron. Pure, unadulterated iron that he let rest upon the floor. From a bar, it became a brick; from a brick, a small sphere that began to grow in size, suspending itself just above the ground as it accumulated mass. Satisfied with its girth, he smirked and stuck up the thumb on his index finger.

The air around the sphere grew wavy and Emmett felt himself lose contact with the substance. Suddenly it began to emanate light, and a minute later it was gone. *Standing across from him was a slightly pudgy Black man with tufts of white hair covering his otherwise-balding ears, and a black mustache.*

"Done," Jethro Marx stated bluntly. Only then did Emmett seem to recall that he was in *a room; it was large and laced with cinder-blocks and lead-lining. It was the definition of non-descript, a secret place in a secret wing of a secret facility.*

A third man in the room, one wearing a black business suit and a red tie, nodded approvingly. His voice was friendly; too friendly. "Very good. And there it is."

Emmett ignored the conversation, turning his attention to a television screen. It was focused upon craggy, gray dust at a distance far exceeding any that Jethro had attempted to breach before. For this experiment, Emmett was just the source of ordinary, albeit extremely dense and pure iron; Geddy's job was the hard one; after little more than four seconds, a metallic sphere appeared on the TV screen.

"Congratulations, gentlemen, we've just---"

Alarms went off, screaming their direst warnings. "Blast Door Breach, Blast Door Breach. Level Three Emergency, Level Three Emergency. Blast Door Breach..."

Emmett looked up, eyes wide, and he saw the image of Erica Hall stepping up to him. She wasn't as he remembered her; she was a little older, now, wearing a familiar black dress and looking upon him with pitiless eyes.

"Hello, murderer," she accused.

He faltered. "I...What?"

"You killed her, Emmett. And your suffering has only just begun. Your violence," she condemned, "tore us to shreds. It tears you to shreds, still."

He stepped forward, his fists clenching as he felt the atoms around him begin to move more rapidly; the temperature was increasing. "I have no idea what you're talking about, Erica! Where's Geddy, where's..."

He blinked as a red-headed woman emerged from seemingly nowhere. She was maybe eight years Emmett's elder, just by looking at her, and she was quite beautiful in her own right. Oddly enough, however, she was also familiar to him; even more-so than Erica's dress, and then even more-so than Erica herself, now. His eyes widened as the strawberry-headed girl grasped his chin and pressed her lips to his. Then, suddenly, Erica was positioned to the left of him and within inches of his figure, in for the kill as they said, and his life flashed before his eyes even as the light bouncing off of the night grazed his pupils before he---

Was staring a hole through Sonia's eyelids, which began to flutter open as the alarm clock in her room began to buzz. He breathed a sigh of relief as his heart rate began to return to normal.

"Hmm?" she sighed as her eyes fluttered open.

"Nothing," he whispered in return, sliding his still-gloved

fingertips through his hair. She set her sights upon them for a moment, then smiled. "Is something on your mind?" he asked her.

"No, not really. I didn't expect the gloves, I guess, but it was still a good time." She grinned, her eyes half-open as she slowly rolled over toward the window and stretched. "It was great; y'know, there's a reason I like older men."

Strangely, this left Emmett unsure of how to feel. On one hand, it was a definite indicator of his prowess; on the other, however, it made him little more than a particular preference, perhaps even a peculiar fetish of the woman laying across the bed before him. As she sat up, he admired the curves of her spine as they flowed in line with her slender figure - and, instantly enough, he just couldn't bring himself to care.

"Well, I can't say I've ever been with a younger woman. I'm not really *that* old, either," he added with a casual laugh, standing up and sliding some undergarments over his form.

Sonia looked over her shoulder at him and nodded a bit. "Thirty-seven, thirty-nine tops I'd say."

"Two year range of error?" At her nod of agreement, he gave her a thumbs-up. "Close enough, then! I'm thirty-five. I'm gonna get ready and head out, if you don't mind?" His tone was casual and aloof as he gathered his things in anticipation of his departure. "We'll talk later, I promise."

The girl shrugged as if she didn't quite believe him. Emmett started off through her living room and into her bathroom. As he splashed water on his face, he gazed up into a mirror and fondled his chin softly. Stubble was growing, but he didn't have a razor to shave it - never mind the fact that he wouldn't have time before class, anyway. "Oh, fuck it," he muttered to himself and splashed his own face again.

When it was time, he turned on the shower. The hot water ran over his face and he found himself eyeballing his first major choice of the day - and of the post-coital situation he found himself in with his student: Did he use her shampoo, complete with her scents and soaps; or, did he simply trust that the water would eliminate the lingering smell of sex? He opted for the latter, letting the warm water run through his hair unaided. When he was finished, he simply turned the flow off and began the arduous process of drying off.

"Finished?" he heard Sonia's voice call over the sound of his hair ruffling in his hands.

"Just about!" the physicist answered calmly, looking at himself in the mirror one last time.

As soon as he opened the door a minute later he felt her grasp him by the hip and pull him close. Flesh brushed over flesh as her lips met his once more. He was paralyzed by the sudden aggression. Then, she leaned up and whispered delicately, "See you in class, Professor," before she delivered a good, hard swat to his rear and sent him on his way.

Chapter Eight
Time Dilation

His footfalls brought him toward DuBois Hall once again, with his Introduction to Physics class next on his agenda. He looked forward to it with a mixture of optimism and anxiety; Sonia was there, for better or worse, and he had made no actual resolution to his problems. Instead, he'd only deepened them. Now he was officially a cheater, even if his relationship only officially existed because it hadn't officially been called off. Maria's lack of an answer to her phone might be interpreted as just that, but it wasn't iron-clad. *"Women are like that,"* he mused. If she returned and then discovered last night's actions, well, chances are she would *make* it iron-clad and blame him for the affair. *"Worse,"* spoke a devilish voice in the back of his mind, one he could identify as his egocentric nature, *"she could out you to the college and cost you your cushy job."*

It wasn't as if Emmett hadn't been jobless before. While he'd never had trouble providing himself with furniture and other material resources, official currency had the nasty little problem of serial numbers; counterfeiting was a risky proposition even under the best of circumstances. Furthermore, while hard metals were a nifty thing to be able to conjure up, there's only so much gold and silver that a man could have in his possession at any given time, and it wasn't exactly a widely-accepted medium of transaction in the 21st century United States. Getting through college had required some clever applications of the term "garage sale," but Emmett eventually raised the funds to avoid substantial debts; then came his time at Connor Point, when money was of no concern.

These days, however, the money flow only held steady as long as he had his job. Teaching was fun, and it just went from "fun" to "lots of fun." Now, he needed to make sure he wasn't going to be in trouble for that fun. Sonia was equally threatening, in fact! How could he not have seen this? *"Calm yourself,*

Emmett," he rationalized; she hadn't threatened him, and had in fact been more than cordial after their exchange. Was blackmail a possibility? *"Anything,"* he rationalized, *"is a possibility."*

As he entered the classroom he saw three of his students discussing the latest intramural flag football match at CCC. Apparently they all played together, and from what he overheard they could use a new receiver - one of theirs couldn't catch worth a damn, or so it seemed. Emmett didn't really understand, since he was abjectly miserable at sports. He smiled politely and went about setting his class-room up; he fumbled about in his shirt pocket for his USB drive and plugged it into the school's computer, then proceeded to quickly check out his lesson plan. It was all intact, as expected, and everything technical seemed willing to work.

With the touch of a button on the console, he activated the Smartboard and its companion projector, even as more students began to filter in. He'd begun to worry she might not join them, but Sonia, with many compliments for the newly-implanted highlights in her hair, sat down and relaxed in the front row. He smiled at her, and she at he - and then, much to his surprise, he found himself feeling genuinely alarmed when one of the sporty men in the back asked her to join them! She declined, however, and earned a sigh of relief from the deviant professor.

"So!" he began with a smile. "Class!" The room grew quiet, and the boys in the back stopped encouraging the girl to leave her post. It was all he could expect, as the demonic little voice in the back of his head remarked with self-satisfaction - he was, after all, in charge here! "I'm sure you've all been running late to something important before! Probably work, maybe to a doctor's appointment, or - I know this is a stretch, here - school." A soft chuckle from the students, all of whom had been late to some class at least once. "And I bet you'd all wished for something that could fix this little problem, some way to get more time, or to slow it down." He got some sympathetic nods. "The fact is, there *is* just such a thing in the world of physics. Its a little side effect of Einstein's $E=MC^2$ equation, actually, and we're going to talk about it today."

With the rap of a knuckle he brought up the familiar formula. "Its a little strange, but as you increase in speed - or mass, in fact! - you end up getting closer and closer to that upper universal speed limit. Anyone remember what that was?" Sonia raised her hand; when nobody else did, he called on her. "Miss Monterrey?"

"The speed of light, E...Professor Eisenberg," she corrected herself, quickly. He paled for just a moment, then - adjusting his glasses with his gloved hand - turned away before he could begin to blush. His phone buzzed, as if making its own thoughts clear about what was running through his own mind. He ignored it, despite its continued presence - whoever it was would just have to leave a message.

"Correct!" he announced, looking down for a moment. "So as you get faster and larger, you can't exactly go past the speed of light. But! Imagine you had a space ship that could get close, and could keep trying to push its way there. How does the universe stay in place, without breaking its own rules?" He smirked, then, and turned back to the class. They all scratched their heads. "A phenomenon called Time Dilation, that's how. To the people moving at high speed, time progresses at what appears to be the normal rate. However, to outside viewers, the travelers appear to move incredibly fast. So, lets say you're in a space ship; what you count as ten seconds might actually be fourteen to those of us hanging out on planet Mars - or, wherever we might be!"

He laughed softly, shaking his head. The rest of the class seemed much quieter than usual. "Now, this effect mandates that a journey which takes a voyager forty years might perhaps, to everyone not taking the trip, really take fifty. It makes space travel *slightly* more feasible, but it means that when you return after what seemed like a decade, you're coming back - perhaps - fifty years later."

At a raised hand, he raised his eyebrow; "Yes, Mister Wilcox?" He was quite amazed that the aquatics expert was asking a question, or offering a comment, in his class - at least, of his own free will.

"Okay, so as somethin' goes faster, umm, it starts warping time? How does that happen? How do you actually prove that it works?" Disbelief was rife in the man's voice - and this was just disbelief of a scientific principle! Imagine what he'd think if he knew the truth about Emmett!

Nevertheless, the physicist smiled politely. "How many of you have ever used GPS tracking software?" At the universal raising of his hands, Emmett folded his own behind his back. "The satellites used to make the system work are, in effect, moving much faster than we are. Orbital speed is, what, at least 18,000 miles an hour?" As if anyone else in the room would know. "And furthermore, in orbit they experience much, much less gravity - meaning they experience different time dilation effects from the Earth than we do."

Brian looked dumbfounded, as if the connection wasn't crystal-clear to him. Emmett continued to explain. "The GPS system constantly has to update itself to keep itself in synch, otherwise you'd start seeing your directions getting even worse. Its one thing to get led onto a road that doesn't exist, but another to be told that the road is six miles to your west, and that you're in a farm!"

After the soft laughter died down, he continued his lesson, describing in slightly more detail the different experiments that had been done to track time dilation's effects. He figured - correctly, most likely - that this would keep the students' attention far better than throwing mathematical models and scientific proofs at them. He talked about rocket ships carrying watches, and not equations carrying decimals over. He eventually brought in the fact that general relativity was responsible for this effect; that time and space are tied to one another and the transmutation of one could effect the outcome of another. It was complicated material, even for the physicist, but he got the bulk of his class through it unabated.

Once the lecture finished, he started his normal routine of

packing up. He caught a look from Brian Wilcox and gave the student a smile; the boy smiled back, of course, but it was clear that he still felt like much of a fool for being shown up, earlier.

"Its alright," Emmett considered, *"because if I listened to him talk about the butterfly stroke, I'd probably drown in confusion just like he's flapping about right here. Poor kid, its kind of messed up, making him take science to get a Phys Ed degree."* Unplugging his USB drive and pocketing it, he looked up and caught a grin from Sonia. He returned the smile, giving her a slight wave; and her eyes clearly craved another encounter, one the carnivore within him was more than happy to embrace.

On his way out of DuBois Hall, he checked his voice-mails and found, much to his surprise, a message from the chair of the Physics Department. He'd been hoping for something from Maria, but what he got was far more interesting - and worrying.

"Emmett, its Bill," the message began. "After your introductory class, today, I'd like you to come by the office. We have an investor here wanting to speak to you about your submission to *Interaction Monthly*." He raised an eyebrow at this, seeing as it was more than unusual to have any sort of investors actually contacting his institution about an article he'd submitted; even upon publication, it was a rare experience. He sighed, familiar suspicions growing in the back of his mind.

He turned around and headed back into the science building, marching up a staircase and into the main science office. The receptionist, a nice lady named Shelly, looked up at him. "Doctor Eisenberg," she began.

"Hi, Shelly, I got Doctor Samuels' message." He gazed around, curious as to the fact that the reception area of the Physics department was completely, thoroughly empty. "What room is he in?" Emmett asked politely; he managed to do a half-way decent job at masking his concern. He still wasn't James, but he was at least capable of deception in its most basic forms, such as misleading.

The older, glasses-wearing brunette smiled warmly; she was always friendly. "Mr. Curtis said he would be right back, actually. He was getting a bottle of water at the vending machine down the hall. I'll tell him to meet you in your office?"

"Excellent," Emmett both thought and said; what he didn't say, however, was the rest of the train chugging through his cranium: *"And lets just hope Mr. Curtis is really what he says he is. An interested investor. Right,"* his thoughts ran towards the sarcastic.

Into his office Emmett went. It was Spartan enough, with an assortment of physics books chosen half at-random and a far greater number of journals splayed on his desk. He quickly cleared this off, making room for his coming conversation partner, and tossed them in an appropriately-labeled box with the year that they all originated from. He withdrew a pair of coasters, one for himself and one for the drink the man was bringing back. Emmett reached out and seized a fresh glass of icy water, taking it for his own. He drew a sip of the liquid into his lips just as he heard a knock at his door.

"Enter," Emmett beckoned, carelessly placing the glass upon the coaster.

A tall, perhaps six foot two inch man opened the door to the physicist's office. He had a dark complexion, and was most likely of Hispanic descent. His hair was kept short, and it manifested as tiny black spikes which matched his dark brown eyes - eyes that were hardened far beyond the gentleman's ostensible age. He was no older than twenty three, as it looked, and almost certainly too young to be any sort of big-wig at a physics publication. Then again, Emmett had certainly met stranger folks. To top things off, the man was clearly muscular, despite the black business suit and red tie the man wore to blend into the professional world. He had a half-empty bottle of water in his hands.

"Doctor Eisenberg, I presume?" asked the tall man with a barely noticeable accent. Perhaps if he hadn't been tipped off by the man's skin tone, the physicist wouldn't have noticed it. He set the bottle down onto the coaster Emmett had prepared.

Rising to his feet, he extended his hand with the best

knock-off of a business professor's posture he could manage. It seemed to do the trick, because the newcomer shook his hand firmly. "That's me," he responded, gesturing to the seat behind him.

Smiling, the larger man took it and both sat down. "Alejandro Curtis, its a pleasure to meet you." Alejandro placed his briefcase on the desk, just off to the side.

Emmett watched as the man fumbled with a four-cylinder combination lock, going over his intended number more than once. Finally, he seemed to have the pass-code in order as he reached for two latches on either end of the container and flung them open. "Doctor Eisenberg," he began, "I came across your most recent article in *Interaction Monthly* and I was really astounded by the theory you presented."

"Thank you very much," Emmett replied cautiously, leaning back in his seat. "It took an awful lot of research to put together my ideas about Muons, for that particular piece. I take it, then, that its already been accepted?"

Alejandro's head dipped to the side for a moment, then he nodded. "Yes, Professor Eisenberg, it will definitely be in our next edition. But what I wanted to ask about, on behalf of my superiors, was, to be blunt, *how* did you research it?"

Emmett blinked his eyes twice. "What do you mean by how, Mister Curtis?"

The man folded his hands together and pressed them on the physicist's desk, leaning forward slightly. His eyes were ominous, and within them seemed to be everything that Emmett had been dreading for ten years. "I mean," Curtis began, "to ask exactly how you managed to perform this research. You discuss the movement of subatomic particles, yet I do not believe you have access to such equipment at this fine university."

"As you can see in the footnotes," the physicist countered, having rehearsed this situation in his mind a dozen times, "I attributed most of my raw data to CERN. I especially appreciate the Large Hadron Collider that our European colleagues have developed." CERN, the central research body of the European

Union, was indeed a major investigator of subatomic particles - and, indeed, CERN had certainly duplicated Emmett's own 'research,' so it was not entirely unjust to attribute them with the otherwise impossible-to-discover science.

Worryingly, that seemed to be exactly the answer Alejandro was looking for. "Doctor Eisenberg, while I appreciate your skill in the fine art of citation, my colleagues and I looked through your previous research and found that it made predictions that could not have been found accurate at the time. We traced your publication history," he whispered quietly - he might as well have been screaming it, "and discovered that you did indeed have access to such resources at your previous facility of employment."

"Connor point," Emmett concluded dryly. He, too, leaned forward on his desk like a Lion challenged. "And what did you think of the old work?"

Alejandro smiled a bit, but it was the kind of smile that held a great deal of threat within. "It turns out that you were decades, literally, ahead of your time. The research you did there will likely be used for the next half a century. What really puzzles me, however, is the way you used the reactor there to generate Trans-Uranics."

The Spaniard continued. "Any reactor that uses Uranium is prone to throwing them off, as you know. Its part of the fusion process, really. You combine the atoms, you get elements heavier than Uranium. But you were generating Californium in large quantities. You were producing Einsteinium, and you even had working theoretical models of Ununseptium nearly a decade before its formal discovery by the American and Russian experiment at Flerov. Forgive me, but you have a steady record of access to the inaccessible."

Emmett sighed, rubbing his forehead as the man continued his speech. "In fact," Alejandro remarked, "I would assert that much of your work was more like science fiction than fact, if it weren't for the inconvenient truth that your research was all spot on, even beyond our wildest dreams. That's why I dug into Connor Point a bit more deeply."

"And what did you discover?" asked Eisenberg, his eyes leveling with Curtis'.

The businessman never once blinked. "I discovered, coincidentally enough, that my father also worked there. Well, really," Alejandro self-corrected, "he funded your projects. His name was Richard Trujillo." Emmett's eyes widened, his instinct toward secrecy failing to suppress his mind's recognition of the name. "He died when I was younger, he committed suicide. He jumped off of his company's building, thirty stories up."

The flash of a thirty-year old Black man with tufts of white hair along his ears, a bushy mustache, and the beginnings of a beer belly flashed into Emmett's mind, and he closed his eyes to shut out the image. He cast his gaze downward, opening them and exhaling softly. "I'm sorry to hear that," he offered sincerely.

Alejandro merely laughed. "I appreciate that. My dad was never really around, you see. Always busy, always working on his pet project. My mother, who I take my last name from, raised me. But once I discovered you were involved in the same project my dad was, well, I felt I had to meet you."

"Umm," Emmett began hesitantly, "I don't know what I can really do to help you, Mister Curtis. Once the project shut down, I didn't really hear anything about the aftermath. I wish I had the facts to be more helpful."

Alejandro's dark eyes gazed into Emmett's again, then, and they seemed to finally find purchase upon something. "You do not," he said flatly, "for you are lying to me. You know precisely what happened. You know what my father was involved in because you were not part of the Alpha group. You were part of the Omega. You were special."

Finally, Emmett sighed with resolution and took a sip from his glass of water. He kept his eyes on Alejandro's the entire time he sipped, then he set it down carefully and ran his fingertips through his hair. "If you've got files on Omega Division, then you've just wasted about five minutes of my time by not calling me out on the truth. What is it you want from me? Money to be quiet?"

"I would have figured," Alejandro dodged, "that you wouldn't be satisfied with the life you're living." He reached into his briefcase and withdrew a small folder with the words *Confidential: Omega Division Only* on it. He opened the pale paper to reveal Emmett's picture and various biographical data including his date of birth, family history, medical records, and the like. "Your psychological report indicated you had every inclination to help make the world better. What went wrong?"

"You don't already know?" the physicist answered calmly. "Interesting. I suppose you've seen the profile for Sari already?"

Alejandro nodded grimly. "Yes. She was a tragic case." He looked as if a worm had crawled down his throat.

Emmett leaned forward, glowering slightly. "Exactly. That tragedy went against everything that Connor Point stood for. The people I worked for - your father, included - were monsters. That's why he---"

"Jethro Marx dropped him off a building. My father," Alejandro continued without a moment's pause, "lost his way. He lost his soul, as did the rest of his colleagues. He didn't understand what it meant to have the powers we do."

Emmett narrowed his eyes. "What we?"

Alejandro shrugged. "I had to do much searching to find the records that Jethro moved. I had to go to the very bottom depths of the ocean. No normal man could have done that, so you know very well what I mean when I say *we* have powers. Now then, as it so happens I have my father's wealth and my mother's sense of conscience. I would like you to join with that formidable combination. I would like to reform the Consortium."

"No chance," Emmett remarked. The chunks of the puzzle started coming together, with the physicist suddenly wondering whether James had already been contacted - whether this was the source of the mooted job offering. "And the others won't be interested, either, I'm afraid."

Alejandro shrugged casually. "I've already spoken to some of the others, and so far you're right. Only Mister Lowery expressed any interest at all, and he did not trust me so far as he could throw me."

"He wasn't wrong to have that opinion, no offense," Emmett retorted neutrally.

Alejandro shrugged. "So you will not save this world, then? You have the most power, and you have the most potential. I know you are capable of solving this Earth's problem of limited resources without even breaking a sweat. Within a day, you can transform the world for the best." Alejandro laid his case out, but his final question was genuine - puzzled, in fact. "Why would you *not* do it?"

For just one moment, Emmett considered the proposition. It was indeed everything he had ever wanted for the world, but something got in the way. It was, much to his surprise, the image of Erica standing before him ten years ago in tears. "Because the last time we tried that," Emmett answered, "it failed. We failed. I can conjure up enough water to fill the deserts - but what happens when it evaporates, and the rain floods cities? I can summon enough Thorium to power the planet until after our sun dies. I can even whip up material so strong and energy-efficient we can use them for space travel."

Alejandro's eyes grew bright, but as Emmett silenced himself the younger man frowned. When he began to speak again, they were worrying words, indeed; "I'm a walking nuclear bomb, Mister Curtis. I'm a walking nuclear bomb that can rearrange matter to make armor that's bullet, rocket, and everything-else proof. There's no chance in hell that the public wouldn't panic - or start worshiping me like an ancient god. Hell, that's probably how the very insipid idea of a God even got started!"

The Hispanic man glowered for a moment, then quickly snatched up the copy of Emmett's file and put it back in his suitcase. He slid the physicist a card with his name and phone number on it. "For when you change your mind," Alejandro stated flatly - then, with a huff, he left the physicist's office without so much as a goodbye.

Emmett tucked the card into his front drawer and sighed,

turning around to face the shelf of books nestled behind him, each within a comfortable reach of his distance. Had he made the right decision? *"Is it really so impossible for us to change the world? Last time,"* he mused, *"we were so close. Is it possible to fix things? Or would history repeat itself? I guess we'll have to see."*

A knock at the door was followed by Emmett's casual, "Come in!," and he turned around to see Shelly, the receptionist, enter into the room.

"Doctor Eisenberg? I saw Mister Curtis leaving; he seemed upset about something. Did everything go alright with the meeting?"

Laughing to himself, he took a sip out of his glass and shrugged. "I think he got the answer he expected, he just didn't like it. Tell me something, Shelly - do you think that one man can save the world?"

"Ever hear of Hilary Koprowski?" Shelly lobbed forward as a loaded question.

Emmett, for the life of him, couldn't make a guess. When he shook his head, the receptionist continued. "He was the man who developed the first effective Polio vaccine. He set the trend for disease eradication, or, well, at least the field of immunology. He kind of did save the world." His eyes widened - of course! Emmett sighed loudly. "Ummm, Emmett? Why are you so worried about it?"

"What if you had the chance to change things? Like, if you could solve the energy crisis?" He wasn't entirely sure why he was asking her this; perhaps because the trusty secretary was such a cliche super-hero ally, or perhaps just because he felt like she had enough worldly experience to make a decision. Clearly she wasn't some dumb book-keeper - one couldn't be, and work at a college as a department's receptionist of choice!

"A lot of people think they can fix things, but no two of them agree on how, so that's your problem. Its all about how you want to change them. That's where you run into problems."

Emmett sighed and looked toward the ceiling of his office.

"But you would, huh?"

Shelly nodded. "Of course, I would. How could you not try?"

"And what if," Emmett intervened, his eyes returning to the receptionist "it could go wrong? What if you thought you might hurt someone in the process, or a lot of people?"

"Emmett," she said with a sigh, "if there's something bothering you, you should head to the psychology department. They--"

"They're half my problem," he blurted out. At Shelly's insulted gaze, he frowned. "I'm sorry. I am - was, I don't know anymore, dating one of them." The receptionist gasped, looking half-surprised and half-impressed. "So they're no help to me right now. Plus, I mean, its kind of a personal issue."

Shelly shrugged. "Sometimes, when there's no other person you can turn to, there's always God. I know, I know," she held up a hand, "most of you physics guys don't believe in that. I do, and I think God's always helped me out. Of course, I also like to think God's a woman just as much as she's a man, so your mileage may vary."

The receptionist clicked her tongue, once, then left Emmett to his thoughts. She gently shut his door behind him, and Emmett gazed up at the ceiling against. "Mileage might vary, huh," he whispered to himself, closing his eyes and meditating on the nature of his own existence. Would God help him? He - or She - certainly hadn't explained why he existed, so far. Free will practically dictated that God couldn't!

"*But then again,*" Emmett pondered, "*perhaps - as with Constantine - there will be a sign. On that sign, that mileage might just be posted.*"

Chapter Nine
Wormholes

Two days can be a lifetime; but in Emmett's case, the time between Tuesday and Thursday was only long because of the void it existed within. Insofar as nothing can happen in a life, nothing happened to the physicist. There was no call - happy, angry, forgiving or furious - from Maria. There was no contact from Sonia. There was no feed-back from Alejandro Curtis. There were classes! But they were uneventful in the extreme. The students asked questions, learned appropriate facts, and went on their merry ways.

It was unbearably dull.

Emmett couldn't stomach the normalcy. About the only thing that was out of the ordinary was that a cold snap crossed over central New York, with temperatures dropping into the high thirties at times. It was hardly a recognizable change of pace, and the building feeling of anxiety had him losing grip on himself at times. He considered starting a fraccas with Dr. Marceau. He contemplated quitting the university entirely. As he grew more and more unsettled, he thought about driving by Sonia's, taking her in his arms, and repeating the transgression he'd committed earlier in the week with twice as much vigor. It was all *too* calm, and it spoke to a nasty finish to the teaching week.

But first, there was Introductory Physics. Thursday afternoon he skulked into his class-room and began to set up his computer equipment. He was earlier than usual, and was the only one in the room at the time. He sighed and gazed toward the ceiling, his lips forming words to mumble to himself.

"Doctor Eisenberg?" he heard behind him; he spun on his heel, eyes blinking twice as he took Sonia's form in. She wore a comfortable set of blue sweat pants and a Catskill Community College sweater - standard student attire.

A weakened smile touched his lips. "Sonia! Hi! How are

you?"

She glanced over her shoulder for a moment, then flashed a wink toward him. "I was looking forward to class. We'll talk after it," she half-ordered, stepping toward the desks and taking her usual front row seat. Then, she proceeded to stare at him intently, watching as he adjusted his gloves and the collar of his shirt. He began to meddle about the computer console, plugging in his thumb drive.

The students began to filter in for what had just become a very interesting session, indeed. They wore their usual assortment of jeans and sweat pants, sweaters and light jackets, and hats of at least two colors. Autumn was indeed in full swing; still warm at times, but giving way to the wintery months as November was nearly upon them.

"So," Emmett began with a smile that defied his depressed attitude, "Today's lesson is all about getting from where you *are* to where you want to be. Or, at least, some place other then where you are. Today, we're gonna talk about a phenomenon that Einstein described called a Wormhole."

"We've learned that time and space are a kind of fabric, right? And, as you've learned, various forces in physics can bend this fabric in different ways. Time dilation can be caused by speed and gravity. The weight of a planet can effect how objects move around it. But, what if that fabric wasn't just bent? What if it caved in on itself?"

The students all stared at each other, and they didn't quite seem to grasp a thing Emmett said. He struggled to find less convoluted terms. "The mass of a star, for example, can sometimes compress itself into a 'black hole' - an area where gravity is so strong that not even light can escape. What happens to objects that fall into it?"

Again, stunned silence. Emmett sighed. "Who knows?" When not one hand ventured upward, he smirked a bit. "Exactly - nobody. Some people think it gets crushed and added to the mass as a whole, while others think that, at some other random point in the universe, a 'hole' opens up and spits the matter back out. A 'white' hole to go with a 'black' one."

At a hand being raised, the physicist managed to conceal his internal cheering. "Mister Wilcox," he stated without even a hint of hesitation at the fact that it was the sub-par academic asking the question.

"Umm, Professor? I think we're all a bit lost." A cadre of nods accompanied the swimmer's statement. "Could you start over, maybe? We kind of skipped over all the black hole stuff."

Emmett was stunned. His silence was only disrupted at a very loud, purposeful knock at the door of the classroom. Looking toward it for a moment, he fought the urge to take it apart atom by atom. Instead, he put his index finger toward the class. "One moment, then I'll try to start over with it."

He opened the door and, in a polite tone, asked, "Can I help you?" Any other words that might have escaped his lips died the minute he actually *looked* at his guest, and he suddenly wish he had done so before he spoke. "Umm. Class! I'll be...Back." He paused awkwardy, then looked over his shoulder. "Actually, everyone, class is canceled." He slammed the door behind himself, leaving his belongings behind.

As the students inside the classroom stared at one another, wondering what could possibly be so wrong, Emmett locked his eyes upon Jethro Marx. The pudgy man looked absolutely exhausted, his shirt stained with still-wet red liquid, a neat hole going through the front - and back - of it. "We need to go see Sari!" he exclaimed, concern rife in his eyes.

"Already did, she was my first stop. You number two, we're goin'." Before Emmett could respond, however, Jethro's hand reached out and snapped hold of the physicist's.

"Where?" Emmett stated - and then he saw, looking around, that he was in a house. It was a well kept living room he'd emerged in, well kept except for the fact that the white rug was drenched red with blood. Looking behind himself, he saw the young Hindu girl he had worked with in the past. "Oh."

"Doctor," Sari whispered weakly, frowning a bit. "It...It was bad...Very bad," she said, her lips trembling. She ran to

Emmett, who opened his arms and pulled the girl into a tight hug.

Making soft hushing sounds with his lips, Emmett's eyes locked upon Getty's. "Was it...?" The indictment of their new 'friend' was clear.

"Yeah. It was. I dropped his ass off in Siberia, if you wanna go take care'a him with me?" It was a grim offer; Getty said it with a heavy heart, but he sounded as determined as the older man had ever been before.

As for the physicist, he had to think. This was certainly a sign, and there was certainly a mileage painted on it. He bit his bottom lip. "Sure," he finally announced, "I'm in."

Sari's eyes widened. "Doctor! No! You can't!"

"Sari, shh. We're just going to settle this. I don't..." he searched for the words. "I won't do anything harsh. I promise." He looked over at Geddy. "Do you have a hat?"

The old man shook his head - Sari quickly rummaged around in a closet and found a baseball cap. Emmett nodded and stared at it casually, stared at every inch of Jethro's clothing. "Flexible but armored. I think you'll appreciate it. A fifty caliber round couldn't get through this cloth, now. Sari," Emmett said as he brushed his fingertip over his glasses. "I'll be there, and I'll be in the same stuff. Trust me, we'll be fine. And we can always get back to you."

Sari sniffed once. "Okay, Doctor. Just be safe, please. Be very safe."

"I will, Sari. I promise, we'll be back before you know it."

Geddy reached his hand out again. Emmett took it, this time, and his eyes widened as he felt the cold chill of autumn in Russia. He quickly shook it from his and his companion's shoulders. Gazing about at the tall trees, the physicist frowned slightly. "Its quiet." Sadly, that wasn't the disturbing part - the large red splotch where Jethro had been just before he jumped to their mutual friend was far more alarming. Briefly, he wondered exactly what the students at Catskill Community College were up to. That thought quickly left his mind.

Suddenly, four gunshots rang out. The first slammed into

Emmett's chest, square over his heart, knocking the wind out of him and eliciting some loud cracks - the rest struck the air before him, or missed him thoroughly. "I had a feeling you would return," whispered a familiar, accented voice. Emmett collapsed to a knee, breathing heavily; he checked downward quickly - no blood. He heard the sound of a gun reloading, and he gazed upward to the form of Alejandro Curtis. Fifty yards away, the large man emerged from behind the concealment of a snow-covered tree walking at a calm, but quick pace.

"Nice shot," Emmett whispered, meeting with an intense amount of pain from each breath, before he raised his hand. Unarmed, Alejandro gazed down at his fingertips, then back up at the physicist. Adrenaline quickly masked his pain. "Now, would you kindly explain what you're doing?"

Growling, Alejandro continued his slow, methodical advance on Emmett. "We have the power to change the world! To rule it! And you would use it to disarm me instead of make us kings!? You cannot be negotiated with - you must die!"

It was as if an invisible brick wall jumped up; Alejandro walked square into it with a dull thud. "Please," Emmett stated dryly, determined to retain his composure while ignoring both pain and pumping hormones, "I'm not interested. Just being an idiot is one thing, but trying to murder my friend? No way. You should be in jail!"

With a relentless fist, Emmett's barrier was broken and Alejandro continued to close the distance. Forty yards, now. "Jail? I'll break out! They cannot hold me. You cannot harm me."

Thirty yards. "Stand where you are and lets talk this through," Emmett declared - it was a patience that he simply never used to have. Furthermore, at the too-close-for-comfort distance of twenty yards, now, the man continued his advance. "Listen!" Emmett shouted, "Don't make me have to do anything harmful! Please!"

Ten yards. "We can talk about this!" Emmett threw up another barrier. "We can settle this like adults! We're past the time when using these powers was just for fun! We can discuss this!" After three punches, each with relentless strength, his barrier failed. Five yards. A fist flew straight at this face. Reason failed, instinct won.

Emmett's body was, without warning, encased in obsidian steel that stole what little moonlight broke through the woods. It was armor much like a knight's, only with jagged metal edges that no blacksmith could forge and no eye-slits to see from. The metal was capable of absorbing and transmitting light one way - and within it, Emmett could see just fine. The inbound fist slammed into his razor-sharp armor, deflecting off of one of the many spikes. It should have been sliced by a blade, it should have been broken upon impact.

"*Interesante*," whispered the pseudo-businessman. He punched Emmett again - the physicist didn't budge. "You truly are a master. As am I." The large man was unfazed, though the blows sent Emmett backwards despite his protection. Each strike should have caused his enemy massive damage, but surprisingly did him no harm.

The physicist narrowed his eyes, deducing his opponent's nature and announcing ominously, "And you, I take it, are super-humanly strong?" He flexed his steel-plated fingers and between them emerged the handle of a long, crystalline blade. A jeweler would have been dumbfounded at how perfectly nature had created the sword of diamond; its edge was as sharp as any known scalpel, and its hardness made it more than capable of cleaving through solid concrete. He swung it with a surprising degree of confidence, as if the professor actually had taken fencing lessons at some point. The blade should have cleaved the brute in half - it didn't even scratch him, didn't even push him back one inch.

"Not really," Alejandro remarked, "but I *am* invulnerable. I suppose that helps," he quipped, moving with unexpected speed and delivering a brutal round-house to Emmett's armored head. The physicist fell to the ground, upon which he was kicked twice - and he learned, to his displeasure, that Alejandro had steel-tipped boots on.

The impact didn't really injure Emmett, but it *did* cause some scrapes and bruises as his heavy armor clanged against his figure. Moving quickly wasn't an option within it - in fact, just to get back to his feet required him to thin the steel until it was ineffective. With a thought, he constructed a metallic beam right before the foot that threatened to deliver a third brutal boot toward his ribs. The two steel bits collided with a bang, and Emmett entirely dispelled his armor in time to get to his feet and prepare to defend himself from a further assault.

Its a good thing he did - a knife was already aimed toward his eye! It struck his glasses, but the eyepiece was only knocked out of alignment as the blade bounced off of it. Emmett narrowed his eyes and the air around Alejandro began to shimmer. The transformation of molecules into thick chlorine gas generated enough heat to create a bluish steam, and by all rights Alejandro should have doubled over immediately upon inhaling the toxic substance. It was a potentially-fatal weapon of Emmett's arsenal.

And, perhaps predictably, it had no effect. "Fascinating," Emmett muttered as he retreated, Alejandro charging after him. He wasn't going to come close to outrunning the athletic man. He chose to do the next best thing - the best defense being, of course, a good offense. Sparing a thought for his friend, he roared, "Look away!" With that, and without checking to ensure Geddy actually obeyed the command, Emmett raised his left hand.

Flames emerged. This fire spawned from more than just heat - it was contained in a small sphere, suspended in the air and embraced by Emmett's hand. The plasma almost immediately vaporized the snow around it. He did nothing more than point the orb in Alejandro's direction and the woods burst into ash and dust, energies emanating from the microscopic solar flare before it died down. There wasn't even time for combustion-fueled fires to start.

As the dust cleared, Alejandro's clothing was reduced to ash much like the woods - but not even one strand of the large, now-nude man's hair was seared. Emmett's eyes widened as his advance hadn't even slowed, and he paid for his delay with a broken nose. The punch sent him tumbling backwards.

The invulnerable man merely roared. "You bastards killed my father! My mother, she was destroyed! And you have such power, just to let others suffer? We should rule this world, Emmett Eisenberg! We must *make* it right, even if it means killing you, you who once played god yourself!"

"Your mileage may vary," Shelly's words called out to him. Emmett rolled out of the way of another boot toward his chin and lifted a hand. The same obsidian alloy that had once comprised Emmett's armor emerged - but this time, it emerged in front of Alejandro. The large man walked into it, blinked dumbfounded at the barricade. and swung, punching it as if he could break through.

"Your tricks cannot save you, Eisenberg!" he turned to his left and attempted to side-step the barrier, only to walk into another one. He backed up - another. The look on his face transformed from confident to confused. He reached his hands above his head and found solid matter holding him within. Now there were no arrogant remarks - only a desperate cry for understanding. "What is this?!"

Emmett lowered his head, rubbing his bloodied nose, and he looked to his left. His friend, Geddy, was standing with his eyes shut. "Its over," Emmett declared. The portly teleporter looked over his shoulder at Emmett. "Come over here, Geddy, please."

Jethro walked over and looked at the large, black cube that had appeared from thin air, replacing the angry Hispanic. His shouts were still audible, even through the one-way visible alloy. "Let me go!" roared Alejandro.

"As I said," Emmett spat, his eyes welling with tears while blood dripped down his face, "you are being sentenced to prison. Not, unfortunately, by the authorities - but by us. You can survive in the face of a star, Alejandro. Maybe a few years hanging out near this planet's might change your attitude!"

Jethro turned to Emmett, stunned by this pronunciation. Then, his eyes narrowed, he nodded. "We ain't keepin' him there that long, you understand? Emmett?"

"Everyone deserves a second chance, Geddy," Emmett declared arrogantly. He closed his eyes, and he saw Erica Hall before him, crying - much like in the dream he'd had at Sonia's apartment. "Vengeance can tear people to shreds, you see. Both the ones seeking it, and the ones effected by it. We're just as guilty. But we never tried to take over the world, either," he finished, folding his arms over his face.

Alejandro pounded fruitlessly against the metal, watching as Geddy extended an arm to his prison. "No! No! You bastards, let me out, let me--" and he was silent, because as soon as Geddy touched the cube he was face-to-face with flame. Nothing but flame. He could look out and, when squinting, make out a small, gray, red-glowing sphere not far from where he stood. It was hot, but the heat wouldn't effect him. He was invulnerable to external forces, and could survive the greatest forces of nuclear fusion unscathed. No, nothing - not even starvation - could effect him; and he would remain that way until someone released him from his new home, or until he died of old age.

*****

The two men stared at one another for a moment before, finally, Emmett spoke with a pain-laced sigh. "I should see Sari. I have some broken ribs," he stated to himself, keeping his focus as far from the pain as possible by analyzing it in a logical fashion.

"You jus' sent a man t'float around the Sun, Emmett. We has bigger problems then a boo-boo!" Geddy fumed, glaring at the man. "How we gonna get 'im back? *When* we gonna get 'im back?"

Emmett frowned, but his ire was directed more toward himself than his friend. "When? A few weeks, maybe months. I don't care. How? You can call it back, right? And if you can't, I can, since I made it. Who knows?" The physicist looked skyward. "Maybe it'll melt and he'll start drifting through space?"

The dark-skinned elder wrapped his arms around his chest, shivering slowly. "Its cold, man. And we're cold. It's like fuckin' torture, man. We're broken."

"We aren't," Emmett replied, gazing at his friend. He snapped his fingertips and the area around them began to rapidly warm - the only sign of anything unnatural was the quick but mild change of pressure around them. "We did what we had to do."

Geddy's eyes narrowed and he stormed over to Emmett, grabbing him by the wrist. Without hesitation, he concentrated - and the two were back in Sari's house. The girl was busy scrubbing the floor clean of the blood-stains Jethro had left about her living room. Upon their appearance, she screamed and grasped the both of them at the same time. Emmett winced.

"Easy, Sari, easy," he cautioned, his hand traveling down to the place where the bullet had smashed into his jacket. Her eyes widened and she rapidly began to tear at the clothing, pulling it apart and placing her hands over the area. With a grimace, Emmett felt his bones crackle and snap back into place - and his breathing was immediately relieved of the pain it had caused.

She looked up at Emmett, her eyes filled with emotions, then hauled off and slapped him in the face. The sound echoed deafeningly off of the walls, eliciting a nervous wince from Jethro as he watched the scientist's head reel around. His hand snapped up at the wound. "Don't you *ever!*" shouted Sari, "*Ever* do something that stupid again! If he'd hit your head, then what?! You would be one dead doctor!"

"Jesus Christ," Geddy remarked, rubbing the top of his fully-bald head anxiously. "Didn't expect to see you get smacked like *that,* man." He lowered his arm, gazing his friend over. "But you deserved it. You fell right back into that 'right at the time' horse-shit you gave me about Garrett."

Emmett blinked his eyes, rubbing his rapidly-reddening face. He gazed down at the young girl in front of him, then back up at his friend, perplexed. His silence was filled in by Jethro, then. "And that's jus' it - it *wasn't* right. It was *wrong*, Emmett. You was wrong. You still is. You wanna know you problem?"

Geddy gritted his teeth, focusing his thoughts. "*That's* you problem! You might'a thunk it was right, but it was wrong. You don't get to walk away from that kinda business, an' you don't get to walk away from Alejandro's shit, either."

Now, the physicist's eyes narrowed slightly. "Alejandro and me? We aren't the same."

A soft whisper broke his thoughts. "Are not you?" Sari looked up at Emmett and shook her head. "Not fully, but a little. You both were wrong, Doctor Eisenberg. I know you were lost and confused ten years ago, but you are not now. He is lost and confused *now*, and you confronted him in a mad rush. What happened to him?"

"Eisenberg stuck him in a rock an' I stuck 'im around the sun for a bit," Geddy said; his tone was heavy, but his words showed no attachment to the incredible feat he'd done. No, only an attachment to the fact that Jethro clearly didn't like his choices. "Its a jail sentence. It turned out that his thing is invincibility. It took a lotta tryin' to figure that out," he concluded ominously.

Emmett looked down, his lips tightening. "He tried to kill me, and I..." he trailed off, remembering the impact of his sword against the man's skull. "I would have killed him, if I could have. I tried, three times even. I failed."

Sari's eyes grew wide, and a maelstrom of emotions overcame her for an instant. "He is immune to harm? Very cool!" She hardened, then, regaining her focus. "But even still, Doctor Eisenberg, could you not have just imprisoned him to begin with? Could you not have protected yourself without harming him? That is what you must consider, Doctor. He is evil now, but may not be tomorrow - just as you once were."

Maybe it was the particular voice that issued the condemnation, but his usual self-righteous defense just didn't manifest itself. His shoulders slumped instead of rising; his eyes lowered instead of glaring. His heart beat and he felt its throbbing at the sore spot on his face. "Evil?" he whispered to himself. "Was I really evil?"

"Were you? Because what you *did* was, Doctor

Eisenberg," Sari declared forcefully. "Even if you, yourself, were not."

"Not for nothin'," Geddy added, "But you was plannin' to destroy *everything,* man. This whole world. People who ain't ever heard of you, or the Consortium, or Connor Point. You snapped, an' we all get it - we all went bad, for a bit. But you was the only one who was gonna get innocent people involved. Tha's why you was wrong, Emmett. That's why you was evil. Now? Now you ain't evil. Now, you's got hope of bein' a good guy, again. Marge saw that in you."

Emmett looked skyward for a moment, then. A million thoughts beat themselves to death against his skull like lemmings leaping over a ledge, but only one made it to his larynx. "Mileage may vary," he muttered to himself in distaste.

"What did you say, Doctor?" Sari queried sincerely.

"A friend said something to me, the other day. She said, basically, that I might have a different idea of God, but that God might exist and show the way. Maybe you guys are kind of like my guiding light."

Sari seemed momentarily confused by this statement, then reached up and tapped the markings on her forehead. "I am of the priestly caste, Doctor. I do believe in the divine. I do believe we represent that. Am I your light? I do not know. I could never say such a thing, for it would be presumptuous in the extreme. I can say, Doctor, that you have work to do here. I can say you have done much to redeem yourself, but that it takes a lifetime to complete the path you walk. You are a good man, Doctor. You must continue being good."

"I gotta get you back to your school," Geddy advised suddenly. "An' when all's said an' done, you need t'think about your future, Emmett. I think we all do, since Alejandro Curtis coulda come for any one'a us, an' its a cut'a sheer luck that it was me."

Emmett nodded his head and the two gentlemen hugged Sari goodbye. Then, Emmett reached his gloved hand out to Geddy. "Thank you, both of you," he said with a deep meaning.

Jethro took Emmett's hand and focused for a moment, and before he knew what happened he was standing in the hallway of the same classroom at Catskill Community College's DuBois' Hall that he'd left from.

Chapter Ten
Redemption

He was fortunate in that his students were lazy, but honest. His materials were right where he'd left them, but said students had long ago departed from the room, it seemed. If there was a class after his introductory physics one, it hadn't started yet - and that gave him all the help in the world. He briskly walked to his bag and checked to ensure his journal was still present and intact; it was. Deftly, his gloved fingers grasped his memory stick and shut down the still-active computer console. The electronics caused his mind to momentarily consider cameras, but Jethro was the escape artist - he assumed his friend would have dealt with it.

Without complication, therefore, he'd returned to his school and made a clean escape! He quickly ruffled and straightened up his clothing, attempting to smooth over the external scars of battle even as he knew he couldn't ignore the internal ones. Slinging his laptop bag over his shoulder, he moved over to the door and turned the knob. It opened obediently, offering to let him loose into a sparsely crowded hallway. With all the tact of a truck horn, he cast his eyes to the left and to the right before he set one foot out of the room.

And that's where the aforementioned, intentionally ignored complication emerged; or, rather, looked over her shoulder and blinked her eyes. Standing right outside of the doorway was Sonia Monterrey, and she cocked her head to the side as Emmett's poked through the doorway. "Umm...Doctor Eisenberg?"

His eyes widened. "Ah, hello, Miss Monterrey. I came back for my things."

"What *happened* to you?" she asked, looking him from head to toe. "You look exhausted! And how did you get past me? I've been standing at the door since you disappeared! Well, it wasn't just me, a few other guys were hanging around too. We wanted to keep your stuff safe. How did you get here?"

He looked off to his left as his mind raced for an

explanation. All he heard in his subconscious was a soft, south-Asian-accented voice reminding him not to be evil. He closed his eyes and exhaled in resignation. He made a decision. "I'll tell you, but not here?"

Sonia raised an eyebrow and nodded. "Mine?" the implication was fairly obvious. She took a moment to think it over, then sighed. Now it was her turn to glance around the hallway, and she spoke only after a nearby pedestrian passed them by. "Fine, but we're doing pizza and you're paying for it."

They smiled at one another once, then went their separate ways. Emmett drove back toward his own apartment and stepped inside, flicking on a light switch. He set his laptop case down and pulled out his journal. A sigh of resignation accompanied the clicking of his custom-made locks opening themselves up, and he reached onto a table to retrieve a pen. He glanced over at a large, red, three-piece sectional couch that he and Maria had gotten together, and grumbled as he walked over to it and sat down.

I'm not sure, he wrote on a fresh sheet of paper, *that the truth is the only answer. Lies have always done the job for me, and half-truths have covered up the facts when they're needed. But, I can't forget Sari's words. She's right - I was evil. I did evil things. I'm good, now, but only because I try to be good. Good people shouldn't lie, sometimes even when its the right thing to do. I'll call Maria. I miss her. I'll tell her the truth. But, I can't wait for her forever. When she's ready, I hope I will be, too. Until then, there's Sonia.*

Sonia is infuriating. She likes older men. There's nothing criminal here, but there's definitely something unprofessional. Either way I don't think I will be a professor for long. Disappearing from classes is a quick way to get fired, and I'm willing to bet Marceau has already made a move against me. That's fine. But Sonia? If she's going to be around me, I need to be straight with her. So, that's what I'll do.

I just hope that not being evil doesn't lead to evil outcomes. I hope the truth is benign.

He put his book down and looked at his watch. He set his alarm clock, slipped off his clothing (except, of course, for those brown gloves) and laid down. He dreamed of stars - their births, their lives, and ultimately their deaths. He watched the universe's birth unfold before his eyes, an experiment he'd never quite worked up the courage to perform himself. He understood "bubble theory," the idea that there were multiple, potentially-touching or even overlapping universes which could "pop" just as easily as new bubbles could form in the fabric of space.

It made him think of children's bath soaps, however the technical features of the theory probably could be - with nothing more than his willpower - proven or disproven between his fingertips. All it would take would be a moment's inflection of matter; though, to be very blunt, he was far more adept with atomic transformations than the transmutation of different forms of energy. Could he create such a demonstrative model? Perhaps. The issue was safety - the Large Hadron Collider was actually sued based on the incredibly unlikely chance that it could create a miniature black hole that, due to a failure of foresight, became unstable and swallowed the Earth up. This eventuality was as close to impossible as an unknown element of physics could have been, but it was enough to prompt cries of 'Doomsday!' across the world. Mechanical problems were chalked up to time-travelers and universal self-protection. All kind of quacks came out of the woodwork.

Clearly, despite the system's activation, the world continued to turn.

He awoke to the sound of his alarm clock.

Slowly, Emmett re-dressed himself, taking the time to change his pair of gloves from one to another. He then set out on a quick course for Sonia's apartment. It was in the same ramshackle condition it had been in the last time he'd visited, and he sent a simple text message to his student; "I'm here."

A few minutes later, the girl emerged from the stairway and the door clicked open. She smiled politely. "Hello, Emmett."

Today, she had blue hair; she'd dyed it again, changing up her demeanor. The hair matched her eyes - and it made looking at her much, much less stressful.

"Hey, Sonia. You did great with the hair," he complimented. "Mind if I come in?"

She nodded softly and threw the portal open for him, leading him once more up those stairs. She unfurled her set of keys and selected the appropriate sliver of metal, unlocking her apartment and stepping in. "Can I fix you a cup of coffee?"

"Sure," he answered, "I usually abstain, but I think tonight we might need it."

She raised an eyebrow and reached over to her counter-top. Two cups sat there, ready to go. He smirked slightly at her preparation. "How do you like it?" she asked politely as she turned around - then, as she saw him, her eyes widened with mock anger. "What's so funny?"

"I just appreciate someone who is prepared," Emmett answered, "and I'll take it with cream and some sugar."

She added the requested ingredients and handed him his cup. He looked it over; there was nothing more complicated than the usual array of molecules one might expect in a cup of coffee, even as the sugar began to dissolve into solution and the milk, water, and coffee components blended into one exquisite drink. A single sip confirmed his suspicions - she was an expert coffee-maker.

"Its very good," he complimented, stepping over to her sofa and taking a seat. The cloth covering it was ragged and worn, lending a nostalgic comfort to it that served as an acceptable alternative to fresh cushiness.

Sonia brushed her newly blue locks from before her face, nodding at his compliment. She seemed intent on studying Emmett for a moment, as if trying to read his mind. Slowly, she sat down next to him. "Lets get it out of the way - what happened to you, today?" She was at arm's length, perhaps, but she wasn't crammed into the arm of the couch. "Why'd you bail out of class?"

Her rhyme brought a slight smile to his lips, one he concealed by sipping at his coffee. After a sufficiently long, weighty pause that made it seem as if he was sincerely contemplating his answer, he set the cup down. "The truth is a little bit complicated, but I need to follow an old friend's good advice and the only way to do that is to tell it."

Now, the girl cocked an eyebrow. "Okay," she stated tentatively, scrutinizing the man she'd made love to half a week ago. "So, start talking."

"The long story is, my friend was shot." Her eyes widened; he'd expected that, as well as the hand that quickly rose to her mouth in shock. "He was shot by a man who is very, very misguided and who I hope will learn from his mistakes. I made the same ones, years ago."

The sorrow in his voice, as well as the implication of similar actions, caused Sonia to lean away from him. She rose to her feet. "You, wait, what? You *shot* someone, Emmett?!"

His eyebrows raised. "No, no, not exactly." He ran gloved fingers over his glasses. "The world, well, its strange. I can't really explain what happened because its a very long story, and a very weird one. We don't really understand *how* it works, or why we can do them, but---"

"You're scaring me," Sonia declared aggressively, looking him from head to toe as if seeing a different man before her than the one she understood. "Stop talking around things and just say them."

He sighed and nodded, a look of intrigue coming over his face. "Actually, to hell with it, I can show you." He removed his left glove slowly and held his naked, sun-deprived hand's palm toward the sky. His eyes closed and he concentrated. Water began to emerge from it - bubbling as if from a fountain spring and falling over the tips of his fingers only to drip into oblivion, unmade as it was made.

"What the hell are you doing?!" Sonia shrieked, sounding half-amazed and half-angered. "How are you doing that? Is this some kind of magic trick?"

"Physics," Emmett answered in a soft tone. The flow of water ceased and he put his glove back on, fingers flexing as if they had been on fire. "I can manipulate atoms and molecules."

Sonia backed up against her kitchen set, grasping the counter in an effort to slow her spinning sense of reality. "How? How do you do it?"

"I've undergone every genetic and physiological test you can name, and there's no answer. Everything is in the median areas, CAT-Scans, MRI's, and I - I just have this talent. I don't know how, I just *feel* the atoms in the air. I feel them in the space around me. I'm not the only one--"

Sonia's eyes grew wide. "Other people can change matter, too?!"

"Not quite," Emmett answered carefully, "but other people *do* have these kind of gifts. My friend who was shot has the power to move anything, uhm, pretty much anywhere. The guy who shot him, well, he was..." Emmett trailed off. "The very pissed off son of a man that we kind of, uhh, killed." At the girl's look of disgust he held his hands up. "We were wrong! We know that now!"

He sighed reluctantly. "The people that we worked for ten years ago were doing a lot of experiments, and we found out that some of them involved torturing a young girl who could heal any wounds she saw. They killed puppies, strangled kittens, and even maimed people - and her - in order to see just how much she fix. To test her limits. It was fucked up, Sonia, and we all just snapped. We went *evil*." He closed his eyes, clenching his fists against the memory. "To see Sari in that wheelchair was too much, and I snapped, too. They stopped me before I did some very, very bad things - I didn't keep my revenge just to the bastards that performed the experiments. After that, well..."

He felt a pulling at his eyes, a sensation similar to drowning that compelled him to rub the sockets of his skull softly. "Ten years later, things came back around. Connor Point--"

Sonia's eyes nearly bulged out of her head. "*The* Connor

Point? The nuke facility in Africa?!"

　　"The same," Emmett responded. She gasped, he sighed.
"It came back to life. I'm not happy with what I did, and I'm not
even happy with who I am! I hate myself, sometimes! But my
department's secretary said God shows herself in mysterious
ways," the girl scoffed at the reference to a female deity, "and
said that my mileage would vary in how I was guided. You knew
me before you knew what happened today, and you know what I
can do and what I was involved in. Sari, my friend, told me that
the only way not to be evil is to be good. Do you think I *can* be
good, Sonia?"

　　She stared at him with wonder, now, walking forward a
step. "Good? I don't know! I hardly know how to take this.
You're Doctor Eisenberg. Emmett! You're gentle!
You're...Wait." She paused, blinking her eyes with astonishment.
"So, like, physics? *Anything* to do with physics?"

　　"Almost." He closed his eyes again and exhaled; slowly, a
thin line of dark material began to form in the air between his
eyes. The substance quickly began to expand vertically, moving
upward until it began to splinter off into small wafers of material.
It grew further, then, forming a long neck and, finally, black
crystals at the head.

　　Sonia stared in wonder. "What's--"

　　"Lean back, please?" whispered the physicist. She
complied, and he creased his eyebrows. Suddenly, before her
very eyes, the substance went from black to gray; then from gray
to white; and finally, it became crystal clear. He grimaced, as if
the process took effort, then ran his gloved hand over the space
above the creation's crown. Finally, he extended his hand.

　　She gasped in wonder at what was clearly a rose formed of
diamond, with red-tinted crystalline petals. Her quivering palms
reached out and took the proffered faux flower and rubbed it, as if
to test its sharpness and its substance. Surprisingly enough, the
object was real. She looked up at him, then, and bit her bottom
lip. "Does it hurt?" she queried in a quiet tone.

　　"Huh?" He was confused. It was a question he hadn't

been asked in a very long time - perhaps not since the earliest days of his tenure at Connor Point. "Does what hurt?"

"When you use your ability? Does it hurt?"

He blinked his eyes a few times, the question taking a moment to make sense; finally, he laughed and shook his head. "Unless I'm doing something *really* difficult, no. Its just something I do, I guess. I feel it, I control it."

Suddenly she squeaked - it was a gleeful sound, and she wrapped her arms around him. She rubbed his back for a moment. Then, she suddenly pushed herself away from him and grabbed his shirt. "So you control physics?" He nodded his agreement. "And your friend? He can move anything anyplace?" Again, a nod. "And that girl, Sari you said? She can heal anyone's sickness?"

At this, Emmett shrugged. "I don't know if she can cure sickness. Something like cancer is the body turning on itself. She might have limits with her talent, but I don't know for sure."

"Don't know?" Sonia asked in astonishment. She cast her eyes on the movie poster in her room, and its cloaked protagonist. "Well," she concluded immediately thereafter, "it doesn't matter! That's soooo cool! You're like a real live super hero! When you were at Connor Point, did they inject you with anything? Were you exposed to radiation or something?"

Emmett shook his head. "No," he explained, "I was recruited to Connor Point precisely because of my abilities."

Her eyes went wide - then she began to laugh. "That is soooo awesome! Are you still out fighting crime?"

Without meaning to, his hand reached up and rubbed his forehead for a moment. Suddenly, Sonia's age was showing - though, he had to confess, he had felt much the same way, at first. "Listen," he stated heavily; her excitement died down a touch. "What I can do is pretty cool, but its led to some very dark places. They *experimented* on Sari." His restatement brought a frown to his lips. "Not with her, but on her. It left her crippled for years, and it turned ordinary people with extraordinary talents into murderers." Sonia blinked, now, totally stunned.

"What happened was sick. I almost killed you, Sonia - I almost killed everyone because I lost control over my emotions and I decided it would be better to watch the world burn then see another single child hurt in the name of profit. I was sick!" His fists clenched and he stared at her with complete exhaustion in his face. "I was sick and I was twisted. I was evil. I'm trying very, very hard not to be, anymore."

Sonia frowned slightly. Emmett briefly considered the notion that he'd terrified her, or shocked her into silence. This was quickly canceled out by her arms wrapping around him once again. She whispered quietly. "Emmett, Emmett, there's no reason to think you're evil! You're sweet! You've come a long way, and you've grown up. Its okay! Its really okay. You're a good man, and Emmett?" She pulled away from him, then, to lock eyes with him. "Its never too late to try again, Emmett. You can always try again - and again if you need to."

He cocked his head to the side, then, and slowly pulled her toward him. Perhaps her immaturity could be a strength, too - optimism was a nice little ally, after all! She moved toward his lips, but he cupped one hand behind her head and stroked her hair gently. He guided her into a tight hug and he whispered ever so softly into her ear, "Alright." He conceded something deep within himself toward her young vigor, so much like his once had been. "You're right."

*****

11:00 AM meetings were some of the worst one could imagine, but at least this particular client wasn't so bad. They were beyond the initial contracting phase - the one where she had a lot of technical work to do - and were mostly covering results of the company's initial evaluation. Half of the money had already been exchanged, and while the final check would be a burden, it was also her bread and butter. She propped up a book, slipped off her socks and drew out her nail polish. One foot and one toe later, the phone rang. The polish was set down and the receiver picked up.

A soft, sultry Russian accent danced over each word. "Lowery Security Services, Katrina speaking. How may I help you?" It was her standard greeting, and when projected over her client base it usually got a very hesitant male's response. This one was not. Her eyes blinked twice, and she began to furiously blow on her toenails, hoping to dry the paint before she had to re-clothe her naked foot. "Ah, yes sir. One moment, please." One hand deftly triggered the hold button.

Deciding she'd sufficiently solved the problem of toenail paint, she slipped her socks and her four-inch heels back on. Quick footsteps took her down the hallway and toward a large, fogged-over door. She knocked three times, then waited. After three seconds, she knocked three more.

"...Remains that yer company has very good internet security, but miserable countermeasures against physical intrusion." James Lowery's voice was just barely audible through the door, growing louder by the second. "My initial assessment o'yer situation is one o'serious concern, an' if w' move ahead wit' the second phase I can prove exactly how easily I can extract yer research. Miss Lark'ill take y'through my initial plans; I have t'take an urgent call, I'm afraid. Ladies, gentlemen."

A second later, James was out of the room. He nodded to Katrina and whispered a simple question; "Which?"

"Doctor Eisenberg," she replied. James looked mildly confused and definitely concerned.

He took quick footsteps to his office and closed the door, then walked to his desk. It was, all in all, a comfortable location - the desk was made of black-stained mahogany and was more than sturdy, and his chair was a rolling, felt-covered luxury model complete with built-in massage probes. Taking a seat, he spun his chair to face outside and look over the city streets so many stories below. He grabbed his phone, dialed in three buttons, then pressed the hold key.

"Physics boy!" James exclaimed with perfect happiness. "How ya doin'?"

The voice on the other end of the phone was grave. He could hear the man's heartbeat; it was slightly elevated, calm but concerned. "I have a pair of problems, Jim," Emmett declared grimly.

James sighed softly. "I 'ave a bit'o time, but I'm supposed t'be in a meetin'. What's on yer mind?"

"First things first, someone tried to kill Jethro."

His pupils dilated. In the comfort of his own office he could afford to show such emotional signals. A quick lap and he soothed parched lips. "That so? I take't they failed, 'course. Who was it?"

Emmett sounded sad. "The culprit's name is Alejan--"

"--Dro Curtis? Son of a bitch! He visited me, tried to talk me int'a restartin' the Consortium an' some other shit. He tried to kill Geddy? It fuckin' figures, Geddy killed 'is old man. Alright, so I take it y'killed the bastard?"

The physicist sighed. "No, but not for a lack of trying. When restraining him failed, he told me that he was like us."

"You have t'be fuckin' kiddin' me. What'd he do?" The spy rose from his seat and walked over to a picture. Applying pressure to the bottom two corners of it, the painting creaked and lifted itself up.

Emmett's shrug was audible on the other end of the phone. "Alejandro can't be hurt."

"Ge' out." James spun the dial of a concealed safe, now, while pressing down on a small thumb-pad. The safe's combination reset upon confirming his identity. It was only through sound that one could decipher this phase of locking mechanism, and it would continually shift combinations if his thumb-print didn't register.

"I wish. I hit him with chlorine and a taste of the sun, not to mention a sword. I think he is unaffected by external stimuli, but I'm not really sure *how* he works."

James next slipped his eyes before a small pop-out panel that scanned his pupils. A third contraption, a keypad, popped up and he entered in an identification key. Finally, the safe gave way and he reached into it to reveal a two racks of files; one white and one black. The first was ignored; it was the second he wanted. He flipped past the next collection of files (nine, to be exact) and withdrew the tenth - a blank. He began to write, furiously.

"Are you there?"

James sighed. "Yeah, Em, absolutely. Jus' makin' a note. What happened with th' bastard?"

"I imprisoned him, Geddy moved him."

"T'where?" Jim's tone held mild interest.

Emmett hesitated. "Umm. To the sun?"

James nearly dropped the phone; his pen clattered against the desk. "Wait a minute, Emmett, y'wrapped 'im up, probably in yer pretty lil' black rock, then y' had Jethro ship 'im off t'the sun?"

"Yeah," Emmett admitted.

"As in the big yellow ball in th'sky that all th' planets revolve 'round!?"

Emmett was quiet for a moment. "Yeah, that's what we did."

"My god," James stated, growing silent. For a moment, it seemed like a chastisement; it wasn't long before James began to laugh. "Tha's brilliant! Genius! 'E's invincible so le' 'im get a taste 'a hell! Y'plannin' on releasin' 'im any time soon?"

Emmett's fingertips, even gloved, made scratches on his forehead that were audible over the phone. "Yeah, probably after a few weeks. When he's had time to cool off."

James' fist hit his desk. "Fuckin' brilliant! Coolin' off at th'sun! Only you, physics-boy, could make tha' joke!"

"It wasn't a joke, James, I'm serious. The guy is up revolving around the sun. Its kind of a messed up situation. In fact, I'm wondering if he saw Erica."

James' mirth drained out of him as if he'd sprung a leak in his humor containment tanks. "T'be honest with y', Emmett, I don't know if sh'could have made 'im feel anything he didn' already. Maybe she set 'im off on a crash course, maybe not. I'll look int'a it, see if there's any phone records, see if they made contact face 't face. I might not even be able t'get an address on 'er, if she's half as smart as I think she is. 'Course, that ain't her field o'expertise, an' my Lark is better'n just 'bout anyone in th' business." Then, without warning, "Was that th' other thing you wanted t'talk about?"

A long pause accompanied the question, and was only eventually broken up by a soft, "No."

"Well, man, what else is up?" James asked, a hint of impatience coming across in his voice. In his mind, Emmett had always suffered difficulties with confrontation - but this was extremely drawn out even for 'physics-boy.'

Eventually, though, Emmett did respond. "You offered me a job. Seeing as I'm probably going to lose mine, soon? I might just take you up on it."

His eyes widened once more. "'Tha so? That's great! I mean, I don' know what y'could really do for me, but---"

For once, Emmett interrupted someone else. "I was thinking; a good friend said God would show himself in mysterious ways. Another said that its never too late to try again and make things work. Maybe - just maybe, Jim - we can make things better after all."

"Wait, Emmett, wait a second. You're suggestin' what, exactly?"

Emmett switched hands with his phone. "I think that as long as we can keep our perspective, and as long as we keep it small and the ones running it are the ones who are doing all the work, we might be able to make a new Consortium."

James didn't answer; somewhere in the back of his mind he was cursing the physicist out. Somewhere else, he wasn't aware exactly *what* he'd been told that had been so agitating. The silence was deafening, and Emmett wasn't used to it. "Jim? Are you there, Jim?"

"Yeah. Yeah. I'm thinkin'."

At further silence, Emmett again spoke up. "I mean, the money can come from me if you can keep it clean."

A flat tone. "Launderin'."

"What?" Emmett asked in puzzlement.

James sighed, fingertips finding the back of his neck. "Yer talkin' about money launderin'."

"I guess I am," the physicist admitted; more to himself than to his friend. "But its not like its the result of a crime. I'm making the money with my own effort, you know?"

The security expert laughed softly. "Emmett, yer great. If we do this - if, 'cause I haven' decided t'do it, yet - then we need Jethro and we need Sari. Erica I can take or leave, an' I suspect you'd be quicker t'leave 'er than I would."

Emmett's exhalation was one of deep sadness. "I should make things right with her, shouldn't I?" His voice was strained.

"Physics-boy," Lowery countered, "I don' think tha's possible. I think she's as busted as anyone could be, an' if she do'en't look for an answer'erself then she'll never find one. She hates y'for what happened, an' I don't blame her, but y'couldn't'a known any more'n she did. I know y'feel responsible for wha' happened, but y'didn't know everythin' that she did. Y'couldn't'ave. It isn't all yer fault."

Emmett's voice sounded as if he were conflicted, but relaxing slowly. "Yeah, I guess you're right."

"Quit bein' a pussy," chastised James. "Now, I've got'a run. I've go' 'a deal t'seal. You man up an' we'll talk about yer idea later. Toodles."

*****

He hung up the phone and slipped it back into his pocket, then stood up and brushed his hair back over his ears. Black eyes gazed over the door before him and he resentfully walked toward it. Fingers stretched out, grasped the knob, and pulled it open. He peeked into the living room and looked to his right and left, then smiled. "I'm done."

The sound of a pan colliding with a pot was heard; he'd shocked the girl in her own kitchen. "Really, Emmett? That's great! How did it go?"

"My friend was, well, I guess we'll just say he's gonna

think about it. I don't want to worry too much about he's going to take it."

Sonia leaned back, her head popping clear of the apartment's sharp edge as she gazed at the physicist's eyes. "So what are you going to do now? What's the next move?"

Emmett shrugged his shoulders. "Before I make any decisions," he declared proudly, "I'm going to enjoy some pasta. That sounds like a plan."

She stepped away from the kitchen, surprising him as she walked over to him and looked him in the eye. "And what about your ex?" Her hand slipped up to caress his face softly.

His eyes widened. "Uh, Erica, you mean?"

"Who's Erica?" asked Sonia, her hand leaving him just as quickly as it had arrived.

He winced internally, and the cock of her eyebrow indicated he'd done so externally, as well. "Erica's my ex. She's like I am, you know. She's the worst person you'd ever meet."

Sonia's eyes grew wide at the implication that this woman, too, was 'gifted'. "What's she do?"

"Emotions; she changes peoples' emotions."

"So she messes around with people's minds? What was her job at Connor Point? I mean, you do physics. Your pal does moving stuff around. That all makes sense - what'd she do to fit in?"

Emmett looked skyward. "Her official title was as a psychologist. It fits - she knows how people think about stuff. Her job was to keep us all together in the head, and I guess I appreciated that, so things happened between us." His intentionally vague description didn't seem to please Sonia very much. "Then, when we found out about Sari..." He sighed despondently. "She had to use her talents to keep me from doing something really, really bad."

"I know, you covered that whole killing people thing," she remarked with distaste. Sonia shook her head, then. "But I was asking about your other ex, the one you were dating who isn't returning your calls. What's your deal with her?"

He raised an eyebrow. "I, uh, I never said she was my ex, Sonia," the man answered cautiously. It was exactly the kind of question he should have expected out of an English major; exactly the kind of question that someone trained in logical progression might throw at him. "I'm still dating her, technically, I just haven't heard from her since we got back from New York."

"So you still love her?" his student queried with reluctance.

Emmett's heart froze. He sighed and looked to his feet. "I do love her, Sonia. I just don't know if that's gonna matter at all to her, anymore."

"If you love her," the student stated flatly, "Then you need to make a play. It'll have to be big, and if it works? Good for you, bad for me? If it doesn't?" She leaned into his ear and whispered delicately. "Let me give you another taste of what's in store."

It certainly made his next task much harder to focus on. The Pasta? Forgotten.

Chapter Eleven
Settlement

He slept.

Sonia looked precisely as she had on their first 'date,' from the unfortunately-colored hair down to the blue dress. The student was flirtatious, gently brushing his arm in a way that the one her visage replaced hadn't done in far too long, now. The two relaxed on her old, beaten-down couch and watched a movie. There were words on the TV screen, black text scrolling across white static-induced snow, but they came out alien to him: "In Hoc Signo Vinces." *He was puzzled; it wasn't English, and though it looked familiar he couldn't make out what it meant.*

"Sonia?" he asked.

The student's mouth moved, but the words were distorted. "Your violence tore us to shreds," *she declared.*

His eyes widened. "How did you kn--Wait. Wait. Is this?"

Sonia grinned cruelly, lifting one leg and straddling him, pinning him to the couch. Despite his best intentions, despite his superior physical strength, he couldn't seem to muster up the will to shove her away. "Do you like this, Emmett? Does it entice you? It should. Its exactly as demonic as you are. And demons?" She reached behind her, slipping fingers along her buttocks and removing them with a loud, sharp snap. *She held a switchblade knife up, one hand bearing down on Emmett's forehead.*

He gritted his teeth. "What are you?!" It didn't take long to realize this wasn't Sonia, after all.

"Goodbye forever, Doctor Eisenberg!" she roared, thrusting the weapon down.

"Erica, wait!" he screamed, hand finally snapping upward with the intent to defend himself. He could hear the sound of wood collapsing and blinked the sleep clear out of his eyes; the darkness was overwhelming. He struggled to make sense out of the scene before him, and that's when he grew worried - the street-lights cast just enough illumination for his glasses-less eyes to conclude that he'd conjured a wave of air pressure. One that had buckled Sonia's ceiling.

"Oh, shit," he whispered, whipping his arms above his head frantically. As one hunk of lumber collapsed he patched up another that threatened to slam down on his forehead. A good five minutes later, he'd collected himself.

It was only then that he noticed the soft, terrified panting of the woman in the bed next to him. "H...Holy shit!" she hissed out, staring up at Emmett. "What the fuck happened?!"

"I had a nightmare," he responded stoically, looking back up at the ceiling. "I fixed the damage and reinforced it," he added in an attempt to make up for the entire incident.

She glared at the man. "You had a nightmare and you so devastated my apartment? Wow. Really fuckin' classy."

"I'm sorry, I really am," he stated; he looked at the clock and it appeared to only be four in the morning.

Sonia exhaled slowly, her breathing finally coming under control. "I guess I understand. I mean, I don't, but you've got a power and you had a nightmare, so you just reacted. But it was about your ex? What did you wanna kill her, for?"

He studied her slowly. "You don't want to know."

"I do," she firmly answered.

Emmett looked to the repaired damage - one couldn't even tell it had ever been scratched, much less crumpled under the weight of sudden burst of gravity. "She was you. She took your body and tried to stab me with it."

At first, she looked completely insulted. Then, more than angry she looked thoughtful. "It was a dream, Emmett." He was silent; she insisted. "It was just a dream, wasn't it?"

Slowly, he turned to her and measured her. "I'm not safe, right now, Sonia," he cautioned, throwing his covers off of him. "I think I know what's going on, and I think it needs to come to an end."

"You're perfectly safe, Em. Lay down, go back to bed."

He closed his eyes; his adrenaline was pumping ferociously, but he was indeed tired and there was nothing he could do to confirm his theory at the time. He laid back down and slipped an arm around Sonia; it was a subconscious gesture, one she initially hesitated to embrace but ultimately accepted. He drifted back to a dreamless, but fitful sleep.

*****

Mansions were rarely located in cities, these days; they existed in large, semi-suburban counties that had incredibly high tax revenues despite incredibly low populations. Westchester County was exactly that kind of area; oh, it had its suburbs and its densely packed areas, but once one moved further away from the cities there were plenty of large spaces of land available for the taking.

He hadn't announced he'd be coming; hadn't made any effort to get in touch with her, at all. In fact, he had only gotten the information from Jim earlier in the day and he'd taken his jaunt east with an unreasonable haste. Sonia had asked to come with him - and it was a request he chose to deny on the grounds that, simply, he couldn't be sure what would happen.

Slowly, his car rolled into the driveway of the large, multi-room house. He stepped out of it and, looking at the vehicle, decided to leave it behind. After all, there was a small garage nestled at the end of the driveway with a limousine resting astride it. He walked forward and placed a hand on the door; it was locked. That didn't last for long.

His entry was only stopped by the worst-timed phone call ever.

"This is Doctor Eisenberg," he answered quietly, withdrawing the small electrical device and holding it up to his ear. He turned away from the building.

He could feel the speakers vibrate as electrons dictated the sounds it should make. Fortunately, nobody would hear the conversation if they weren't him - a lovely area of silence just happened to surround him. "Doctor Eisenberg," began the French-filled voice of the caller, "this is Doctor Daniel Marceau from Catskill Community College. Have you rethought our previous conversation?"

"Yes, I have," Emmett responded. "And frankly, I don't think I'm too worried. I've already made plans to take another job if you try to sink me. I'm getting Maria back."

The psychologist on the other side laughed. "So that is what this is about, to you? Doctor Montclaire? Whatever happened between you two is in the past. She's hurt. You need to let her get over that and stop trying to contact her."

"Blow me," Emmett retorted, hanging up his phone, returning to the house. He exhaled, and he blinked once as the sound of the breeze again managed to reach his ears. Slowly, then, his fingertips brushed the metal facade right underneath the doorknob. Gears turned, latched activated, and very slowly the metal scraped against itself; it was inaudible. He watched the space between the door and the wall with caution, and when he saw air pass through he gently tugged the door open.

The welcoming room was posh to say the least, with two chairs and a walk-in closet nestled behind a second, mercifully-opened glass door. He crept through it, listening as carefully as he could for any signs of life. He observed none, so he stepped inside of the living room. This was quite the extravagant part of his victim's domicile; dark red walls and rugs, dark red couches, and pink, heart-shaped pillows with black frills. A large picture of herself and her band hung along one wall, with a huge HDTV adorning the other. She was expressionless in the image; a completely different look than the rest of the Wildcats had on, each of whom attempted to fulfill their own appearance-based niches. A staircase leading upward was nestled into one corner of the room, with a doorway to what looked like a linoleum-tiled kitchen was tucked into the other. He turned toward the kitchen, eyes glaring into the empty room.

A loud clack, the sound of a hard substance striking wood, resonated behind him. "Anxiety, then irritation, then determination, and finally back to anxiety; all with a fine coating of guilt. Breaking in without making a sound, but using the door to do so. I have narrowed you down to three people. Only two should have had my address, and I sent the other away packing with his pretty voice'd tail between his legs. James Lowery," the malice-laced voice came closer to declaring than querying, accusing instead of asking, "have you come to die, today?"

Suddenly a wave of despair crept over Emmett; forget about using his abilities! He knew damn well his best option was to run. Yet, all he could do was clench his gloved fists defensively. Further steps drew the pale-skinned figure down the stairs. She had on sandals - and nothing else, for her hair was still covered in soap-suds. Her hollow eyes stared into Emmett's.

"Well," she declared without any evident surprise, refusing to cover herself up even now. The only movement she made was with her left hand, which trailed slowly over her stomach. Emmett couldn't help but avert his eyes as he was suddenly awash in self-hatred and poisoned memories. "I stand before my worst enemy. Doctor Eisenberg. I take it you have come here for a reason?"

He searched around for a knife, for anything - not for self defense, but to apply to himself! He gritted his teeth and closed his eyes; his fingertips flexed and he raised a very poor barrier of compressed air around himself. It was just enough to blunt the worst of her depressive rage, though he could feel the unbridled hatred burning around him, hammering away at his defenses harder than any foe had ever dreamed of.

"I..." he began, gulping once. "I'm here to talk, Erica. I want to fix things."

"Build a time machine, Eisenberg. Change your past. Since you know you cannot, do you have any last words before you commit suicide?"

He crumbled to his knees, extending one arm over his face to ward off what might as well have been a blinding spotlight of self-hatred. It was overwhelming, and before he could react he found himself forging a smaller version of the weapon he'd wielded against Alejandro; a crystalline blade as long as his hand that he held toward himself, staring at it contemplatively.

Was this the way that so many of her previous victims had gone out? The thought gave him just enough internal balance to raise stronger defenses. He lowered the weapon and gazed up at Erica. "Yes...Yes, I do. I'm sorry, Erica, I'm so sorry."

"You said that already," she concluded. He looked up toward her; her eyes were completely dead, her expression was passionless. Those downright skeletal orbs locked upon his without compassion or pity, and her hand only then managed to lower itself from her abdomen.

Emmett gritted his teeth. "We all messed up, Erica. I..." he groaned softly, struggling to find the words. "I have nightmares about it, that's why I came to iron this out!"

"Of course you have nightmares, Eisenberg. You're smart enough to have figured it out." His eyes widened. "You know the extent of my abilities. I can do more than plant conscious emotions. I can destroy your very subconscious. You will learn this soon."

He gathered enough foresight to take the knife in his hands and throw it across the house. It skittered along the floor of her kitchen, scraping the linoleum and etching a clear path until it finally slid point-first into the bottom of a cabinet, puncturing it with a dull thud. The woman before him didn't even look up to notice. "I will!" he concurred. "But I also know you're limiting what I feel right now. I'm not feeling what you are - just what you want me to."

"Oh?" Erica remarked, her head turning ever so slightly as if she was intrigued by the idea. It was a fleeting emotion. "And why does that matter?"

It was a difficult gambit, but so far he was finding success. He looked downward, the intensity of Erica's emotions fading slightly. It was clear she wanted him to continue - otherwise she would have kept cranking her powers up. "Uhm..." he took a deep breath in, the first solid O2 intake he'd had in the last five minutes. "Think about it. If I was, you know, to feel the way you feel? *That* would be justice. That would be the only fair thing, right?"

"Quaint," she pronounced, glaring down at him suspiciously. "You are not just saying it to save your own life, either. I would know. You really do wish to experience how I feel. How I felt. Fine. I'll grant you this wish. It does not make us even, Eisenberg. Nothing can. I can taste how conflicted you are - your precious, yet lost girlfriend or that new, adorable fuck. Your optimism and your pessimism." She continued to look down at him with hardly a scrap of emotion in her eyes. Soap suds continued to drip down her body as she judged him. "Even your little self-doubts, the fear that you're just as evil as you were ten years ago. You're as pathetic as you ever were. Do you have anything else you want to say to me?"

Emmett winced and looked to the side. "Not really. I'm just very, very sorry; I hope that some day you find an inner peace, because I think I'm really close."

"Oh?" she laughed a mirthless laugh. "Inner peace is a lie. You won't find any - and as to being close? Enjoy this, Doctor Eisenberg. If I ever see you again, you'll kill yourself, for sure. It will be just like in Oceania - you will realize your sins, now, and repent for them. Some later day, a day of my convenience, you will die for them." With that ominous declaration she closed her eyes and extended a palm down toward the defeated Master of Physics.

Emmett's eyes widened. His heart raced so quickly it was threatening to explode. He scrambled to his feet, crawling like a dog for a moment, then ran for the door. He didn't hold anything back, and the wood burst into splinters as he tore its molecular bonds apart simply because it would save him a few seconds over fumbling with the knob.

His feet slammed against the small pebbles of the driveway, sending them spewing in all directions as he found his car door and began to frantically push the remote-control lock device while ripping at the handle. He managed to finally activate the devices properly and jumped into his seat, starting his vehicle. The open door hung out until he backed up and stopped, closing it; he slammed his foot on the accelerator and topped out at a hundred miles an hour heading downhill - a true feat for his hybrid, one probably only possible thanks to the power of gravity. It was a miracle that he didn't lose control of the car; and he only slowed down when he realized he needed to merge with oncoming traffic and that his speed would get him killed.

Once he'd put some distance between himself and Erica, he realized exactly what he'd experienced - her true feelings. Or were they? *"Is she just playing a game with me? Did she just choose to scare me off?"* he wondered to himself, *"Or does she really feel this feeling every second of every day?"* He managed to reduce his car's speed to a respectable seventy five miles an hour by the time he hit the highway; still more than illegal, but at least he was only slightly outrunning traffic.

"Dear god! How can I have been so stupid as to go up against her? How could I have hoped she'd see reason? I really did break her." He grit his teeth and tapped his brake, reducing his speed to an acceptable, if still 'too fast' level. His eyes took in the trees as he flew by them, and he changed lanes to dodge a slightly-slower vehicle. *"But, well, at least now I know. Now I know how she feels. Oh god, no wonder she doesn't show any emotion but hatred."*

His gloved fingers ran over his face slowly, and he trembled as he recalled the wave of terror that rush through his body. With a conscious effort to draw in a deep breath, he relaxed into the drivers' seat and continued his trek home. His heart rate began to slow when he was around twenty miles from Erica's, and he was home almost before he knew it.

*****

The phone rang.

He glanced at the number displayed on the Caller ID and, with resignation, hit the accept button on his phone. "Hello," he offered. Soft footfalls carried him to his couch.

"Doctor Eisenberg," the Russian offered politely, "This is Katrina. Hold for Mister Lowery."

With a pair of quick beeps, the Irishman's lilt echoed into his ear. "Hey Emmett, jus callin' t'see how things went."

"I'm still alive," the physicist responded. A peek at his alarm clock revealed it to be 9:47 AM; far, far earlier than he'd intended to get up.

James' voice was calm and genuine. "Well, that's a surprise. I figured y'for a dead man. Think she knew I gave y' 'er address?"

"She thought I *was* you, at first. And," he added, "it was really, truly bad."

Jim actually laughed at this. "Good, then; y'lived and i't'was only bad! Th' bad news is that she'll probably declare a holy war on me. Did y'find out if Curtis was in bed with 'er?"

"No. Wait, actually," the physicist struggled to recall, "she mentioned someone she sent packing. It was probably him; she said he had a pretty voice, so it was probably him."

"Probably a yes, then. Alrighty, Physics-Boy, tha's good enough fer me. Have y're-thought yer offer to me?"

Emmett knew exactly what this meant. "Not really. I got another threat from the Psychology head, and I think he's gonna have me fired soon. Chances are I won't have a job next semester."

James chuckled once more. Before Emmett could protest, he managed to form giggle-distrubed words. "Oh great, he's that big'o a dick, eh? Well'en, you're in luck! I've decided I'll help y'start up yer own lil' research corporation!" Emmett's lips curved into a grin. "I've got enough weight in the financial world thanks to Lark's great accountin' skills tha' I can create a small channel for raw gold an' other materials t'be redistributed t'high bidders. Its a seller's market, right now."

"What would I ever do without you? Wait, don't answer that," Emmett decided, a smirk touching his lips. "How about Geddy, is he interested?"

"'Ol Jethro said he wants nothin' t'do with it," James

stated; Emmett was stunned. After all the talk about being on the path to being 'good,' Geddy had decided to stay out of this project? Emmett understood, but he didn't expect what came next. "O'Course," Jim added, "his old lady told'im to quit bein' a coward and t'give it a crack. He's in, but he's gonna wanna take it slow."

Emmett nearly applauded to himself. "Great!" he remarked, leaning back in his seat. "Did Sari have anything to say about it?"

"I haven't been able to get in touch with 'er, actually. She's on vacation, I think, but I'll hear from her soon. I'm sure o'that."

The physicist nodded to himself. "Alright, excellent! Then I'll talk to ya soon?"

"Absolutely, Physics-Boy. Get tha' first shipment of gold ready t'go. Be safe."

He laughed gently. "Alright. See ya, Jim." He hung up the phone and stared at it for a moment, halfway melting into his couch. Then, casually, he tossed it across the sofa and, after a pair of soft bounces, it nestled itself right into the crook of the furniture's arm. There was something innately satisfying about the return to constructive business; "*I guess the days of pretending to be a normal person are coming to an end. And thank God for that.*"

His thoughts were interrupted by a loud buzzing sound coming from his phone. A text message, most likely - he decided to check it. He flipped his phone open and his eyebrows raised slightly. The name on the caller ID was Maria Montclaire.

"Meet me at the Coffee Hut in an hour if you want to talk."

Gloved fingers ran through his hair slowly; he shivered, once, as he contemplated his next move. Would he text her back? Of course. Would he go? Almost certainly. But, what would he say? Moreover, what did she want? How would she react to the events of the Midtown Ballroom? He stood up and went to his closet, throwing on a nice pair of pants and a suit-jacket to match his brown gloves; gloves that he replaced with an identical pair.

Before he left, he took the time to withdraw his journal from its resting place.

Erica is dealt with. Her greatest emotion, according to what I felt, was fear. Horrible terror that couldn't be escaped no matter how fast I drove. If she's trapped with that, if she's been trapped with that for ten years, then I really didn't do right by her. She could have killed me. Maybe she should have, but she didn't.

Otherwise, I've decided to give saving the world one more try. I think that my friends and I can keep one another honest. I think we can work it all out. I'm being optimistic, I know, but its worth a shot. At least I feel anchored, now. It has to be - natural resources are scarce and will only grow scarcer. If I can find a way to help change our fate as a species, then maybe it will make up, in some cosmic sense, for the crimes I committed ten years ago.

Finally, Maria; she wants to talk. I don't know why. I'm going meet with her now, and we'll see what happens.

The trip to the Coffee Hut was short; it was in town, after all, within a Triple-C student's walk from the campus. The building itself was a renovated house and its exterior was nothing fancy, with simple wooden panels coated in white paint and large windows permitting a view of the changing fall foliage. Its interior? Well, that was another story; walls had been strategically knocked down to create an open atmosphere while couches and large, cushioned chairs were arranged in such a fashion that it created small nooks that, when sitting with friends, created a sense of seclusion. It was paradoxical and effective, making for a neat little place to get coffee, tea, or some snack-style foods.

Stepping inside, he glanced around and quickly identified the strawberry-headed woman he had an appointment with. Soft steps took him toward her and, perhaps more importantly, around a small but tightly stacked line. Consequently, he was quickly intercepted by a hostess.

"Hello, sir, can I help you?"

Emmett studied the girl; she was tall and husky, with black hair tied back in a bun, and most likely a student at the college working a job to get by. She had a name-tag that read, "Happy to Help!" and, on a second line, "Lisa!" He gestured toward the table Maria sat at. "I'm meeting up with that lady over there, actually."

"Oh," the hostess answered flatly, as if her authority had somehow been surpassed and she was spiteful about it. "Okay, then, go ahead," she attempted to permit.

Emmett politely nodded. "Thanks, Lisa," and ignored an irked glare or two from other patrons as he strolled past the crowd, navigating the different curves of the couches as he finally approached Maria. His eyes met hers' for an instant, then looked down at the relatively simple chair before him. A metallic frame with a pad on the seat? It would have to do.

Relaxing into it, he looked up at the psychologist once more. "Hi," he offered politely.

"Hey," she responded in kind, locking her green eyes with his gray. "Know what you want, already?" she asked swiftly.

He gazed down at the menu; the Coffee Hut had plenty of special, nifty names for their drinks. One, for example, was the "Whip McCinny," a lovely drink consisting of Irish Cream flavored coffee, whipped cream, and cinnamon. This was only obvious because its ingredients were listed underneath the name, all followed by a fairly substantial price tag for a single cup.

"Y'know," he briskly concluded, "I'm gonna go with a Raspberry Tea. Simple, default, but there's no way I could run through all of these choices and settle on just one. I think I'll also add..." he flipped through to the baked-goods section. "A chocolate chip cookie sundae. Sound good to you?"

"Whatever works, Emmett," Maria replied distantly. She raised a finger.

Sure enough, Lisa walked over to the group and pulled out

a green pad with a red label reading 'guest check.' "Hi! I'm Lisa, and I'll be your server?" She gazed down at Emmett. "How can I help you?"

"Umm, well I'll take a Raspberry Tea--" he began.

She interrupted. "Large or small?"

"Whatever, I guess large," he answered indifferently, refusing to be goaded. He gazed up toward Lisa, then. "And a Chocolate Chip Cookie Sundae."

"What kind of ice cream would you like with that?"

Emmett shrugged. "Vanilla, I guess. Hot fudge if you have it."

"Sure. And what can I get for you, miss?" she asked with a much less hostile tone.

Maria smiled. "I'll try your Mocha Meltdown." Emmett began to navigate quickly through the menu; he determined that this was mocha coffee with no milk; instead, a scoop of vanilla ice cream was added to the concoction, and a shot of espresso was poured over it.

"Alright, sounds good. I'll bring that right out for you," Lisa said, practically snatching the menu out of Emmett's hand while he was still reading. She traipsed off, and the physicist gazed over at the psychologist and allowed his shoulders to rise and fall meaningfully.

"I wonder if she makes good tips?" he asked idly.

Maria couldn't fight back the hint of a smile, but she quickly used a loose strand of hair as an excuse to obscure her face with her hand and tuck it back behind her ear. "I've decided," she declared without any opening fencing, "that you've got one chance to explain to me exactly what you want from me. Daniel was crushed when I took my leave from the college."

Emmett sounded stumped. "Who is Daniel, again?"

Maria raised an eyebrow. "Daniel Marceau, my supervisor. He said you were rude to him in person and on the phone, actually."

Emmett clenched a fist under the table, masking it from his girlfriend - or, at least, his *official* girlfriend. "He basically threatened my job." The strawberry-headed woman's face contorted in disbelief. "That's alright, I guess, because I've been thinking it over and I think I need to go back to doing something with my talents."

She leaned back in her seat, almost baiting him. "Come again, Emmett?"

It was only then, when he recognized the thoroughly disenchanted tone in her voice, that he realized he hadn't at all meant to open their conversation this way. In fact, he concluded almost immediately afterward that he hadn't planned it out at all - he had absolutely no idea what to say to her, no matter how often he'd called her and offered to discuss things over!

"Maria, I've decided I'm going to work with Geddy and Jim again"

She stared at him disapprovingly. "Like ten years ago, you mean." It was a statement, not a question, and she didn't like it either way.

"Yes, but no. We're going to try it again, and we're going to do everything in our power to keep from going back to what we were." Emmett whispered in a hushed voice. "I think its too important for the future to let our abilities go unused."

Maria continued to stare at him. He looked back, and there was no shame in his expression - only, strangely enough, hope. Finally, she looked down at the table. "You're insane. That's *my* decision, Emmett. You're crazy. You people - these *friends* of yours - are playing some kind of sick game. Hell, I should put you in my book - you're delusional, Emmett, and you need help."

He leaned forward in his seat and reached for her hand; she avoided the grasp of his gloves and folded her arms over her chest. He sighed and tapped the table softly. "Maria, I'm not crazy."

She pursed her lips and leaned forward, practically hissing her retort in an afterthought toward their privacy. "You people talked about blowing up the world!" she hissed. "You were like some super-villain with a doomsday machine! Its madness,

Emmett! I don't know why you had to involve me in your little game, but you're a sick, sick man."

"Maria, its real." He flexed his fingertips and produced a tiny green stone; an emerald, one he conjured by altering air molecules into vital components and shoving them all together. His heart beat quickly. "See?"

"See what?" she looked at the gem, then tossed it casually to the floor. His heart sank even as the logical part of his mind was stunned that such an expensive stone could be discarded so callously. "You pulled it out of your gloves and tried to pass off some slight-of-hand as magic. You're just like all the other mentally incapacitated people I've met. I bet that when the reactor at Connor Point got messed up, you guys all snapped and this is the best you can do to explain what happened to yourself."

Emmett opened his mouth to speak. "Its like all of the gods of the ancient days, Emmett," she blurted out over him. "Lightning strikes so there's Zeus, floods happen so there's Poseidon. You can't explain it, and you rationalize it. You're like the priests, Emmett - giving doubters something to believe just to trick them into paying a tithe."

For a moment, the physicist contemplated the otherwise-unthinkable. He considered conjuring his diamond sword, suggested to himself that he should summon a sphere of glass larger than the table and fuse it to a wall. It would certainly prove his point! Of course, it would also undermine every last hope he had of starting a new life for himself.

"Maria," he responded with an exasperated tone, "if you'd just come back with me to my apartment, I could show you. I could prove it."

Maria and Emmett had been a great pair because they thought alike. They both understood the value of research, both understood the way the other thought. That's why his plea met exactly the response he feared. "Why not now, Emmett?" she retorted dryly. "Why not prove it to me right now? The answer is that you can't! You'll give me some story about how it would put peoples' lives in jeopardy and how it would reveal your dark little secret to the world. You'll peddle some snake-oil excuse for a trick at your apartment, something where you look one way and something just happens to take place. I don't buy it, Emmett, and if you want to throw your job away to live in some fantasy land then-- what?"

Maria's tirade slowed as he pointed behind her; approaching quickly was their unhappy hostess, Lisa. She set a tray down on the table and stepped away without a word; on it was a pair of gray clay cups, one filled with a fusion of ice cream and coffee with the second empty. Additionally, a large black tea kettle and a metal tin with melting vanilla ice cream and hot fudge, along with whipped cream and a cherry, topped the meal off. The psychologist tilted her head back and sipped at the concoction, and her eyes visibly softened at the mere flavor of it.

"Alright," she continued, her voice noticeably calmer but incredibly stern, "listen. If you want to throw your life away, then you're throwing me away, too. Is that really what you want?"

He winced; she was dropping an ultimatum she had no idea of the circumstances behind. To top it off, his phone buzzed. The latter was ignored, but the former was addressed simply. "I'm not throwing it away, Maria. Its real. I promise, I can prove it."

The woman closed her eyes and shook her head. "Emmett, you're going to be fired. Do you understand this? Fired. You hung up on Daniel, insulted him, and told him you planned on causing problems for our department. You don't have tenure!"

"I think he likes you, Maria," Emmett stated at random. He took the kettle and poured the red liquid into his cup, then added two spoonful's worth of sugar from a large glass container.

The psychologist's eyes widened and she blushed for an instant, then looked away from him. "Maybe he does, Emmett, but that's not what this is about. This is about you messing with my head and talking about being a killer. Em, you're sick. Please," she half-pleaded, "don't push this."

"Maria, I'm sorry. Its the truth. If you don't understand, then I don't blame you. I'm..." he sipped at his tea. "Wow, this is really good."

"Isn't it?" she countered, sighing gently and looking around. Emmett, in the lull, looked down at his phone. It was another text message; and his teeth found his bottom lip as he read the name: Sonia Monterrey. He clicked on accept.

"Saw u at the Hut. Montclaire huh? Very cute. Have fun u 2!"

His eyes immediately began to shift around, scanning the house for his student. So far, no luck; from twenty degrees to three hundred and sixty, he couldn't isolate the blonde. That was unsettling enough, but as he put his phone away he looked up to find Maria's eyes closed in contemplation. "Umm," he struggled to begin, "what's bothering you?"

"I hate to have to do this, Emmett, I really do, but I have to. Goodbye" She stood up, set down a five dollar bill, and started out of the door.

Emmett stood up. "Maria! Wait! I promise you, just come by my apartment and we can talk about it!" His voice drew the attention of half of the room; Maria's shoulders rose as her height diminished and she marched dutifully out of the coffee hut.

Lisa strolled past and gave Emmett a dirty look. "Sounds like someone said the wrong thing," she chirped in a cheery tone, an inauthentic attempt to seem reassuring. She also handed him the green check from earlier along with a polystyrene (so often generalized as Styrofoam) cup and box, then briskly walked away. He gazed it over; twelve dollars and twenty seven cents. He put down exact change, poured his tea into the cup and rolled his ice cream dish over into the box, then marched out of the Coffee Hut and glared around for a sign of either of the two women in his life. No such luck.

He gazed down at his cell phone and typed back a quick response to Sonia: "It went poorly. Sorry you had to see us together."

The walk to his car was relatively quick, seeing as he was parked just outside of the building, but by the time he returned he had another message from the student; "Want 2 talk? Come 2 my place." Grumbling internally about today's youth and literacy, he stepped into his vehicle and began to drive. This trip was completely uneventful; no speeding, no larceny, no deception and no supernatural combat or explosions. It was a simple jaunt through the countryside.

Arriving at Sonia's apartment, he was greeted at the door with a warm smile. Today, her hair was black; he wondered exactly how much money she'd been spending on dye, lately, since he'd never observed this trend during the first half of the semester. Shrugging the curiosity off, he made his way upstairs. "I take it you don't want coffee," she remarked at the sight of his upheld cup and chilly, condensation-covered tray. "But sit down, lets talk! I didn't know Maria was Montclaire Maria!"

He took a seat and whipped out a plastic spoon, taking a bite out of his sundae and shrugging indifferently. "She thinks I'm crazy," he offered openly.

"You are crazy. But, I'd have sex with her too, so you aren't *that* crazy," she countered with a laugh. Without requesting an invitation, she reached out and seized his spoon, chomping off a bit of that ice cream and cookie combination for herself. She blinked to herself, grinning as she chirped, "That's really good! I worked at the Coffee Hut for a while, actually."

"*That explains her talent for making coffee,*" he thought with a grin to himself. "I could tell," he added carefully. "Did you happen to know Lisa when you worked there?"

"Lisa? Yeah, I knew her. Kind of a bitch," she took another bite, "Really missed the ice cream she makes, though."

His brows rose. "*She* makes this stuff?" Suddenly, he wanted it a bit less - or, perhaps, he liked her just a little bit more than the 'not at all' he previously had.

"Once in a while," Sonia answered. "Anyhow, your girlfriend thinks you're crazy? Couldn't you have just proven things to her right then and there?"

The physicist sighed and rubbed his forehead with gloved fingertips. "I tried. I formed her an emerald and she thought it was a prop that I pulled like some crummy stage-magician playing a card trick. She tossed it across the room."

"Shit!" Sonia exclaimed in astonishment, "George is - oh, he's the owner," she filled in. "he's gonna be rich if he finds it! Awesome! Oh, yeah," she calmed down at a baleful glance from Emmett, "I'm sorry it didn't work out. Really, I am, because you really loved that woman. Its rare to find that sort of thing; and I know, I can tell."

Emmett studied the student, trying to gauge whether she was about to burst into laughter at her statement or whether she was actually serious. When no mirth was forthcoming, he took a sip of his tea and smiled a bit. "Did I? I guess I did."

"Then again," the girl countered as she took another bite of Emmett's ice cream, "what would I know? I'm just the girl that fucks her professor. And the best part? I'm not even doing it for a good grade!"

Emmett smirked dryly, setting his cup down. "Actually," he offered, "they're different categories. You would have gotten an A in Physics, anyway."

"Oh? And what about this?" she queried as she unceremoniously stood up, walked toward him and sat down in his lap. Her legs dangled off his thighs as she turned her upper torso to face him.

Emmett smiled, relaxing into his seat; one hand darted up to her head and dragged fingertips through her hair slowly. "So far? Maybe a B-." She swatted at him - he grinned and ducked out of the way of her hands. "But you're quickly gaining more points!"

Chapter Twelve
Successful Schemes

If he had placed a bet on it with himself, he would have won; the phone call came on Monday morning, right when he'd expect it - at 9:00, when the office opened. He woke up lazily and checked his voice-mail; he greeted by Shelly's warm voice. "Doctor Eisenberg, Doctor Samuels has asked for you to come in today and have a talk with Doctors Marceau and Montclaire from the Psychology department. If you can, make it in at one PM; if not, call and let us know."

Emmett sighed; things weren't looking up. Excusing himself from Sonia's place, he retreated swiftly to his own apartment before taking care of business matters. After the short journey, he picked up his phone and called to confirm the appointment. Following the first, he placed a second call to a different party. The dial tone buzzed twice. He was greeted by a now-familiar voice on the other end of the line. "Lowery Security Services, Katrina speaking."

"Hey Katrina," he stated calmly and politely, "its Doctor Eisenberg. Is Jim available?"

She sounded strangely pleased to receive the call; far more happy than she usually came off. "Good morning. Hold for Mister Lowery." Then, he was treated to a lovely, gentle click. After about seven seconds of boring lounge music, the receiver clicked once again.

"Physics boy!" Jim exclaimed excitedly, "How are ya?"

Emmett smiled to himself, finding humor in the fact that his tone of voice was going to finally be a source of confusion for the spy. "I'm probably about to be fired, Jim, so I hope everything is well on your end!"

James chortled. "Y'sound happy about that! Yer timin' couldn't be better." he silenced his laughter with some effort

"Check yer mailbox. If me calculations're correct, ye'll have a check book an' a bank account statement t'look over."

Now, the physicist's eyes blinked. He shifted his phone from one shoulder to the other, threw on a pair of pants, slippers, and a robe, then headed down to his mailbox. "Hold on a sec," he requested, walking over to the receptacle and opening it. His fingertips flipped through the documents enclosed; a statement from the Grummit Capital Bank, a major multi-national corporate credit network, thanking him for his opening deposit of $100,000. Furthermore, there were checks in his name! With his address! Everything was signed off by managers and vice-presidents of business accounts; everything was legal and legitimate.

"Nice as always, Jim, downright perfect," Emmett remarked as he skimmed the other documents; most important of them was a confirmation letter from a gold purchasing company that provided the opening deposit and, more importantly, a promise of nine times that amount upon receipt and approval of his first shipment of raw gold.

James echoed his thoughts; "According'to officials, only about twenty percent o' that money's actually profit. Most of it is earmarked for shippin' an' production. In reality, since y'produced it all yourself, all yer doin' is payin' fer shippin' yer sample; I figure you'll need somewhere around thirty G's t'ship securely. Lark's prepared all th' documents you'll need - an' you'll find 'em comin' yer way about tomorrow'r so. Until then? Spend th'rest wisely an' remember tha' when yer done, there's more to come!"

Deep inside, Emmett felt just a tiny pang of guilt over his fund-raising methods; then, of course, he consoled himself with the knowledge that it was all going to something greater - it was all going to the construction of a new future for the world. Then it hit him: He still had a loose end to tie up!

"Oh! Hey, Jim," he began hurriedly, "did you manage to reach Sari?"

His friend sounded confused for a moment. "Huh? Who? Oh, right, Sari! O'course! Yeah! She's in; she said she wants an equal share for her time, both in profit an' in authority, because if we start turnin' on ourselves again sh' wants t'be the first t' know so sh' can stoppit. Its the opposite o'Geddy, who wants to be on th'outside t'start with until we prove ourselves. Both of 'em are afraid of this. It isn't unreasonable of 'em."

"I don't blame them," Emmett answered sincerely, "it went really badly last time. I don't know if it'll work this one, even. We might fail completely."

"What was that?" Jim asked; Jim never mis-heard him on the phone. When Emmett drew a breath in, he could make out the sound of the phone scraping against James' head. "Sorry Em, not you; Katrina? Yes, yes." The spy exhaled slowly, sounding almost bored with the explanation the Russian had given him. "Anyhow, Emmett, it'll work. I'm sure of it. Just let me know when you've signed off on th' shipment, an' we're good to go. Alright? Great."

After hanging up the phone, Emmett tossed on a brown suit-jacket and looked outside of his window at the rolling hills in the distance. The middle part of Autumn had given way to the later, now; he was being treated to a classical November collage of red, yellow, green, orange, and brown shades. He selected a blue undershirt and a brown jacket to wear on top of brown pants. His gloves were replaced delicately. A plan hatched in his mind and he retrieved a trio of plain, white envelopes. He walked out to his car and drove through the colorful roads to Catskill Community College for his greatest show-down yet - a duel of the minds with Daniel Marceau.

*****

Entering into the Physics Department's waiting area, he turned his eyes upon his favorite secretary and smiled. "Hey, Shelly," he offered politely, along with a casual wave.

"Doctor Eisenberg! Hi!" she stood up and walked over to the physicist. She gave him a hug; a pretense that excused her soft whispering. "Is everything alright? This meeting is rather sudden!"

Emmett laughed and smiled to himself. "We'll talk afterwards, Shelly. Everything is good." She patted her on the back once, then - without warning - stepped back toward the conference room. As expected, the door was open; though he could see through the glass panels that his boss, Dr. William Samuels, was sitting across from Maria and Daniel. He was a five foot, three inch chubby man with no hair and a beard growing from his chin. The room they all sat in was decorated with glass-encased paintings of atomic structures and astronomical phenomenon; the Horsehead Nebula, to be precise.

He offered the three gathered educators a smile and a wave, then closed the door behind himself. He took a seat on Bill's right, gazing the three over and folding his hands in his lap. "Hi," he stated politely.

Marceau's eyes moved to Emmett's with displeasure. "So, Doctor Eisenberg, we're here to talk about your behavior over the last two weeks." He exuded an authoritarian tone, one that offered false permission and dictated the future. "Where do you think it would be best to begin?"

"I don't know," Emmett responded, giving a deferring glance to his boss, Bill. "Wherever you've decided is best?"

"Well," his superior opened hesitantly, "Doctor Marceau says you've been harassing Doctor Montclaire. He said you've been calling her a lot, trying to talk to her even when she doesn't respond, and he said that when he asked you to back off your pursuit, you were rude in your refusal." Bill sounded worried; not so much for himself, but for his colleague.

Emmett opened his mouth to defend himself, but Maria beat him to it. "Actually," the surprised-sounding psychologist said, "I just want to make clear that he wasn't harassing me. Not *really* harassing me, anyway. I mean, we had just broken up, so he wanted to explain himself to me. He might have gone too far, but I'm not really mad about that."

"Umm, sure, we can go with that," Emmett concurred; and his eyes drifted to Daniel. "And Doctor Marceau, I tried to be polite with you, but you couldn't let up. You got into my business and I didn't appreciate it. If that was rude, I'm sorry, but I'm a fairly private man."

The somewhat muscular professor looked back at Emmett, eyeball to eyeball, and shook his head. "Whatever you did or did not appreciate, Doctor Eisenberg, your response of - quote - 'blow me' - unquote - was unacceptable. You were bothering my colleague, and I tried to reason with you. That went poorly. You're hardly one that I see having a future at this institution, with your behavior."

"You might be right," Emmett retorted with a dry tone.

Bill glanced sideways toward his subordinate and held a hand up. "Now, wait just a minute Doctor Marceau. You aren't pushing to have Emmett fired, are you?" He laughed as if the mere idea of signing off on such a pink slip was comedic gold. "He's one of the most promising scientists in this country. More to the point, its *his* personal life, not yours. You chose to get involved, you deal with the consequences."

"I was protecting Doctor Montclaire, Doctor Samuels," the Frenchman psychologist interjected, looking the elder physicist dead in the eye.

The female raised an eyebrow. "I was never in any danger, Daniel. I was stressed and upset, but I don't think he was ever going to hurt me. I'm more worried about Emmett then I am mad at him, to be honest."

Now, Bill scratched his head. He looked at Emmett, who merely smiled back at his boss, and then turned to Maria. "Please," the director requested, "elaborate a little. Why are you worried about him?"

"Emmett's not okay right now, Bill. Lets quit the professionalism for sixty seconds - Em." She stared at him. "You need help. You're going to jeopardize your career over your daydreams about doing the world some good. You're doing plenty of it here! You just need to get some therapy, to clear your mind. Do you know what Emmett experienced when he worked at Connor Point ten years ago, Doctor Samuels? Didn't you talk about it when you hired him?"

At this question, Emmett actually frowned; Bill rubbed his chin thoughtfully, then shook his head. "There was a reactor melt-down. It was very troubling. It was a huge crisis, and the stress on a nuclear engineer facing those kind of conditions will definitely take a toll." It sounded almost, for just a minute, as if Bill really understood where the younger physicist was coming from. "Emmett took a few years off to get his mind together, then he went about rebuilding his life. I didn't ask for specifics because I looked at his track-record as a physicist, and he's the best in this business. We're not firing him, so take that off the table right now."

"You're right about that," Emmett remarked with a grin; a grin that clearly began to infuriate Daniel Marceau the longer he kept it on. Slowly, the younger physicist reached into his suit-jacket's inside pocket. As the silence left behind by his retort started to age, Emmett withdrew an envelope from his coat.

"What is that?" asked the male psychologist with a hint of impatience sewn through his voice.

Emmett appeared to ignore him, running his fingertip underneath the glue seal of the container and withdrawing a small slip of paper. He took out a pen and applied it to the colored sheet within. "This," he stated just before Marceau had a chance to explode. "Is a check I am signing for twenty thousand dollars." The room grew suddenly silent, as if breathing were a sin. "I want it to go to renovations in the physics department laboratories. I know we could use new equipment."

"Where the hell did you get this kind of money?" exclaimed Maria with surprise in her voice. "Have you started selling your belongings?" It was one of the most classic signs of a psychological break-down; large gestures which could even end in suicide. "Please, Emmett, don't do this!"

The physicist merely handed the check to Bill (who seemed as confused as humanly possible as he accepted it) and laughed off her concern. "Maria, I loved you. I really wish you had given me a chance to prove that I'm not crazy. Some day, maybe you'll believe me."

"Emmett," Bill stated in a worried voice, "what are you thinking? What are you about to do?"

The physicist stood up and extended his hand to his boss; the man rose almost instinctively to take the offered palm. "I'm sorry, Bill. I quit. I have a calling to follow."

"Have you gone mad?" Daniel remarked. Then, he looked thoughtfully to the ceiling. "I suppose that's a terrible question - you *are* mad."

"Emmett, you can't really want to quit? What are you going to do for a living?" Bill queried again, holding his colleague's hand as the younger man tried to withdraw from the exchange.

The now-former professor merely shrugged. "I have some arrangements worked out with two companies - Lowery Security Services, and Construction Connections. They're both grade-A organizations that I'm happy to be affiliated with."

Maria stormed across the table and stared her ex-boyfriend in the eye. Her body blocked his access to the doorway. "Your friends are insane, Emmett! They've got you deluded into thinking that they can somehow save the world."

"Save who now?" Bill interjected, puzzled at the exchange.

Emmett laughed and seized his hand back in order to softly pat Maria on the shoulder. "We will. It'll be different this time, you'll see. Maria, Dan, Bill - I'll see you around, I promise." Before any further protests could take place, he gently guided Maria to the side and started walking. By the time they even raised a voice to object, he'd cleared the doorway and started walking toward the front desk.

Shelly stood up and cocked her head to the side. He seemed entirely too cheery for a man who had just been chewed out. "Doctor Eisenberg, are you okay? I was worried!"

"Actually, Shelly, I took your advice." At her puzzled look, he held up a finger. "Remember when you told me that my mileage may vary? About God?"

"Yeah, I do," she conceded after a moment's thought.

The physicist shrugged his shoulders. "I might not have found a speed limit sign quite yet, or any other markers, but I think I found the road I need to be on. I think I got some little clues to tell me what I need to do."

"That's wonderful, Doctor Eisenberg! But what happened in the meeting? Marceau seemed really mad about something, he really wanted to get your goat." Emmett just laughed in face of the psychologist's threat. "Why is that funny?" Shelly asked him with an askance glare.

His response was to reach into his coat and withdraw a second envelope. His pen was utilized as an opening device and he looked her over briefly. "Because it is," he acquiesced vaguely, setting his newly-freed check on her desk and quickly signing it.

"What's that? Wait," she commanded. "That's a check. Why are you? Huh, that's my name. And - Emmett, no. No, Emmett."

He looked up and presented her with the small slip of paper. "Shelly, listen. This is for you - for all your help and your good advice. Buy something that will make your life better."

"Its five thousand dollars, Emmett!" she protested loudly.

"So find a mutual fund for it and invest it; something for you or your kids, something that will help you in the long term. Believe me, this isn't a lot of money for me, anymore. You helped clear me up when I was confused, so now you get a bit of the reward for it. You've earned it, Shelly, and don't let anything convince you otherwise. I'll be around once in a while, since I have to clear out my office."

She looked the document over again and again, rolling it between her fingers as if she were a child contemplating a new toy she'd come across. The implication of his statement was crystal-clear - he was quitting, or fired, and he was going to leave her with this parting gift. Finally, she sighed. "I hope you get a mileage sign soon, Emmett."

"I hope so too, Shelly, but for now at least I know I'm on

the right road. Goodbye! Oh, and thanks again," he offered, strolling out of the Physics department he'd called home for the last chunk of his life and kissing the past farewell; even as he kissed the future hello.

Speaking of futures, the next destination he had in mind was a small apartment building in the central part of town. He pulled his vehicle up in front of it and dashed off a brief text-message. A moment later he was escorted up and into his mark's room.

"Coffee?" Sonia asked politely, pouring herself a cup. Strangely enough, she still had black hair; she hadn't redyed it, indicating that perhaps she'd found a new preference.

Emmett nodded. "Sure, Sonia, that sounds good."

"Same as always?"

"Yeah. I actually have to talk about something pretty serious, right now, Sonia."

The girl frowned; she quickly distributed two cups and saucers, one to each of them, and took a seat on the other side of the table. She exhaled slowly and took a slow pull from the very top of her drink; it was steaming, but not so hot as to burn her lips. Emmett mimicked the motion, then she looked him in the eye. "What's on your mind?"

He set his cup to its coaster and shrugged. "I've officially left the college; I just had a meeting to resolve it."

Sonia scratched her head confusedly. "I'm sorry? I mean, you were planning to move on, anyway, so I don't see why this is such a surprise to me."

The physicist sighed. "True!" he concurred, "but then you have to factor in the idea that I was going to be chased out by the head of the Psychology department, anyway. One way or another it was happening."

"So how are things with your friends?" she asked, "are you ready to make a move? Start savin' the world again, Emmett?" she questioned with a teasing tone, her head lolling to the side slightly as she spoke.

His response was to withdraw a final envelope from his

pocket and unseal it with his pen. A quick signature later and he produced the check to her. "Already made it. Sonia, this is a check for--"

"Twenty grand!?" she exclaimed, looking at the document then back up to the professor. "What's this about?"

He blinked, perhaps not having expected such an energetic reaction. "Its for your schooling, and as a down payment toward working at the company I'm forming up."

"Is it?" she stated speculatively, doubt creeping like a vine into her voice and entangling his good intentions, "or is it a bribe? Is it hush money for being the girl you fucked on the side? That's a lot of dough, Emmett, so tell me what this is about."

Was he hurt? He wasn't sure; but there was definitely a pain in the center of his chest. He'd considered this little more than generosity - and in exchange, he found himself challenged by someone he was stunned to be so effected by. "Sonia, no. No! Its not like that."

"Then what is it?"

He leaned forward in his seat, resting his chin on his hand. "What I'm suggesting is that you're one of the only people in this world that know about us. I trust you, and you're extremely promising as a human being, as a whole. I need you to work with us."

"Twenty thousand dollars, Emmett! That's a ton of cash. What is it all for?" Her fingertips slowly brushed over the check, as if verifying that it was real.

The physicist merely sighed, gloved hands reaching out and taking her's in gently. "Sonia, its for you. If you're going to be finishing your degree, then you'll need the money. I can promise that if you choose to work with me, it won't be that hard."

She exhaled slowly, closing her eyes and growing extremely still for a moment. When she took in another breath, her eyes snapped open and she nodded. "What would I be doing?"

"Your schoolwork, mostly. I might need a hand with

setting up my office and organization, things like that, and correspondence, since you're a writer," he admitted; he was never the most organized man on Earth, after all, "But otherwise?" His head shook, "There's nothing much I'd need you to do. For now, I'm just making the gold and shipping it off - once I have some finances built up, I can establish a larger research venture."

Sonia closed her eyes again, her lips pursing as she concentrated on finding an answer. "I mean, we don't have to continue the physical stuff if that would be awkward, you know," Emmett began tentatively - and reluctantly.

"Shut up, stupid, you and I know damn well that's not true. I don't know how I feel about you, but I know I want to stay with you." His dark gray eyes widened. "I don't know if I love you, and I don't even care if you love me back, but I want this to work. You're not like anyone I've ever met, and not just for the obvious reasons. You're a real man - you've fucked up, but you've tried to make it right. Not a lot of men can say that, Emmett."

She pulled her arms away from him and, without warning, wrapped them around his shoulders. She tugged on him tightly, so hard that he nearly coughed from the pressure. Then, she tore away from him and looked him in the eyes. "Just promise me you won't ever go back to being the man you were a decade ago."

He couldn't lie; "I think that if I have you in my heart and if I have my friends by my side, then I won't ever come close."

Chapter Thirteen
Destiny Ex-Machina

She woke up; with a yawn and a stretch, she rose to a seated position in her king-sized bed. Fingertips ruffled her short, curly, gray hair and she stood up. A robe was quickly grabbed and draped around her shoulders, and she took soft footsteps toward the large curtain adorning her wall. She pulled down a cord and revealed a dazzling view of Manhattan. Judging by the sun, it was about 11:00 AM; it was just short of its peak, after all. She smiled as the rays struck her dark skin - but, on the fortieth floor, it was always a slight bit unnerving.

She took a casual stroll into the living room of the penthouse suite and glanced toward a large map on the wall. There it was - the entire Earth laid out before her very eyes. Along it were clocks indicating what time it was across the world; New York indicated 11:22 AM. She followed the list to the right; sure enough, a line drawn right across the area she was searching for indicated that it was 6:22 PM.

She set a kettle of water on her stove and turned the electric on. While she waited, she walked back into the bedroom and looked toward her phone; a small red light on it blinked, indicating there was a voice-mail awaiting her. Striding over to the device, she pressed the play button and listened to the robotic narrator drone on about how many - one - messages she had coming up; and that this one was going to be the first.

"Hey Geddy, its Emmett," the physicist's recorded voice indicated, "if its alright with you, I'd like to go about gathering the group up, real quick. Jim and Sari are already willing, so we just need your help. Thanks, take care - and say hello to Marge for me!"

The aforementioned woman smiled warmly, walking back

to her tea kettle just before it began to whistle. A bag of Earl Grey was opened and placed in a cup, and she poured the water into it. A touch of sugar and honey were applied and a wooden stirrer was used to mix the concoction just right. Taking a sip to confirm her culinary prowess helped jolt her awake. Fingertips reached for the phone a second time, dialing in a number she knew by heart.

The voice on the other end sounded relieved to hear her. "Hey, Marge, how you doin'?"

"I'm good, Jethro, and yourself?"

He laughed softly. "That deal is done, got the contract an' everything. Good money, even if it bes risky because its in Iraq. What 'bout you? Need anythin'?"

"Oh, no, honey. I'm fine. Our friend Emmett called."

"What he want?" Geddy responded curtly.

"Now Jethro," she chided him, "Doctor Eisenberg was perfectly polite. He jus' wanted to get the group together, said he's got Jim and Sari lined up t'help out. I think you should do it, Jethro. Think you can find the time?"

The sound of static overcame the phone; the signal was lost. Marge hung it up and smiled contentedly; Geddy's voice came from directly behind her, now, and his arms enfolded her. "I always find the time, honey. In fact, I think I might know what Emmett wants - there's one more man we gots to bring on board."

*****

Catskill Community College's Cuomo Concert Hall, named after the former Governor of New York (As opposed to the current), was hosting a choral performance on that particularly chilly night in the second week of November. The music students of the school were in particularly rare form, that night - their song echoed off of the walls of the chamber and warmed every heart in the audience. In a world so focused on academic achievement and turning out scientists and math teachers, it was downright relieving to be reminded of why exactly the arts were funded by the state.

At least, that's what she thought as she listened from the back of the auditorium. Nobody noticed her, of course; she wouldn't benefit from that particular happenstance at all. As the songbirds moved from one tune to another, she applauded; gently, of course, and politely. She appreciated it. Each song set her adrift on another sea of emotion; some waters were calm and brisk, while others were tumultuous and powered by tiny squalls. The waves washed over her own, barely-bulwarked fears and anxieties, helping her to think more clearly. Her piercing blue eyes relaxed as the performance continued; but, sadly, the operatic finale - a rendition of the so-called "*Toreador Song*" from *Carmen* - came to a conclusion far sooner than the aficionado within her had wished.

Her applause was loud, upon the concert's conclusion, and continued until the performers left the stage, returned for an encore bow, and departed again. It was only then that she conceded to herself that her marks had, at least, chosen a good show to attend. For now, however, she waited; she watched. As the theater thinned out, she disappeared behind a trio of "Goth" students. In her outfit - a black, frilly dress and a black halter top, paired up with knee-high leather boots with sharp stiletto heels - she fit in surprisingly well. That was key to her plan, after all; she wanted to emerge from nowhere.

It couldn't have gone any better, in fact! Outside of the theater and its immediate vicinity, the large trees blotted out the moonlight while the campus' street lights were sparsely positioned. Oh, never enough that a security risk was posed - but just enough that there were shadows which could be moved within, when necessary. Without hesitation, her human cover marched right toward the two she intended to intercept. The first wore a knee-length, shoulder-less red dress and an artificial rose upon her left wrist. The male in question had on a black suit-jacket over a red button-up shirt, one that concealed a fairly muscular frame, and he wore a hat with the back rolled down to cover up his over-muscular neck.

"I didn't think Cynthia was telling the truth about how good they were, but she's really improved her program over this semester." The man's statement was ever so heavily accented with an Algerian tone.

The woman responded with a chuckle. "She's gotten some good talent in, I guess. Last year, they sounded - and I love our students to death - like cats getting strangled." The man joined in the laughter. Laughter was good, the onlooker reasoned - it meant they weren't paying attention.

She peeled off of the Vampire Trio (as she called them in the back of her mind) and approached them from their mutual left. The woman was closest, and she was too caught up in the man's muscular chest to notice. As to the man? His date provided a visual screen, and he was similarly affixed on the woman's cleavage.

A smile cracked over her pink lips - ten yards, five, two; she was on top of them! All it would take, now, was for the girl to look even straight ahead and she would discover the intruder. That's why it was time to give up the ghost. "Good evening," came her emotionless statement.

The two suddenly stood erect; the man looked at the interloper as if trying to figure out if he knew her while the woman's eyes widened in recognition. They narrowed briefly. "Oh, great, its the tart," she muttered derisively.

"The what, dear?" the male offered in his French accent.

The obsidian-wearing woman clicked one of her high-heeled boots. "Hello, again," the indifferent tone intimated, "Doctor Montclaire. And you must be...?" she asked, not at all holding her hand out in introduction.

He, however, did just that; "Daniel Marceau," he stated politely. His eyes drank in the woman's proffered figure and couldn't help but think deviant thoughts. She almost felt her lips twitch, either in disgust or amusement - she couldn't be entirely sure which she felt more, and that was a rarity! "And yourself?"

"Erica Hall," she pronounced, looking down at the hand as if it were extending out of a filled, fly-crowned dumpster. He seemed mildly insulted and withdrew the offered appendage.

Maria curled her lips into a frown. "This is one of Doctor Eisenberg's so-called friends, Daniel. She's his ex-girlfriend, actually. What did you want, now, Erica?" the psychologist asked in a disdainful voice.

Erica, on the other hand, simply stared blankly back at her. In the back of the singer's mind, she realized the two now belonged to an exclusive, small club of those who Emmett had dated and broken up with on unfortunate terms. "In a sense," she thought out loud, "we are sisters. Both his ex-girlfriends."

He slipped an arm onto Maria's shoulder protectively; the red-head didn't seem to react. "Great, you've solved our sleeping life crises!" the red-dressed woman declared with sarcasm dripping from her larynx. "Can I get back to my crazy-free evening, now?"

If Erica was amused, she didn't look it. If she was offended? Also, she didn't look it. She looked nothing more than a walking corpse. Slowly, her head wilted to the side and her shocking blue eyes matched up with Maria's green. "And I will harden Pharaoh's heart, and multiply my signs and wonders in the land of Egypt," Erica declared neutrally and ambiguously.

"Come again, lady?" Maria queried impetuously, folding her arms across her chest and staring daggers at the singer standing before them.

Daniel Marceau, however, finally stepped forward and took a good look at the girl. He studied her expression and the psychologist part of his brain actually kicked in and started doing its job. Furthermore, unlike Maria he actually understood the statement; his lips quivered slightly. "It is from the Bible, no?"

Erica nodded; it was a slow dip of her chin, a zombie-like movement. "Exodus 7:3. It describes what I did to you, Doctor Montclaire, very w--"

"Shut up, Hall, because you're even more crazy than Emmett is." The condemnation was firm, and coming from the psychologist it was certainly an educated assumption about her mental state.

Softly, downright sadistically, Erica laughed. The chuckle was inward, the amusement meant for herself. "I certainly agree, Doctor," the singer concurred crisply, a taunting tone intended to strike the woman's very heart.

It required a great deal of effort to restrain Maria at that point; and that's probably why Daniel stepped forward to get between the two. He gave a glance over both his subordinate and date, one that held a hint of displeasure at her lack of restraint. The gaze was passing; he was quickly focused back on the blonde before him. "I must ask, Miss Hall, what are you talking about?

Erica gazed about the darkness and raised an eyebrow slowly. "She hasn't told you, has she?"

"Cut the mystery out, already, you crazy bitch," Maria declared with a strange ferocity in her voice. She clenched a fist. "You ruined everything!"

Once more, the singer began to laugh softly. The muscular man had suffered enough. "Enough, miss," Daniel interjected with his colonial lilt, doing absolutely nothing to make her grow silent, "What did you come here, for? Why are you stalking us? Or, must I call security?"

"You...Doctor Marceau. Let me taste you." At the man's incredibly disturbed look, she raised her fingertips to her lips and continued to chuckle sadistically. "Not like *that*. Your feelings."

"You're absolutely insane, Erica. You need help. If Dan doesn't---"

Erica cast her the most horrifying, sudden, unexpected gaze she'd ever experienced. It silenced her instantly. "I am working, woman," Erica asserted, returning those penetrating blue orbs toward Daniel. "Yes. You looked at me, and that was something even an ape could read. You wanted my body more than you could admit. You want this woman before me just as badly - yet underneath, you feel guilt. You have a loved one - a wife, no doubt - that you still love, that you cannot bring yourself to ignore. I know this," the vocal vixen explained, "because you feel it. That means I may feel it."

Daniel narrowed his eyes; he was a practiced student of

the human mind, after all, and he was not about to let some girl talk down to him when it was his job to know how people thought. She could have seen his reaction anywhere in the world - he redoubled his efforts to appear completely neutral. "You, dear girl, are truly insane."

"Am I? Let us play a game, then!" Erica announced with a sadistic glee plastered on her overjoyed face. "I will make a statement, and you may call my bluff; I not only can feel your feelings, but I can control them to such an extent that I can make you believe, fully and whole-heartedly," she said as her index finger rose to point toward a distant street-lamp - and, more precisely, the garbage can just barely visible underneath its far-off light, "that fornication with that receptacle is the most important and all-consuming task you will ever undertake."

"That's obscene!" Maria declared; she made a move to step past Daniel but he didn't even flinch. Not to hold her back, nor to challenge the blonde.

Her head twitched; her chin tilted from one side to the other. "No? Not going to call my bluff?" Erica's voice held no triumph within it; merely amusement. "It is because you know deep down that Emmett Eisenberg, that pathetic disgrace of a would-be savior, was the better man in the end. You played politics against a man who could have destroyed you with but a thought - and your victory, as I taste, was stolen from you by his...Resignation?" Her eyebrows wriggled as she lectured. "No, dear doctor, I am not reading your thoughts. I am reading your feelings."

"Destroy him?" Maria interjected; finally, she shoved Daniel out of the way and reached both of her arms out; she grasped Erica by the shirt and came quite close to lifting the slender woman off of her heel-adorned feet. "Emmett is insane. *You* are insane. You're pretending to be some kind of, of, of psychic! Its sick. You're sick. Go away! Please! Just go away, already!" She was on the verge of tears.

Erica shook her head. "Maria Montclaire. I hardened your heart." The reiterated reference caused Maria to turn as red as her hair with rage. "You are a woman of science. Do you not believe yourself to have been capable of giving the master of physics a chance to prove he was telling the truth? Use that rationality - why did you resist letting Emmett prove himself to you?"

Suddenly, it hit the psychologist; Emmett and her had their disagreements, but they'd been happy together - why wouldn't she give the man a chance? The feelings raced through her mind, and in spite of her self she experienced a very new, very real concern: That those feelings were being intruded upon. They were; Erica could virtually smell the woman's self-assessment, her analyzing of every conversation she'd had since she first met Jethro Marx at the Jazz club called X-Quisitie. There had been signs; and they only grew when she met James Lowery and Sari. She'd been curious, she'd wanted to learn, and there was no chance of her missing the next clue about her boyfriend's past. He was eccentric! But he was reasonable!

When she met Erica, her reaction was anger and betrayal - and never, ever contemplation. It took weeks for her to call him back. She ridiculed his attempts to explain himself, accusing him of being nothing more than a nickel-and-dime-store quality charlatan! There was no research, no assessment of a patient's emotional or psychological distress, no verification! There was, as Maria realized, only her fury at what Emmett had done.

"Or *was* it your fury?" Erica echoed as if pulling the next line of reasoning out of the red-head's mind. Her tone changed ever so slightly; it was still emotionally distraught, but it sounded as if there might just be some small part of her that didn't appreciate the circumstances - no matter how amusing it was to torture those who actually held the degrees she'd claimed to possess ten years ago. "It was. However, that is all I allowed you to feel."

"If admitting one has a problem is the first step toward recovery, then I am taking it, now." Her voice was cold, but contemplative. "I used you. My revenge against Eisenberg would not have been as complete without destroying what you two had. In the process, I hurt you, and you were innocent. That makes me little better than he is. *Our* violence - all of ours - tore us to shreds" Her confession was accompanied with her closing her eyes.

When she spoke next, she brushed a hand through her hair and took on a saddened tone. "They will fail. It will happen again, you know.   Kennedy - both of them - failed. Caesar failed. Christ failed. They have all failed, in spite of the might they wielded. Even those with power such as Eisenberg's will fail no matter how many times they attempt it. But do you know what?"

Erica's hand moved slowly toward her stomach, over a scar that never manifested itself physically in such a way that it did emotionally. "We only fail because of the actions we take, as they always have unforeseen consequences."

The silence following this statement forced those sharp blue orbs to open once more. She studied the two; and they studied her in response, speechless. She could taste everything - their confusion, their anger toward her, their defense of one another in the face of something they didn't quite understand. They were unwilling to speak for fear of betraying some aspect of foolishness. Slowly, that hand over her stomach rose up and over her voluptuous figure, brushing across her lips and over the bridge of her nose. A tuft of hair was brushed to the side.

"Allow me to prove it. I give you the future. I feel your feelings. Now, feel mine." Her words were accompanied by a well-focused burst of emotional energy. There was a fleeting impulse within the heels of both doctors, an impulse screaming *run!!!* in the back of their minds. It was immediately replaced, however, with exhaustion. It was an unspeakable ache - not of physical stress or even of a lack of sleep, but more of an inability to find motivation to try and take one more step forward for fear of yet another kick backwards.

It faded as quickly as it came, and Maria's hand reached up toward her mouth. "Oh my god!" she exclaimed, astonishment seizing her. "I...I don't believe it! Its true! You really *can!* And that means Emmett! Oh god, what have I done? What did I do?"

"*I* did it, Maria Montclaire," Erica amended for the psychologist. "And in the end?" She gestured toward the man before her. "Unlike the Consortium I worked for a decade ago, you don't undertake a course doomed to failure. You two? You will do very well for yourselves and the world simply by keeping your little mouths shut and keeping your little eyes focused on this school. Congratulations," Erica offered, turning on that sharp heel (and digging up some dirt in the process). "You will do more good than we superhuman fools and our decaying dreams."

Before Maria could speak, Erica held up a hand. "Farewell, Doctor Montclaire. Doctor Marceau." She left the two, then; left them stranded and stunned at the campus of Catskill Community College, where Maria's involvement with Emmett - and, by extension, Erica - began and, as it appeared, ended. "We shall not meet again," she announced as a tree above the red-head shed a reddened leaf, one that caught a glare of light off of its dried husk and drifted to the ground. It was shed after having given its tree a scant bit of strength in its infinitely long life; but even as it descended, lifeless, it would be replaced by another that would, in time, keep the tree alive.

Maria looked at Daniel; Daniel looked at Maria. Their hands brushed over one another gently, and their eyes met. They smiled, and they silently agreed to do exactly as Erica said - build a better world and keep their little mouths shut. Perhaps, after all was decided, by pressing their lips into one anothers'.

*****

Eight people arrived suddenly in the Siberian wastelands. There was a light snowfall, but there was, with ease, a campfire quickly built. It was a coal fire, one buried deep within a pit of rocks to prevent it from spreading.

The one responsible for the fire smiled politely. "So, who'll get him? You, or me?"

The one responsible for the transportation answered gruffly. "I got the prick. You just make sure he ain't gonna hurt us."

"If h' tries anythin'," came an Irish lilt, "I'll find a way t'break 'is arms. One way'r another."

Emmett gazed over at James and shrugged indifferently; Jim, meanwhile, looked over to the black-haired woman who had escorted the physicist. "So you're...?"

"Sonia," the slender girl offered with a nervous voice; the surroundings were clearly alien to her, and the trip? Although they'd been the last ones to travel, she was still incredibly disoriented. Slowly, however, her breathing returned to normal and she relaxed in her posture. "And you three?"

Jim gestured to the women behind him, pointing at the silent Russian, first. "This's Katrina," he offered; then, a movement toward the equally silent Irishwoman. "An' this's Lark. They're my secretaries," he offered without a hint of condescension in his voice (no matter what his diction implied) "an' I'm James. Jim Lowery. I ain't like these three clowns," he offered with a gesture toward Geddy, Emmett, and the Hindu. "I'm a master'o me own senses. Hearin', eyesight, balance."

The youth blushed. "That's so cool," Sonia stammered. "And you're Sari? *The* Sari?"

The Hindu's eyes blinked; she hadn't expected *that* description. "I would say I am simply Sari, my dear." She examined the girl, both of whom were about the same age, with a certain bit of curiosity. "It is nice to meet you, Miss Sonia. I hope we shall make excellent friends." The healer cast her eyes toward Emmett, then, and nodded her head once, approvingly. "I make no promises, Doctor, but I hope it can work."

The physicist returned it. "Alright, then. Geddy, on your mark."

Jethro leaned forward and gave the eighth individual, his heavily-dressed wife Marge, a kiss. Then, two steps were taken away from the group. He shut his eyes and held his hands out. "Aight, first t'find it." He reached out with his senses and followed the 'trails' he'd left. That was the easy part. "Now I gots't correct it. Can't bring it if it ain't corrected." Arresting momentum wasn't a pleasant experience; not because it was difficult, necessarily, but because it required so much focus to make sure that there was no risk of collateral damage.

"Last an' not least..." he began. A blue sphere of light suddenly emerged before their eyes, illuminating the darkened Russian grove. Flecks of snow were caught in it and disappeared. "Emmett, can y' make sure---"

The physicist already knew what he was being asked. "We're good, but make it quick," he announced, sensing the various radioactive particles escaping the glowing area. He could practically ignore the not-so-ionizing aspects, but the quite-so? No; the Gamma rays were the most dangerous at the moment. They required the utmost amount of his focus to neutralize as they escaped the sphere. "I don't know that we thought this one through, Geddy!"

"Ya damn right, Eisenberg!" shouted the portly fellow, his arms widening and rising over his head. The illumination continued to grow brighter, and Emmett shut his eyes to ward off the pressure in his forehead as he prevented the harmful cosmic radiation from pummeling his friends. "I got 'im!" Geddy shouted, "I got 'im! Here we go!"

The final warning was accompanied by a loud thud; the ground underneath them shook for a moment, and it only seemed blunted because Emmett's fists shut and nullified as much of the impact energy as he could.

Sari almost couldn't believe her eyes; and Sonia? The poor girl was staring at the newly-arrived object in wonder. The women bore witness to a large, black stone half-entombed in the ground. One half of it resembled a perfectly engraved gemstone while the other side of it was partially melted and had multiple cavities in it. Sari walked up to the stone and let her tan fingertips hover near it. She felt no heat, none whatsoever, that could be attributed to the sun.

"I am impressed, Emmett. You must remember this trick," the Hindu announced.

Sonia bit her bottom lip. "So, that's him? In that stone?"

"Y'really sent 'im up aroun' th' sun. Sonu'va bitch," Jim muttered, a smile cracking on the spy's face.

Emmett stepped up to the tomb and studied it for an instant. "I know you can hear me. You can see me. I'm going to tear a small part of the crystal away, now. Just enough that we can look at each other, and we can all talk." He had no idea if this would help the circumstances or not; nevertheless, he raised his fingertips and made a gesture as if he was snatching a fly from midair. Without a sound, part of the gemstone broke away.

The heavily breathing man within clenched his fists to retain his balance as he found himself staring at the eight figures before him. He cursed vigorously in Spanish.

"Is'e secured?" Jim demanded, reaching to his boot and withdrawing a long, old bowie knife that had seen many battles, and been cleaned many times. He held it at the ready.

Emmett shrugged. "Seeing as he can't push his way through this material? Seeing what it withstood, in space? He's no threat to anyone, right now."

James nodded, once, and the healer who stood near the stone looked up into his eyes. The man was enraged - perhaps deranged - and she bit her bottom lip softly. "Alejandro, Alejandro," she whispered cautiously, examining his psychological state through his expression. She gazed over her shoulder. "This is not my area of expertise! Miss Hall should be doing this!"

"Blondie ain'' an option, Sari. He's just nuts - she's worse. You can do this, I know it," Jim offered reassuringly. Geddy took the emotional reinforcement to the next level; he approached and placed a hand on the girl's shoulder, smiling down at her. Marge silently took her other side.

Alejandro screamed. "Let me go! Let me go!" The sound of his fists slamming against the metal prison he sat within.

Sari whispered delicately. "Please, Alejandro, breathe for me. Breathe. Let me in. I can see, but I cannot touch. Allow me to touch. Yes, that is it..." Her eyes fixed upon his, and his upon her. There was no outward sign that anything happened to the young girl, but Alejandro began to slow his breathing. His pupils dilated and he slumped against the inside of the cell. James resheathed his knife.

The Hindu stepped away and rubbed the patch of flesh that her *Tilaka* rested upon. "It is quite a headache," she remarked as she looked up at him. "But when he allowed it, I was capable of touching him, a little. His mind is, for lack of a more appropriate term, resetting. He shall recover in a minute. I am only able to change its physical structure - I do not effect his emotions, just the connections they made."

Sonia clasped her hands together and leaned upon Emmett's shoulder, and the Physicist nodded as a result of the explanation. "Great work, Sari," he commended, eyes drifting toward the unconscious man.

"Now we wait," Geddy added. It didn't take long; first, the Spaniard began to purse his lips and rock his shoulders as if he were in the midst of a fitful dream. Finally, with a loud groan, his dark eyes fluttered open and he brought his hand over his face.

"Dios Mio, is this what a hang-over feels like?" he grumbled, reaching his arms above his head to stretch out. They clanged against his metallic bondage, and he gave it a dismissive glare. "Emmett Eisenberg, you are there, no?"

Emmett smiled warmly as Curtis' eyes locked upon the physicist's. "Yes, I am," he answered. "Are you ready to talk about things?"

Alejandro shrugged casually; its was not as if he had a choice as to whether or not the conversation would take place. The metal surrounding him cracked, suddenly, then began to dissolve into vapor from its top to its bottom. Freed, he took a step forward and stretched once more, feeling his muscles relax into place properly. A smile crossed his lips. "Talk," the Spaniard half-commanded.

"Oi! Here's the deal, boyo," Jim announced smartly, "Y'weren' wrong when y'said we shoul' group back up, after all."

The Spaniard blinked; Marge, the older woman with the gray hair, smiled. "Yes, Mistah Curtis," she said subtly, "We've *all* thought it over and we decided to rebuild."

"You...Wait." He hesitated. "You mean the Consortium?" Alejandro's eyes widened slightly. The realization of his father's dream was suddenly at hand - and, unfortunately, his father's legacy was not finished tormenting him.

Geddy approached him and, strangely enough, extended his hand. "I's sorry, man. I's sorry for what I did t'ya, an' what I did t'ya daddy."

Alejandro stared at it with smoldering eyes, and he eventually shook his head. "Not yet, Jethro. I still...I'm not happy with you. I understand it, I understand why you did it. But, I do not forgive you. I cannot. Not yet, anyway. It was my life you ruined."

The older man slowly lowered his hand and nodded. "I'm hopin' that in a few months an' years, maybe, you can see I ain't so bad. Until then, I just hope I can work wit you."

"You're in," Emmett added quickly enough, walking up to Alejandro and offering a gloved hand. Unlike Jethro, this time the invincible man took the palm. "We're all equal, here; Jim is setting me up with a cash flow, thanks to Lark and Katrina. Geddy and Marge going to work on the outside, Sari has a lot of oversight, and Sonia?" He looked over his shoulder at his now-former student, "She's special to me. You've got an equal share, Alejandro. We work together to fix this world up."

"An' don't'cha go thinkin' y'can take it over," Jim interjected, stepping up toward the man and shaking his hand. "This inn'it some Doomsday Coalition or other bull-shit super-group. We're gonna help this world or cut it out - ain't no rulership takin' place."

Alejandro cracked a slight smile. "I think I can live with that. Sari?" he looked over toward the healer, then, and bowed his head deeply. "Thank you very much for helping me see straight."

The Brahman also bowed. She then proceeded to step backwards. The Irishman and the Spaniard began to talk with Marge; Geddy remained distant, not making an effort to engage with the man whose father he had killed a decade ago.

A moment later, however, the healer emerged behind Emmett and whispered into the physicist's ear. "I cannot say Erica was behind this, for certain," the ominous information emerged.

Emmett managed a slight smile in the face of this fact. "That's fine," he responded, turning to face the beautiful woman. "When I saw her," he began, looking over toward Sonia with a smile. "When I saw Erica, well, she made me feel fear. She said that is what she has felt for ten years, ever since things went wrong."

Sonia's eyes grew wide, draping her arm around his shoulder. "Em, fear? What could she be afraid of?"

Emmett shook his head and gently took Sonia's hand into his. "I don't know," he answered truthfully, looking down at his feet. "It might have been fear of giving up her hatred, fear of the reality she lived in, or fear of just looking at me and feeling anything other than rage. I really don't know."

Sari frowned slightly at this revelation, and something within the Hindu girl snapped. "I cannot be silent any longer. I had been with Miss Hall when--"

"Hall? Erica *Hall?*" Sonia gasped, clenching the physicist's hand. "Riki and the Wildcats? When...When we had our first date, my hair, I--"

Emmett laughed sharply as closed his eyes. "I had to fight not to get sick, Sonia, but its alright. I know. You had no way to know, and its fine. Thank you."

"I'm an idiot!" Sonia wailed in despair. Sari laughed, then, as well.

"No, Miss Sonia, you are not. No more than we all are. I was saying," she continued with renewed gravity, "that I had been with Miss Hall when she got sick, months after you disappeared. She was terrified of everything, and she hurt so much. It *was* fear I felt. She did love you, Doctor Eisenberg, but her secrets tore her apart." Sari closed her eyes slowly and began to recall that day, nearly a decade ago. "I did all I could, at the hospital, but in the state I was in, myself, I was of little use. I failed, too. But Doctor, Miss Hall wanted you to know. I know she did. She told me, and I think she wanted me to tell you when the time was right, before everything went so wrong."

Emmett bit his bottom lip. A tear fell from his eye, a slightly saline sliver of silver liquid that splashed against the Siberian snow and almost instantly solidified. The coal-fire that burned was slowly running low on fuel, and would shortly force a departure from the arctic areas. Nevertheless, the physicist allowed himself to drink in its light for a moment. His fingertips moved swiftly; he removed his gloves, exposing his hands to the early, yet frigid Russian winter. They quickly re-grasped his former students', and his eyes moved to the Brahmin's slowly. The Hindu drew in a slow breath and offered the final valediction for Emmett's future dreams, placing a name on the past he'd finally made peace with.

"Jasmine."